D1740119

Apostasy

The Perpetual War 3

LEON STEELGRAVE

ICE PICK

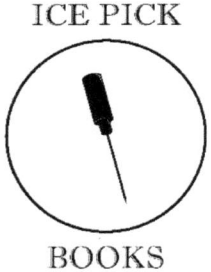

BOOKS

Published by Ice Pick Books

Copyright © 2023 Leon Steelgrave

ISBN: 978-1-7391858-1-7

LEON STEELGRAVE

In loving memory of Hunter.
You were the best, boy!

Books by Leon Steelgrave

Europa City 1: White Vampyre
Europa City 2: Though Your Sins Be Scarlet
Europa City 3: The Violet Hour
Europa City 4: A Life Owed

Europa City One-shot: Cocoa Psycho Killer
Europa City One-shot: Smack Upside The Head

The Perpetual War 1: Crusade
The Perpetual War 2: Resistance
The Perpetual War 3: Apostasy

Darkness Visible: The Complete Short Stories

CHAPTER 1

Pulaski presented her right eye to the eyepiece and initiated the retinal scan. She tapped her fingers against her thigh as she waited for the scanner to confirm her identity. The elevator control panel changed from red to green, revealing an option for Sub-Level C. Pulaski pressed her thumb against it and the carriage commenced its descent into the subterranean bowels of the Eagle's Nest.

The existence of Sub-Level C beneath Free America's underground command centre was known to a select few and accessible to even fewer. Pulaski didn't concern herself with the moral ambiguities of its existence. Her time in the Senate of the old republic had taught her the Bill of Rights, or any other human conventions or accords, did not need to apply everywhere. In the 2040s, they had defended the country against its enemies. Now, almost fifty years later, at the tail end of the twenty-first century, Free America sought to reunite a fractured nation by deposing the leaders of the seceded Religious States. The ends, she assured herself, more than justified the means.

The elevator door opened to reveal the bare concrete walls of a narrow corridor. It was illuminated by the harsh, actinic glare of overhead bulkheads. Pulaski's shadow strobed ahead of her as she marched forward, ignoring the doors to her left and right as she made for the one at the corridor's end. She pressed her palm against the sensor, then heard a hum and felt the vibration through the soles of her shoes as servomotors drew back the locking bars.

The laboratory was Spartan in its decoration and furnishing, with white rendered walls and grey vinyl flooring. A central island of extruded plastic housed a workstation and a trolley holding medical implements rested against the right wall. Its occupant unfolded himself from the room's only chair. Doctor Bendix was a tall, spare man. His white lab coat hung from his shoulders almost like a cape. He inclined his head in the briefest of nods.

'You've sourced a suitable test subject?'

'I have,' replied the doctor.

Bendix tapped a key, rendering the upper half of the rear wall transparent, revealing the execution chamber. The woman strapped to the gurney appeared unremarkable. She was of average height and build, neither young nor old, with mousy brown hair. An IV line snaked away from the cannula in each arm, leading to the execution console, which was loaded with the fatal sequence of drugs. Aware that she was being observed, the prisoner turned her head. Her lips moved silently as she shouted a defiant obscenity.

'Judy Gilmartin. Aged thirty-two. Convicted of a double homicide and robbery...'

Pulaski waved the doctor to silence. 'I'm not here for her biography. Has Project Phoenix been administered?'

'Seventy-two hours ago.'

'Then let's proceed.'

Bendix swiped the workstation screen and an ECG reading appeared. He glanced at the time on screen. 'The execution AI is set to commence the program in just under two minutes.'

Pulaski stepped closer. She had witnessed executions before, but today promised something altogether different.

A successful demonstration of Project Phoenix would be Free America's Rubicon. She allowed herself a brief moment of trepidation before quashing it. They had come too far to stop or retreat. Right now, Judy Gilmartin was just another felon. But if all went to plan, she would enter the history books.

'Thirteen hundred hours – commencement of saline drip. Lines are clear.'

Bendix's voice was dispassionate as he monitored Gilmartin's vital signs. Pulaski wondered if he felt any pang of conscience or betrayal of his Hippocratic oath. Technically, no human agency was involved in the execution, since an AI was responsible for administering the sequence of lethal drugs. Bendix would only intervene in the event of a process failure.

'Pentobarbital administered.' Bendix checked the monitor. 'Subject is now unconscious. Pancuronium bromide administered. Paralysis of the diaphragm and other respiratory muscles confirmed. If the process were to be interrupted at this point, the subject would die from asphyxiation. Depending on results, it might be worth running a second trial on that basis. Potassium chloride administered. Abnormal heart rhythm detected. Full cardiac arrest. Time of death, 13:08.'

Bendix started a timer on his com-unit and walked over to the viewing window. Pulaski continued to study Gilmartin's body. Was that a twitch or just her imagination? The seconds stretched painfully to minutes. Bendix had attempted to explain the science, but she wasn't interested in the mechanics, only the result and what it meant for Free America's rebellion against the Religious States. Her atonement.

This time, the twitch was unmistakeable. It started in Gilmartin's shoulders, ran down her torso, and made her legs kick. A second and then a third one followed, with the speed increasing. Her hands clenched and her back arched as Gilmartin's corpse fought against the restraints. Pulaski glanced at Bendix's com-unit: five minutes, eleven seconds.

The leather straps stretched as Gilmartin's corpse pulled against them with preternatural strength. Pulaski flinched as a steel pin popped free and ricocheted against the viewing window. Another pin went as Gilmartin's reanimated corpse tore her right arm free. She freed her other arm and unbuckled the remaining straps. Gilmartin's head turned, as if looking right at Pulaski, somehow staring through the wall.

Pulaski stepped back. She felt something bump against the small of her back and realised she had retreated to the central island.

'Damn it, Bendix, that's enough! Kill it!'

The doctor swiped his com-unit, dousing the execution chamber with liquid nitrogen. His lips compressed into a thin smile. 'Now I am become Death, the destroyer of worlds.'

CHAPTER 2

Cooper covered his mouth and nose with his bandana and closed his eyes as the hopper dusted down. He kept them shut until the whine of the engine dropped to a low hum. The VTOL craft's passenger slid back the door and dropped the two feet to the ground. Cooper held out his hand and received a firm grip in return.

'Welcome back to the Religious States and Fort Irwin, Sarge. You're looking well.'

'Got you to thank for that,' Jackson replied.

Cooper waved the sergeant over to the waiting buggy and stowed his kitbag in the back. The air-con was a welcome relief after the arid desert air. It seemed to get hotter each year. He put the buggy in drive and watched the hopper lift off in the rear-view as he pulled away in the direction of the main barracks.

He examined Jackson's profile as they rolled along the blacktop. He expected to see evidence of the third-degree burns he had sustained when insurgents had ambushed their JLTV in Damascus, but Jackson's skin was perfect. The lines and wrinkles he remembered had been smoothed away by regenerative nano-therapy.

Cooper pointed to the ribbon of Jackson's Purple Heart

'See you got yourself another oak leaf cluster.'

'Damn lucky it wasn't posthumous. Would have been if it wasn't for you.'

'Guess that makes us even.'

Cooper cursed himself in the awkward silence that followed. Neither man wanted to talk about the role Jackson had played in Colonel Tyler's death. He wondered if the sergeant regretted saving his life. If not his, certainly Lynch's, given the journalist's subsequent broadcasts decrying the war in the Middle East and involvement with the insurgent Free America movement, which was seeking to reunify the former American states. Some would doubtless view it as treachery, but Cooper couldn't help admiring Lynch's unflinching dedication to the ideals of the old republic, however impossible their restoration might seem.

Jackson raised a hand and pointed to the left, towards the chapel. 'I'd like to offer up my thanks.'

'Sure. Whatever you need.'

Cooper angled the buggy towards the extended western wall. Its surface was deliberately distressed in homage to the last surviving fragments of the original Temple in Jerusalem. Sunlight burnished the lead-lined roof; the buttresses cast long fingers of shadow that seemed to move away as they approached. Then the buttresses and shadows disappeared behind the wall as the buggy drew to a halt.

'Do you want me to pray with you, Sarge?'

'No. This is personal. Do me a favour and stow my gear in the barracks. I'll see you in the mess before vespers tonight.'

Cooper stared at Jackson's retreating back. The sergeant's brush with death seemed to have brought him closer to God, whereas all the death Cooper had witnessed only drove God further away. Not that he had ever felt particularly connected. He had thought being home might help, but it only served to remind him how much he hated the war. How little he wanted to return to it. So much for being one of God's chosen soldiers, one of the Templar elites.

Jackson's was the first familiar face that Cooper had seen since his return. After eighteen months on the front lines, the surviving Templars were finally receiving a long-overdue furlough. Some would surely pitch up at Fort Irwin prior to their redeployment. Following Doctor Steiner's assessment, Cooper was assigned to assist with training the latest intake of Templars. Less than seventy of the two hundred and fifty applicants would make it to the end of selection, and they had been drawn from the top three per centile of army recruits. Cooper remembered the physical and mental challenges used to forge raw recruits into living weapons. He didn't envy this latest batch of fresh-faced youths as they assembled before him.

Cooper felt the weight of expectation as the novitiates stared rigidly ahead. Here before them stood everything they aspired to: the possessor of the fabled red cross of a sworn soldier of Christ. A seasoned veteran who had fought the Caliphate in Israel and Syria. With such a man as their instructor, how could they fail?

Cooper knew the answer from bitter experience: in ways too numerous to count. He looked along the front row, taking in the fresh, open expressions. No doubt he, Mackinlay, Walker, and the others had looked just like that. Was it really only two years ago? So much had happened since they'd completed selection and taken their vows. When he looked back, it was like watching a movie, and he was a spectator outside the body of this young man who fought to survive and return home to his family.

He finally focused on his datapad, scanning briefly through the attached biographical details as he read the roll call. He noted the eager barks they returned in response to their names. At 'Porter, Daryl of Jonesboro,' Cooper paused and identified a sandy-haired kid. He had put on muscle, but there was no mistaking the boy who had been two years below him in senior high. Porter shifted nervously and Cooper quickly found his place and moved on.

Having confirmed all were present, Cooper split the novitiates into groups and assigned them instructors. He ensured Porter was in his group for tomorrow's MILES exercise in Razish, the largest of the training villages. The kid could have had a hundred reasons for joining, but Cooper couldn't shake feeling responsible. The thought of inspiring others to join up, of being idolised, made him feel sick to his stomach. He had to get out. Had to.

'You all right there, Cooper?'

Cooper started guiltily at the sound of Jackson's voice. 'Must have zoned out there for a moment, Sarge. Still adjusting to being home.'

'It's the adrenaline. Or, more accurately, the lack of it. You get used to running on it. Makes it hard to settle at first, but it'll pass. Come on, let's get these boys to the quartermaster and get them issued with their kit.' Jackson winked. 'We'll start them easy with forty pounds of equipment and ten klicks. See what kind of material the good Lord has sent us.'

Cooper watched the squad move between the crumbling adobe buildings. He felt the tension rise as they scanned each doorway and window, expecting an insurgent to burst out with murderous intent. Porter tried to hide it, but Cooper could see the whites of his knuckles as he gripped his assault rifle and the way his head jerked in response to the faintest blip on the motion sensor. Young was the calmest, and Ford was a close second; they reviewed their telemetry and acted accordingly. Good prospects, Cooper thought.

Hicks was more of an enigma. He displayed no nerves but equally showed little interest. Perhaps he found it difficult to disconnect from the knowledge that it was a simulation. If so, he would taste Chaplain-Commander Du Pont's whip before being assigned to the box to reflect on his failings. Cooper felt an itch between his shoulders as he recalled receiving his own lashes. Du Pont clearly took no pleasure in the pain he meted out; he really did see it as discharging a holy duty, however unpleasant.

Cooper pressed his finger behind his right ear in response to a dull ache. He blinked as his vision shifted, his perception changing, so that he appeared to be looking down upon himself. Where was he? Damascus? Jerusalem? Hostile territory. Separated from his squad. Surrounded by insurgents. They hadn't seen him, but that could change at any moment. His hands moved automatically as he unlimbered his carbine, backing away to maximise his field of fire. He thumbed the selector switch on his weapon to full-auto and curled his finger around the trigger.

'Enemy contact!'

Cooper jolted at the shout. He stared at the carbine his hand, then quickly dropped the barrel to point at the ground. His hands shook.

'Are you sure?' Young asked.

'He darted around the corner,' Porter replied.

Porter's rifle chattered as he sprayed a salvo toward a group of figures from around the corner of the narrow street. Despite what the rest of the squad saw, he kept on firing until the magazine was empty. Even then, his finger remained clenched on the trigger. A football rolled towards them. Young trapped it with his foot and cast his eyes downward.

Cooper took control of himself. He needed to ignore the episode he had just suffered; the training was being recorded and his own performance scrutinised. He stepped forward and removed Porter's finger from the trigger. The novitiate's gaze remained fixed on the group of sprawled bodies, too small to belong to adults. Cooper swiped his com-unit and opened the casualty probability look-up table.

'Daanish, aged nine, deceased. Absalom, aged eleven,

deceased. Faheed, aged eight, deceased. Jamella, aged seven, deceased. Borzou, aged nine, deceased.'

'Way to go!' Hicks whooped. 'Kill 'em before they're old enough to fight for the Caliphate. That's what I say.'

'That's enough, Hicks,' Cooper barked. 'We're soldiers, not killers.'

'Come on, man. It's just a dumb sim. Nobody's actually dead.'

Cooper tapped the cross on his left breast. 'If you're fortunate enough to pass selection, it will be real. Our duty is to defend the faith, not murder women and children. I can see you're having difficulty with that, Hicks. Hand me your weapon and report to Chaplain-Commander Du Pont for discipline.'

Hicks looked at his squad mates for support. Finding none, he thrust his rifle at Cooper. He lifted his HUD and positioned it on top of his helmet, blinking in the bright sun. Squaring his shoulders, he marched off, muttering under his breath. Cooper gave him two weeks max before he washed out. Hicks wouldn't see it that way, but he would be one of the lucky ones.

Cooper ordered the squad to move out. As they passed the casualties, they saw the children were actually dwarves. Still in character, they offered up the fixed stares of the dead. Cooper wondered how much they were being paid. Not enough, most likely. But there was little enough work for the able-bodied, so what choice did they have? Like himself, none. You took the work you were fit for, no matter how unpleasant.

'Enter,' Willard called.

Cooper took a deep breath and pushed open the door. The colonel sat behind an expansive desk; its surface was covered with holo-projections. Cooper caught some of the proposed troop deployments in Syria before the images winked out. He stood to attention and snapped off a salute.

Willard glanced at his watch. 'Templar-Private Cooper. You requested a meeting?'

'Yes, sir. I was hoping for an update on the status of my request to leave the Order.'

Willard leaned back in his chair, staring up towards the ceiling. 'Ah, yes. You made it following the Jerusalem campaign?'

'Yes, sir. I understand things were tense following President Hamilton's assassination. But we're back on home soil now.'

'I see. Guess there's no denying it was a hard campaign. But thanks to the sacrifices made by yourself and your bothers, we were, with God's grace, able to liberate Israel from the Caliphate and restore Jerusalem as a place of Christian worship and pilgrimage. Few have what it takes to earn the red cross pattée of a Templar. I hate to lose any of them, whether it be to death, disability, or ... disillusionment. This war is far from won and before it's out we're going to need every faithful soldier of Christ we can get. At times, the task God has set us can seem impossible, but I want you to remember you don't have to complete it alone. We're all brothers here, sworn to one another. I know it's been a hard road, what with the death of my predecessor and your own captivity at the hands of Marshal Ismail, but I want you to make me a promise, Cooper. Promise me you'll think your decision over carefully while you're here at Fort Irwin. Do that for me and I'll personally take up your request with Grand Master Vanderbilt. I'm sure, with God's guidance, you'll make the correct decision. Dismissed.'

Cooper turned on his heel and marched from the room, head reeling. He recognised it as indoctrination, a process all the candidates went through, but the guilt at letting down his brothers, living and dead, still felt real. The Templars might be his sworn brothers, but what of his actual brothers? The twins, Dale and Wade, his sister Shania, or his mother and father? Didn't the Bible say he had a duty to them as well?

The military psychiatric hospital occupied the old Marine Corps Logistics Base southeast of Barstow. Its grey and beige plascrete building was shielded from the road by scrub and trees. The road and building were unsigned, adding to the sense of the clandestine because God's holy warriors were not supposed to crack under pressure. But that was what had happened to Cooper's old comrade, Goodman.

Cooper followed Doctor Steiner down the corridor. His eyes flitted up and down as he took in the bright abstract art on the walls. The artwork ended a metre from the reinforced door of the locked ward. Steiner offered up his right palm and then his eyes for verification. Mag-bolts clicked in response and the doctor pushed open the door. He stepped forward and then stopped, blocking the way.

'I'm allowing this visit despite my better judgement. Corporal Goodman remains in a fragile state of mind. Please avoid any topics of conversation that might ... agitate him.'

Cooper, worried the doctor might change his mind, nodded his agreement. Steiner stepped aside, allowing him to pass. The door shut behind them with a clang, demarcating the threshold between hospital and penitentiary. The battleship-grey corridor beyond terminated in a second secure door, in front of which stood a slab-like orderly. At their approach, the orderly unfolded his arms and slid back the door's viewing panel.

'How is the patient today, Lauriston?'

'Docile as a lamb. See for yourself.'

Steiner permitted himself a brief glance at the patient before swiping his ID to open the door. 'Lauriston and I will be outside. Try to avoid raising your voice or making any sudden movements. It can provoke a ... reaction.'

Cooper bit back a retort. He had learned early on during his own sessions with Steiner that puncturing the doctor's self-importance inevitably triggered a fit of pique. The door shut silently behind him. He looked at the figure slumped in the chair opposite the muted holo-screen. Goodman's hair had been shaved to the scalp, possibly to facilitate ECT and his pupils were dilated to the point where only a narrow ring of green showed around them. Tranquilised.

Cooper pulled up a second chair and sat opposite his former comrade in captivity. The corporal's head tilted up. Then, the effort apparently too much, his chin dropped again to rest on his neck.

'Hey there, Pete. How are you doing? It's me, Billy Ray. But you know that, right?'

The tip of Goodman's tongue protruded between his lips. His Adam's apple bobbed up and down as he swallowed several times in quick succession. 'Coop.' His voice sounded dry and reedy. 'Don't tell me they've got you in here as well?'

'No. Just visiting. Thought it might be good for you to see a familiar face. They treating you okay?'

'I guess.' Goodman raised a palsied hand and plucked nervously at his shirt. 'It's the meds. Makes it difficult to think. To remember. But they tell me I get violent without them. A danger to myself and others. But I'm a Templar. I'm supposed to be dangerous.'

Cooper tried to catch the viewing panel out of the corner of his eye. Steiner was listening to every word. He thought carefully about how to broach the subject without upsetting Goodman or giving himself away. Steiner had assured him that psych profiling and scans had not revealed any trace of the kind of programming within himself that had induced Goodman to attack Major Stanley. The incident during the MILES exercise was the latest in a series of blackouts. The attacks started small, with a man finding himself entering a room and realising he had no idea why he was there. The kind of absentmindedness that one would put down to being tired or distracted. Soon he lost ten minutes here, fifteen minutes there, sometimes changing clothes and location. Last night, he had been cleaning his kit in barracks, only to then find himself in the motor pool. Something was wrong, and his suspicions as to the cause terrified him.

'You remember being captured by the Caliphate and taken to Marshal Ismail's compound?'

Goodman's body stiffened and he stopped picking at his shirt. 'Not likely to forget it. When he shot that poor bastard from the Support Battalion, I really thought our time had come.'

'His name was Sanchez. Gabriel Sanchez,' Cooper said. 'I looked him up when I got home. He had a wife and a baby daughter.'

'And that's why we Templars foreswear taking wives and fathering children. Don't stress about it, Coop.' Goodman uttered a forced laugh. 'Or you might end up in here with me.'

'Is there anything that sticks out in your mind about our time in the compound? Maybe things you should remember but can't.'

Goodman went still again, possibly fighting another wave of drug-induced lethargy. He cleared his throat and said, 'It's true what they say: there really is no such thing as a free lunch. Every meal came with a lecture from Ismail on the glory of Islam and its achievements down through the centuries. Enough to give anyone indigestion.'

'No blackouts or lost time?'

Goodman's knuckles whitened as he clenched his fists. 'If there were any, I guess I forgot them.'

'You don't remember anything before you tried to kill Stanley?'

The attack was incredibly swift. One moment, Goodman was slumped in his chair; the next, he was flying towards Cooper. The impact threw him to the floor, and he felt Goodman's fingers wrap around his throat. He tried to prise his hands free, but Goodman had the strength of the possessed. His fingers tightened inexorably. As his vision grew dim, Cooper heard the door bang open and the orderly's shadow fell across him. Then the weight on his chest and the choking pressure about his throat was gone and he found himself gasping sweet air.

Steiner appeared, and Cooper heard the hiss of a needle-gun as the doctor administered a rapid-acting sedative. Goodman relaxed in Lauriston's grip. The orderly carried him over to the bed and laid him down gently. Cooper managed to regain his feet.

Steiner pointed an imperious finger at the door. 'Visiting time is over, Templar-Private Cooper.'
Cooper stood his ground until the orderly took up position at Steiner's right shoulder. He recalled how easily Lauriston had picked Goodman up and restrained him. He raised his hands and backed through the door.

CHAPTER 3

Almost a full day had passed since the broadcast, yet they had received no response from President Gerrard to their demands that he hand over control of the Religious States to Free America forces. No one had expected a bloodless coup, but the silence was unnerving, as was the apparent lack of military build-up along the border, or increased activity within the RSA. But the images on their spy satellites, confirmed by FA operatives on the ground, could not be denied. They were being ignored.

No one addressed it directly, but then they did not have to. It was there in the hooded eyes, clenched fists, and stiff lines of their bodies. Had uncertainty spread like a contagion, or was it endemic? Lynch neither knew nor cared; he craved only certainty. Corroborated facts were meat and drink to an investigative journalist and self-styled political junkie.

Lynch ran his finger along the inside of his collar and exhaled. The briefing room was full to capacity, with the air-scrubbers working overtime to cool and cleanse the air. His eyes flicked up to the cast squares of the ceiling. He felt claustrophobic at the thought of sitting beneath the tonnes of plascrete that formed and encased the Eagle's Nest, the secret underground command centre for the Free America movement. Its location in upstate New York was a closely guarded secret. His admittance was a sign he had entered the FA circle of trust. He needed to stay within it.

Lynch surveyed the room. Pulaski wore an expression he knew only too well; the strong leader feared her authority was being undermined. Her concern was reflected in the face of her top military advisor, Brigadier General Lou Drummond. At forty, he was too young to have fought in the original War of Separation. Lynch pegged him as a man desperate for renown, regardless of the cost. It made him dangerous. Overall, the mood was uncomfortably similar to that of the Templars prior to landing at Palmachim Beach. Only, this time, American blood would be spilt on both sides. He needed to try to cool things down.

'It's only been a day. We've planted the seed with our broadcast. We need to give it a little time to grow. Try to nurture it. I say we cross into Delaware from New Jersey and make for Wilmington. Show the people we come in peace, that our war is not with them. Try to convince them to join us, or at least not actively oppose us. That's the kind of shit you brought me on board for. Isn't it?'

'No.' Drummond shook his head. 'We've shown our hand. The RSA is seeking our bases. We need to take immediate action. Failure to do so could compromise the entire mission.'

Lynch turned to Pulaski. 'Is that what you think?'

The former US senator's smile was cold. 'I think I've been in politics far too long to fall for a play like that. Brigadier General Drummond has my full confidence in all military matters. He was instrumental in designing this base and structuring our forces.'

'I'm not denying it's impressive, but we're still outgunned, especially if the RSA starts withdrawing troops from the Middle East. Relying on military force alone might not get us across the line. And surely, that's what we're all here for at the end of the day: a reunited United States.'

'Says the journalist with no military experience,' Drummond bit back. 'You seem confused as to your role, Lynch, so I'll make it clear. You're to film what we say you're to film and keep the propaganda flowing. Leave the strategy to those who haven't pickled their brains with liquor and drugs.'

'Won't deny I've done my share of that, but I reckon I'm still thinking clearer than you on this one. Doesn't take a military genius to see it's a numbers game. I don't doubt our ability to capture the Capitol, but we'll never hold it if the people aren't behind us. The only hope of long-term success we have relies on winning over the friends and families of the troops. Persuading them to join us in deposing the government in Richmond.'

Drummond waved a dismissive hand. 'Now you're just repeating yourself. And you're forgetting Canada. Once the conflict has started, the Canadians will jump at the chance to join us. The RSA has been a thorn in their side for too long.'

'I wouldn't bet the farm on that. There's a world of difference between covertly arming and supplying us and openly violating their treaty of neutrality. I get there's a time constraint here, but we have a few days to play with. Our stealth technology is good, and the RSA has no means of identifying the source of our broadcast. It must have bounced through a dozen or more satellites. At least let me try to make use of that time while you prepare in the background.'

Pulaski deferred to Drummond. 'It's your call, Lou.'

Drummond fixed Lynch with a withering stare. 'Three days. Not a second longer. Because regardless of where you are, we'll be activating our sleeper agents and commencing the invasion. Once we bust that dam, nothing will hold back the tide of our forces.'

Three days was tight, but Drummond's expression told Lynch it was non-negotiable. 'Three days.'

'And Lynch, I don't what any of that loose cannon shit

of yours. Captain Jones is in charge of the mission. You follow his orders; no ifs or buts. Otherwise, he might just put a bullet in your ass. And I doubt there's many here who'd be sorry about that.'

Lynch walked along the line of JLTVs, at once familiar and different. The latest generation was fitted with infrared camouflage technology, with infrared cameras linked to thousands of hexagonal plates that could be heated or cooled to match the background temperature. The thermal cloaking system also contained a library of images, used to pass the JLTV off as a car, a truck, or other friendly. Travelling under cover of dark, it would shield them from spy satellites, aerial and long-range reconnaissance. The JLTV Mark IV also contained enhanced defensive capabilities, in the form of countermeasures and a turret-mounted heavy machine gun, making them perfect for a fast attack role.

Lynch patted the vehicle in much the same way as he would pet a powerful dog. Speaking of attack dogs, he turned at the approach of Captain Jones and took his measure of the man. He was in his late twenties with a gym physique, brown eyes and buzzcut. He stood just shy of six feet tall. He had Jock written all over him, which wasn't necessarily a criticism. But...

Jones stopped and stood legs akimbo with his fists planted on his hips. 'See you're admiring our ride. Latest gen, straight off the production line in Europa City. The Jesus freaks have nothing like this yet.'

'And whose largesse is responsible for that?'

'Say what?'

'Europa City isn't in the habit of donating lethal aid. Someone bought these, presumably without revealing they were destined to be deployed against Europa City's biggest arms customer.'

'Anonymous donor.'

'And that doesn't set off any alarm bells?'

'Nope.' Jones shrugged. 'Plenty of folks have reason enough to hate the RSA without wishing to show their hand. Vehicles have been fully vetted and given a clean bill of health, so ours is not to reason why.'

Lynch said nothing. He could think of several candidates who stood to gain from a third American civil war, starting with the Caliphate. Then there was the Greater Russian Collective. They might have assisted with the liberation of Israel, but old animosities and distrust ran deep, and they certainly wouldn't be opposed to taking advantage of the economic chaos that would result from war. As to the African Tech Corps, they would profit from supplying both sides. All of them had a vested interest in inciting war and keeping it going for as long as possible. And both sides appeared dumb enough to let them. Lynch found it hard to believe no one else had joined the dots, which made him think they were deliberately ignoring it for the sake of short-term gain.

'Are you listening?'

'What?' Lynch started at the sound of Jones's voice. 'Yeah. We leave at twenty hundred hours. Don't worry. I'll be ready.'

Jones's expression suggested he harboured doubts as to Lynch's state of readiness, but he contented himself with a curt nod before turning on his heel. Lynch watched his retreating back. He had a bad feeling about this. Then again, it was a long time since he could remember having a good feeling about anything. Whatever Pulaski said to the contrary, Free America was on a war footing. Unlike the conflicts he had reported on from the Middle East, this one would be fought on American soil, presenting a real and present danger to the civilian population.

Lynch took out his com-unit and swiped it open to reveal the image of his daughter, Christine. It was an old picture, taken before his divorce. She'd be twelve now, growing up fast. Comms were locked down, protected by layers of lethal Black ICE. Given time, he could probably circumnavigate it, but did he really want to antagonise his hosts? But what kind of father would he be if he didn't try to get some kind of warning to his ex-wife, so that she could protect their daughter from the coming storm?

CHAPTER 4

Deputy Director Hannah scanned through the message on his screen. He read it a second and then a third time, parsing it for some hidden code or meaning. Standard encryption. Low priority. Should he forward it to an analyst, or was he just being paranoid? He read the message again.

To: Grand Master Vanderbilt

From: Colonel James Willard

Subject: Templar-Private Billy Ray Cooper, Service number 26647155

TP Cooper has again expressed a desire to leave the Order and requested a follow-up. While some doubt remains as to his combat fitness following his incarceration by Marshal Ismail, Doctor Steiner has provided him with a clean bill of health. Accordingly, I have assigned him to selection training duties at Fort Irwin. Initial observation shows he is performing this task with all due diligence. As he represents a considerable investment in time and money, my recommendation is that you deny his request and for him to continue in the role of instructor. On completion of the latest round of selection, his fitness for front line duty can be reassessed with a view to redeployment

to the front.
   Yours fraternally,
   Colonel J. Willard

Hannah steepled his fingers. As a rule, he tried to avoid gut instinct. But it seemed as though events were playing into his hands. Cooper was staying in play to execute Steiner's modified conditioning and assassinate Vanderbilt, providing the neuro-link technology Steiner had implanted in his skull performed as expected. The doctor could present as many papers as he liked; the proof would be his ability to compel Cooper to kill the Grand Master in cold blood. Time was running out. Intelligence reports indicated that Vanderbilt was laying the ground for a military coup. His opening moves to unseat President Gerrard were sound enough, but Hannah reckoned himself the real master when it came to game play. And that brought him neatly to his next problem.

He pulled up the files on Gina Pulaski and the Free America movement. Although known to him, Hannah had previously dismissed FA as being largely irrelevant. Pulaski was a three-term senator who had never held any of the great offices of state; her resume reeked of mediocrity. Like others before her, she had risen to the top simply by surviving. The events she had lived through would have toughened her up, but talent, in Hannah's experience, couldn't be magicked out of thin air. Risk taking and creative thinking were not her strong suit, which meant someone else was pulling the strings in the background.

This time, Hannah did key up a request for an analyst. He typed methodically, ordering his thoughts as he went. The first rule remained: follow the money to find out who was equipping and arming the would-be revolutionaries. Next, gather as much satellite intel as possible. He and his peers had grown complacent, taking the agrarian-based states of the former republic at face value. They saw only what they expected to see, while they secretly built an army. Too damned busy worrying about the Caliphate to see what was happening on their doorstep. He wouldn't make that mistake again. This time, they really would bomb the revolutionaries back into the Stone Age, not leaving a single piece of critical national infrastructure standing. The international community could complain all they liked afterwards. The RSA had a right to defend itself.

Hannah read over the message, ensuring there was no ambiguity or room for misinterpretation. The Free America uprising couldn't have come at a worst time. With their lines of supply already stretched to breaking point in the Middle East, a determined counterattack by the Caliphate might well succeed in wresting back the newly liberated territories. Meanwhile, the spectre of Vanderbilt launching a military coup loomed over the home front. Quite the coincidence. Only, Hannah didn't believe in coincidence. He had run enough operations to recognise when somebody was trying to effect regime change. Their enemies were gathering, and he needed to eliminate them. It was his duty, but it was also his pleasure.

CHAPTER 5

Cooper ordered the men to form up in a circle, facing inwards. He walked along its circumference, the gym floorboards squeaking beneath his heels. The novitiates fought to remain calm as they waited for his selection. He went around again, knowing the anticipation would be worse than the pain. It was time. Finally, he reached out and tapped Porter on the shoulder. Porter's body stiffened briefly, but he quickly mastered himself and stepped into the centre of the circle, which closed around him.

Hicks was the first to throw a punch, hitting Porter on the jaw and snapping his head to the side. Porter rode it out as best he could and stood tall again. Young struck next, followed by Diego, whose blow dropped Porter to his knees. Porter climbed shakily to his feet and spat out a mouthful of blood. His right eye was already swelling shut. Thompson dealt the next blow. It looked weak to Cooper, either from sympathy or in the hope Porter would show similar leniency when his own turn in the milling ring came. Dwight, by contrast, put his bodyweight behind the punch Porter staggered into Hicks, who pushed him back towards the centre.

As Hollister prepared to strike, Cooper held up his hand, pausing the exercise. Porter was swaying side to side as if drunk. Cooper allowed him a few seconds to clear his head, then dropped his hand. Bone cracked and blood sprayed from Porter's nose. He held for a moment and then fell to his knees. Cooper counted to ten, but the young novitiate made no attempt to rise. But six was a decent score for a first-timer.

'Hicks. Dwight. Help your brother to his feet.'

The circle formed afresh with Porter as part of its perimeter. His pain was evident, but he showed no outward sign of distress. Templar material, sure enough, Cooper thought. More's the pity.

Hicks, having thrown the first punch, took his place in the centre. Fielding, as the only novitiate not to have struck a blow, took the first shot. Hicks' fingers curled into fists as he fought the urge to strike back. Cooper had pulled up his psych eval after the village exercise. Sure enough, Hicks was registered as borderline psychotic. If he could master his impulses, he would sail through selection. If not, he would be spending a lot of time in the box.

The mill ground on. Cooper noted another lame blow from Thompson. He would be lucky to survive the first week. But whatever hopes and dreams were crushed, Cooper knew it would be for the best. Dwight landed another haymaker and Hicks went down. He shook his head to clear it and pushed himself up from his hands and knees, his pain already mastered. That, of course, was the point of the exercise: to teach the men that the anticipation of pain was usually worse than the pain itself. It was a process of desensitisation; the agony of a broken nose or cheek could be shrugged off while they inflicted worse damage on the enemy.

Cooper ran his tongue along the inside of his top teeth. He had lost three of them during his own selection, which had subsequently been replaced by stem cell implants. The pain from a fractured nose and right orbital had faded to a distant memory; the damage had been invisibly repaired by regenerative nano-therapy.

The mill rotated back to Fielding, who caught Hicks with a brutal uppercut that snapped his teeth together. Hicks' knees buckled as he fought to say conscious. For a moment, it looked as though sheer will would carry him back to his feet. Then he slumped forward, blood dripping from his nose and mouth. Cooper let him have ten precious seconds before ordering Fielding and Thompson to help him up.

Fielding entered the ring without being asked. Diego caught him with a lightning-fast right cross. Cooper felt blood splatter across his cheek and neck. He ignored it. The pace would quicken now; they had gotten a taste for blood and those still to enter the ring were getting in their retaliation first.

Cooper followed the slope of the cargo net from the ground to a height of ten metres, where it connected with a set of parallel beams. The beams led to a rope swing, followed by a three-metre gap, where a short platform gave access to a Burma Bridge. The remainder of the aerial assault course disappeared into the shimmering, hot haze. The sky above was a bright, unbroken blue.

Cooper had slept badly. He'd had the dream about the bus again. Even now, under the mid-morning sun, he could feel the phantom recoil of his assault rifle as he and Mackinlay pumped round after round into the bus. Then, in the ensuing silence, the emergency exit popped open, and a child's arm flopped out. The bead of blood dropping to the ground from a stiffened finger remained frozen in his memory for eternity. It was visible still when he started awake with a scream, body drenched in sweat.

The guilt had faded for a time, but being back at Fort Irwin, instructing the next intake of Templars, had woken it with a vengeance. Cooper looked at the expectant faces and felt his anger rise. Why couldn't these mutts see he was no hero? They queued up, anxious to serve God and country, little knowing it was an empty pleasure. He would show them the error of their beliefs.

'All right! This is the infamous Golgotha – the aerial assault course that has broken over a hundred men. I will now demonstrate, and you will follow me at ten-second intervals.'

Cooper sprang forward, leapt onto the cargo net, and quickly climbed his way to the top. A backward glance showed Hicks midway up the net, with Diego following. He ran along the narrow beam, arms outstretched for balance, eyes focused on the rope at the far end. As he reached to grab the swing, he felt a vibration through the soles of his boots, indicating at least one man in pursuit. Hauling back on the rope, Cooper launched himself, letting go at the apogee of his swing to drop down to the platform below. This time, he spared neither thought nor glance for his pursuers as he made his way along the V-shaped rope bridge, angling his feet across the bottom rope while using his hands to propel himself along the two guide ropes. He heard a series of curses as someone misjudged the rope swing and swung back into those waiting their turn on the short platform.

Adrenaline coursed through Cooper, driving out his doubts and concerns. His lungs burned with the effort as he powered on. The next obstacle, a series of swinging steps, loomed ahead. With his right foot on the first step, he pushed off with his left. He quickly brought his foot forward to gain the next one, back and forth, until he reached the safety of another platform.

A scream, girlishly high, made Cooper turn in time to see Thompson plumet to the ground. He screamed again following the bone-jarring impact. Young, who had just stepped onto the Burma rope bridge, looked down at the stricken figure and then over to Cooper.

Cooper cupped his hands around his mouth to amplify his voice. 'Finish the course, Young. That goes for the rest of you. Last one earns a ten-klick punishment run.'

Cooper moved to the next obstacle. He pulled the end of the seesaw down and stepped on. The wood bowed under his weight. He thrust his hands out for balance as he approached the fulcrum and the plank started to lift. It balanced level for an instant as he reached the centre point and then thudded down. The impact jarred through him, but he kept his balance and stepped cleanly from the saw.

A narrow walkway stretched ahead of him; its surface was rounded, mossy, and treacherous. Cooper pushed himself off, relying on momentum to keep him moving as he churned up the moss. Ahead loomed the leap of faith: a five-metre gap with an angled cargo net beyond. In theory, the farther one jumped, the less distance one had to fall. But Cooper knew catching the rough rope was an art in itself. He also knew thought was the enemy.

Cooper launched himself. Warm air whistled past as he fell, arms stretched outwards. He brushed the netting with his fingertips for half a metre before catching hold. Pain tore through the muscles of his right arm as his body swung into the net. He ignored it and found purchase with his feet and left hand, which allowed him to shake out the abused limb. But there was no time to rest. Hicks was already approaching the leap and Cooper had no intention of being in the line of fire if he missed his jump. He descended the net quickly, angling off to the side, and was less than a metre from the ground when he felt Hicks hit the net.

Hicks had somehow turned around and struck the net with his back. He slid down, arms windmilling as he tried to arrest his descent. Cooper jumped clear as the novitiate finally caught a grip. He hung there perilously for a second. Then Diego crashed into the net and the impact jarred Hicks free. Cooper expected him to crash to the ground, but he somehow managed to thrust a foot through the net and twist the rope around it, swinging himself around to hang upside-down. Diego started his descent as Young hit the net, catching hold with both hands and lowering himself without a pause. Cooper nodded his approval.

Cooper walked back along the course, trusting the remaining novitiates to finish. Thompson's groans of pain grew louder as he neared the vertical beams. Sunlight glinted from the white of exposed bone as Cooper examined the fracture. Both his tibia and fibula had snapped, ripping open the flesh of the shin. Thompson's face was deathly pale, covered in a film of sweat. He stopped moaning as he surrendered to shock. Cooper opened his medical pouch and took out a fentanyl pen. He stabbed the injector into Thompson's thigh, then replaced the cap, aware of the audience gathering behind him.

'Dwight, Porter, take your brother to the medical centre. The rest of you, back to barracks. Clean up and get some chow.' Cooper held out his hand, catching Hollister in the chest. 'Not you. Last man – ten klicks. Remember?'

Hollister sagged, but he didn't argue. He took a moment to gather himself and then started towards the old runway. More prime Templar material.

Cooper pushed his steak away, barely touched. He rubbed his eyes as though it would somehow dispel the imprinted image of Thompson's crippled body. He should have felt guilty, responsible, or horrified. All he felt was empty. War used up his sympathy and ate away his empathy. Thompson should count himself lucky that he'd be going home with nothing worse than a limp. Caliphate would have chewed him up and spat him out.

He dug his fingers into the medium rare meat until blood oozed out. What the hell was wrong with him? That's the kind of shit he'd despised Tyler for. Was he just going to train the next round of sacrificial lambs, grateful it was no longer himself in the firing line? Maybe Goodman was the sane one and Cooper should be in the secure wing.

Cooper pulled out his com-unit and swiped through his contacts. He had put this off too long already, particularly after what had happened during the MILES training sim.

The bright and airy voice of Doctor Steiner's secretary asked how she could help.

'I'd like to book a consultation, please.'

CHAPTER 6

S canners picked up three drones inside of fifteen minutes as they crossed from New York to New Jersey. Last time, the drone came in low enough for them to detect the thrum of its engines. But the Adaptiv thermal camouflage must have held, for death did not rain from the sky. Lynch wiped his palm across his forehead, and it came away wet. Next to him, Jones sat passively, his eyes flicking across to the scanner and back. Fucker appeared to be enjoying himself.

'Christ, Lynch, you're hovering like a bad smell. Try to relax.'

'Can't help it if the possibility of being blown to smithereens makes me jumpy.'

'Yeah? Just remember this whole mission was your crazy idea.'

Lynch refused to bite. It was his idea. He didn't want Pulaski's nascent rebellion descending into a killfest. He'd seen enough death in Israel to last a lifetime. But getting himself killed in the process wasn't part of the plan.

Through the window, the night passed in a series of shadows. Somewhere staggered along the road were another seven JLTVs, all running in stealth mode. Enough to hopefully fight their way out if they ran into trouble. But Lynch had to believe it wouldn't come to that. He hoped he could appeal to the good citizens of Wilmington, Delaware and make them see the justice of their cause. The trouble with the oppressed was they often didn't know they were oppressed and didn't take kindly to being told so.

The low drone of engines sounded again. Lynch looked down at his fingers, digging into the dash, and forced himself to relax.

Mendoza swung nonchalantly from the ladder leading up to the gun turret. His jaws worked furiously as he masticated a piece of gum. Kid looked lucky to be eighteen. He should be indulging in heavy petting behind the bleachers, not mobilising for war. But if his time among the Templars had taught him anything, it was that nobody could convince these young men that peace was an option. They all saw themselves as heroes in waiting, right up until the moment the bullet hit them between the eyes.

Lynch turned away. Sometimes he depressed himself. He polarised his HUD as dark as it would go and stretched out his legs. It was going to be a long drive, so he might as well try to get a little shuteye. And there it was, that low thrum on the edge of his hearing. Goddamn drones were driving him crazy.

Lynch's joints popped as he stretched. He had a metallic taste in his mouth, and a dull throb behind his eyes heralded the onset of a tension headache. The clock on the dash read a little after four in the morning. With dawn fast approaching, Jones was prepping the JLTV to complete the last leg of the journey before the light came in. Lynch checked the nav comp. They would head west along the old Interstate 495, cross the Christina River, take the slip road onto Route 13, then hang a left and cross the river again as it looped back on itself. Then they'd park up on the riverfront next to Hoots Hollow and it would be showtime.

The powerful electric motor hummed to life as Jones put the JLTV in drive. Lynch looked for Mendoza, but his absence suggested he was already in position in the gun turret. Jones would no doubt refer to that as a precautionary measure. Just so long as the kid didn't get spooked and become trigger-happy.

They drove fast, zigzagging across the six lanes as they overtook the early morning traffic, relying on their lack of markings to pass as friendlies. No one would anticipate them operating this far inside the RSA. Accordingly, they had formed up into a convoy, an olive-green arrow of intent.

Lynch powered up his camera drones and ran through diagnostics. In truth, he was unlikely to have an audience for several hours, but he found it easier than sitting idle. He synched his implant. The drones rose slowly from the docking station on his belt and the camera feed went live, automatically transmitting in night-vision mode in response to the low light.

'Quit fuckling around with those things while we're moving.'

Lynch supressed a grumble. Jones was still an unknown quantity; he would be better off not testing him at present. The drones docked with a click. He resorted to staring out the window.

The sullen waters of the Christina passed below as they entered Wilmington. The interstate grew busier with freight trucks and couriers. Jones pressed down on the accelerator, closing the gap between them and the trailer of an eighteen-wheeler. The auto-drive AI responded by pulling off to the left. Lynch wasn't sure of the speed limit, but he was fairly certain they were exceeding it. The stealth part of the mission must be over.

Jones, seemingly reading his mind, said, 'Relax. The cops won't fuck with the military.'

Lynch looked in the rear-view and saw the rest of the convoy keeping pace. His stomach lurched as the JLTV took the curve of the slip road at speed, merging onto Route

13. Lynch's right leg started jiggling up and down and he clamped both hands on his thigh. A cigarette would calm him, but Jones had made it abundantly clear the JLTV was a no smoking zone. He patted down the pockets of his gillet instead and produced a hip flask.

'Pulaski said she doesn't want you getting toasted before going on air.'

Lynch responded by shaking the flask. It gave a desultory glug. 'Ain't no more than a sharpener here.' He put the flask to his lips and upended it. The bourbon formed a comforting ball of heat in his stomach. One that faded all too soon.

The river passed below again, slower this time, as Jones decelerated in preparation for the turn into the park. A pair of pink granite pillars rose before them, bearing a curved metal sign identifying the park as the Jerusalem Memorial Gardens. Jones slowed further as they progressed along a straight drive, which was lined on either side with rose bushes. Then there was the monument: a base formed of Caliphate dead surmounted by three twenty-foot-high bronze figures standing back-to-back, weapons raised. Lynch recognised the helmetless figure in the centre as Commander Maxwell Lewis, martyr of the Fall of Jerusalem. He had it on good authority from an eyewitness that Lewis had, in fact, been machine gunned to death while kneeling in prayer. Presumably, the sculptor hadn't found that a suitably heroic subject to immortalise.

They parked the JLTVs in a line on the south side of the monument, churning up the well-kept lawn. Mendoza appeared from the gun turret and erected a telescopic flagpole. He ran up the flag without ceremony, but something caught in Lynch's throat as its red, white and blue unfurled. The Stars and Stripes. Old Glory. Now there could be no doubt as to whose colours they were riding under.

Lynch climbed up onto the roof of the JLTV and activated the drones. He panned them out, covering the park, taking in the early morning joggers as they approached. The loudspeakers clicked on: 'This is Free America, broadcasting the revolution. Stay tuned for updates.' The message repeated at ten-second intervals.

Lynch checked the uplink. They were spliced into three of the local broadcast satellites, ready to replace the feed with their own. Behind him, Mendoza and his comrades nonchalantly manned the machine gun turrets. Lynch had wanted them out of sight, but Jones wouldn't wear it.

By now, a small crowd was gathering; the joggers and dog walkers were joined by the owner of a coffee concession. Several had com-units in their hands. Lynch panned out and saw a steady trickle of the curious approaching the park along the rose-lined avenue. He let them come and gather, ignoring their restive gestures and calls for explanation.

But it wasn't only the good citizens of Wilmington who would notice. Images were being posted to the socials, from where it would be a short step to government forces noticing and acting. The clock was ticking. He needed to get the show on the road.

Lynch cleared his throat, triggered the broadcast and confirmed the satellite feeds were under FA control. 'Citizens of Wilmington, I'm Jefferson Lynch. You may not know my face, but you might recognise my name or know my reputation.'

A couple of the crowd booed and there was a shout of, 'Traitor!'

Lynch waited for the hubbub to die down, then continued. 'Look around. We've ridden armed and unopposed into your town. We could lay waste to it, if that were our intention. But that's not why we've come today. Ours is a peaceful mission. We're here to offer the hand of friendship, to join that which was put asunder. To build back a better America with opportunity for all. Despite what Gerrard and his goons might say, war isn't inevitable. I truly believe that this can be a peaceful transition, for the benefit of all the American people.'

'Bullshit, man! You're a bunch of heathens in league with the Caliphate.'

'That's propaganda,' Lynch riposted, 'spread by the Gerrard administration to discredit us.'

The shouts grew louder, and a plastic water bottle bounced off the front of the JLTV. A hotdog and an apple followed as the crowd grew more restless.

'The problems facing you in your day-to-day life aren't anything to do with the Caliphate. Decades of slow growth, low wages, and employment insecurity are the result of trade wars, a failure to prepare for automation, and deliberate deindustrialisation. Successive governments have continuously underinvested in public services and critical infrastructure in order to fund their ideological wars in the Middle East. It's the oldest trick in the book – using fear of the other to stoke division and distract voters from domestic issues.'

'I'll live with that if it stops the Caliphate from destroying our country!'

'Goddamn it, aren't you listening? The Caliphate is not your enemy.'

'No, man,' the heckler cried out. 'You are! Let's show these guys how we deal with traitors and Muslim stooges in Wilmington!'

Another barrage of bottles and food struck the JLTV. Jones' voice buzzed angrily in Lynch's earpiece. 'Get your ass back inside, Lynch. They're about to kick off.'

'No. I can talk them round.'

'Trust me, these mooks are past listening. Gunners, fire a warning shot.'

Lynch screamed again, but his warning was lost in the rattle of .50 calibre rounds as the JLTV gunners fired over the heads of the crowd. Panic broke out instantly. Lynch saw a toddler and an old woman trampled underfoot in the rush to escape. He started forward to help them and then stopped as a determined knot rushed the JLTVs.

This time, there was no warning, only death. The bullets ripped through the unarmed civilians, exiting in a spray or arterial red. Lynch belatedly realised he was still broadcasting and killed the feed. He staggered back to the JLTV in a trance and allowed Jones to pull him inside. The other vehicles were already moving, speeding along the avenue.

'There was no need for that. No need at all!' Lynch snarled, balling his fists. 'You're just another murderous swine, like Gerrard and his ilk!'

Jones drew his pistol and pointed it at Lynch's head. 'Back the fuck up and sit down. I get this is a PR disaster – the opposite of what we set out to do. We can hold a post-mortem later, but right now we need to stay ahead of the retaliation.'

Rubber squealed in protest as the JLTV slewed onto the bridge. A pair of police cruisers pulled up at the far end, blocking the exit. The lead JLTV increased speed as the first shots rang out, bouncing harmlessly off the armour. Glass crunched and metal buckled as the JLTV shouldered the cruisers aside. Lynch caught sight of the mangled body of one of the officers as they shot past.

They reached the I-495 unopposed, travelling eastwards. But law enforcement and state troopers would be assembling roadblocks further along the interstate. And Lynch didn't doubt they'd come prepared with tank busters. Total fucking cluster.

Jones, who was surveying the satellite feeds, appeared to reach the same conclusion. A jolt ran through the vehicle as it bumped off the slip road, making for the forest.

'Thermal camouflage is useless until we block line of sight,' he explained needlessly.

To Lynch's relief, a logging path appeared as they drew near the forest. The three lead JLTVs disappeared into the sylvan gloom and then it was their own turn. Jones tapped the dash map display at the point where the path branched off. His finger slid along to a clearing and stopped.

'Won't we be just as visible from the air in a clearing?' Lynch asked.

'No flies on you. But we're not stopping in the clearing. There'll be enough thinning to let us get under the canopy. Far from perfect. But it should buy us time.'

'For what?'

'To engage our contingency plan for exfiltration. No offence, but I wasn't going to bet my life and the lives of my men on your oratory skills.'

Lynch flipped Jones the bird. He'd been crazy to think he could talk people round to a popular uprising. It might not have been his finger on the trigger, but he was no less responsible for the deaths. A brutal and bloody civil war was inevitable. All he could do now was spectate. No, that was bullshit. He had a duty to report the facts, and he would be damned before he allowed the likes of Pulaski or Drummond to stop him.

Jones refused to elaborate when Lynch pressed him as to the nature of the contingency. Whatever it was, it involved the captain sending out a series of encrypted commands while anxiously checking the time.

Lynch thought he was imagining it at first, but Jones' expression confirmed that he also heard the thrum of engines. They were out of time. The wheels threw up clumps of moss and twigs as Jones reversed back into the clearing and spun the JLTV around.

'Make yourself useful and get those eyes of yours in the sky.'

Lynch lowered the window and activated the drones. They flitted up from his belt and out, rising rapidly to clear the canopy of the surrounding forest. The names painted on their sides, Truth and Justice, now seemed like foul mockery. He synched the camera feeds to the JLTV console and scanned the sky. Three hunter-killer drones, flying in tight formation, were closing on their six. Chaff billowed upwards as the JLTVs launched countermeasures, followed by the blazing arcs of tracer fire. The lead drone banked away from it, turning round at an almost leisurely pace as it launched an air-to-ground missile. It streaked straight towards the lead vehicle, which momentarily appeared to rest on top of a fireball before fragmenting in a hail of shrapnel. Jones swore as he swerved past the burning chassis. Another missile streaked past and a second JLTV erupted in a ball of flame.

The first drone loomed up on the console display. Lynch saw the flare as it launched a missile. 'Incoming!'

Jones pushed the JLTV as fast as it would go. But its top speed was no match for a Hellfire missile.

CHAPTER 7

Rivera swiped a finger across her com-link. She had been surfing the feeds for ten minutes, unable to settle on any one article or feature. The initial relief she'd felt when she received the order recalling her stateside had soon given way to ennui. Training exercises were deadly dull, and bar hopping quickly paled. She dropped the com-unit on her lap and looked around the barracks. No sign of Austin or Chappelle; they were probably still in the mess hall. She really should eat something herself, or at least grab a coffee. But she felt nauseous, having slept badly. Truth be told, she hadn't had a decent night's rest since arriving stateside.

The klaxon burst to life, flashing red and emitting an intermittent tone: scramble! Rivera swung her legs off the cot and rummaged underneath for her boots. She pulled them on without lacing them and threw a shirt over her T-shirt. Her exhaustion was forgotten as she pushed open the door and sprinted across the quad to the adjacent building housing the UAS flight pod.

Chappelle spun round at her entrance and gave her the thumbs up and a wolfish smile. Rivera waved back and settled in front of her console, pulling on her headset and

HUD. She quickly ran through her own pre-flight checks, pausing only to acknowledge Austin's arrival. Her lips pursed as she watched the RQ-19 Reaper taxi along the runway, her two wingmen pulling into position behind. As hunter-killers went, it was a well-engineered machine, but compared to the F-27 Hellcat fighter she normally piloted, it was a donkey next to a thoroughbred. But that was all Langley Air Force Base, the nearest operational site to the target, had to offer.

Air Traffic Control gave her clearance to launch and she pulled back on the joystick. The Reaper accelerated along the runway and lifted into the clear blue sky. Rivera checked the position of her wingmen as she flew out over Chesapeake Bay. They were locked tight behind her at nine and three o'clock. Estimated time to acquiring target was two hours. She set the autopilot to destination and reviewed the mission briefing.

Rebel insurgents had launched an unprovoked attack on civilians in Wilmington and were now attempting to flee back to New Jersey. Their mission was to seek and destroy, discouraging any future incursions. Rivera pulled up satellite images on her console. She zoomed in on the convoy of vehicles. The JLTVs were unfamiliar to her; more heavily armoured and equipped with a machine gun turret. But even with these enhancements, they would be defenceless against the Reapers.

Satellites lost them in woodland east of the I-495. Whoever was in command was smart but not that smart. They had gone off-road to avoid being intercepted and taken cover in a forest. But they couldn't hole up indefinitely, and the logging roads would leave them perilously exposed, should they try to exit that way.

Rivera felt a stab of disappointment. This was her first action in weeks, and it was going to be a turkey shoot. She risked a glance around the pod. As expected, Chappelle and Austin were focused on their telemetry. Fair pilots, if a little too rote for her. It was a personal source of pride to her that in almost ten years, she had only lost one aircraft. Others could get complacent because they weren't physically risking their necks. Not her. She ran the footage again, studying each vehicle in turn, gaining an overall sense of their capabilities and driving style.

They were fifty klicks out when the rebels broke cover. They skidded across a large clearing, making, as she had anticipated, for one of the logging trails. She dipped the nose of the drone, descending rapidly in search of a missile lock. Clouds of chaff billowed from the JLTVs, and she jinked out of the way to target the lead vehicle. The Hellfire missile flew true, and the ensuing explosion mushroomed into the sky, black smoke roiling off the tongues of bright flame. Chappelle was also on target, and a second JLTV and its crew met a fiery end. Austin, keen not to miss out, swept in low. The risk proved to be his undoing. Tracer fire shredded the Reaper's port wing and it spiralled to the ground and exploded.

Rivera ignored the stream of cuss words in the flight pod as Austin tore off his headset and threw it aside. She banked slowly, coming in for another attack run. The missile went hot, homing unerringly towards its target, only to detonate in a cloud of chaff. At least one of her opponents knew how to deploy countermeasures correctly. Undeterred, she successfully targeted the next vehicle. Chappelle also hit with his next missile. The JLTV rose into the air on a ball of flame and flipped over, causing the following vehicle to crash into the trees with devastating force. Three targets left in the game.

'Three to two,' Chappelle called across the pod.

'Fuck you. Collateral doesn't count. We're even – for now.'

'Suit yourself, *chica.*'

Rivera pulled back on the joystick, looping the Reaper upwards as she prepared for a fresh attack. Her console went blank as the telemetry froze on her HUD.

'What the fuck?' Chappelle threw up his hands. 'Fuckers

must be jamming the flight-stack. We're blind.'

Rivera thumped the console. Unthinkable as it seemed, the rebels had succeeded in hacking their systems. She could find out how later. Protocol in such a situation was clear; they couldn't risk their technology falling into enemy hands. She armed the self-destruct sequence and, after looking over to Chappelle to synchronise, initiated it. The debrief summons arrived thirty seconds later. If the top brass expected answers, they were in for a disappointment.

Rivera picked up her tray and looked around the mess hall for an empty seat. She spotted Cooper sitting alone and her lips curved maliciously. She hadn't seen him since he rejected her advances in Jerusalem. She should have known she would run into him sooner or later with the Templars recalled from the Middle East.

She sat opposite, deliberately banging down her tray, causing Cooper's water to slop from the glass. 'Hey, Coop, how's it hanging?'

Cooper looked up and shrugged, then went back to staring at his com-unit. Rivera snorted. Indifference irked her.

'Hear you're something of a celebrity now. One of only two survivors of the raid that took out El Zayyoud. A hero of Jerusalem. Of Damascus. Not forgetting your star turn as a captive of the evil Marshall Ismail.'

Cooper placed his com-unit screen down on the table. 'What do you want, Evelyn?'

'Do I have to want something? Can't I just be interested in catching up with an old comrade? After all, we were close once.'

'Keep your voice down,' Cooper hissed.

'Oh puh-lease. You think anyone gives a damn about that? It was before your vows. And trust me, plenty have broken that particular oath afterwards. Celibacy ain't natural. But don't worry. I'm not pining over you. Or looking for a rematch. You made your feelings on that abundantly clear.' Rivera thought she saw a flash of disappointment and turned the screw a little more. 'Got no shortage of offers in that respect.'

Cooper pushed his half-eaten burger away. 'Glad we got that sorted out. Now, I have things to do.'

As he made to stand, Rivera reached out and grabbed his hand. 'Come on, won't you at least give me five minutes? I really do want to know what's happening with you.'

Cooper pulled his hand away. He looked furtively around, taking in the packed tables, before pushing himself to his feet. 'Fine. But not here.'

Rivera let him get halfway to the exit before following. The sport had better be worth it. Cooper was waiting for her outside. He kept his gaze ahead, refusing to make eye contact as he set off down the corridor. Rivera fell in step with him, her long legs matching his pace. She spotted the gymnasium door and gripped his upper arm to stop him, feeling the corded muscle through his shirt. She had forgotten how ripped the Templars were. Rumour had it they were augmented with nanotech.

Rivera kept a hold of Cooper's arm as she executed a half-turn and bumped the door open with her hip. The lights fluoresced to life in response to a PIR sensor. She steered him across the floor to the base of an indoor climbing wall. She pressed herself against him, feeling the heat of his body.

'Alone at last.'

The push had just enough force behind it to suggest a second one, should it prove necessary, would not be as gentle. Rivera stepped back and folded her arms across her chest.

'If you're not interested in hearing what I have to say, just get the hell out!' Cooper snarled.

'What happened to you, Coop? You used to be fun '

'War happened to me. And nothing good ever comes from that. Just pain, suffering and misery.'

'War happened to me too. You don't hear me bitching about it.'

'None of it bothers you? You don't care who you drop bombs on or shoot from the sky? Never wonder about the legitimacy of your targets?'

'Sorry to disappoint, but no, I don't. That kind of shit is above my paygrade. I receive my orders and carry them out. Nothing more. Nothing less. It's called serving your country. It's what good soldiers do.'

'Then I pity you.'

She knew she shouldn't push it, but Cooper's tone burned her. 'Fuck you, you prick. Whatever you want to think is right or wrong about what we've done in the Middle East, I did something good today. And you don't get to take that away from me. Those rebels your old buddy Lynch has taken up with, they attacked Wilmington – killed innocent women and children. I rained hellfire down on their asses. Made sure they'll think twice about attacking again. I did that to protect families. Don't you dare try and tell me you wouldn't do the same for yours.'

Cooper's knuckles whitened as he stepped closer. A murderous light shone in his eyes. 'Everything I've done in this dirty little war of ours has been for my family. Sitting safe in your little pod – you've no idea of the price I paid.'

Rivera felt a surge of relief when Cooper turned and walked away. If anyone had told her she'd be frightened by the boy she'd met during his selection, she'd have laughed in their face. But the anger and guilt she had just witnessed was a deadly combination. Cooper was close to the edge, and she prayed to God she was nowhere near him when he finally went over.

The gymnasium door banged shut, but she gave it a few seconds before moving. She didn't wish to even see Cooper in the corridor. Some games weren't worth the risk.

CHAPTER 8

V anderbilt had retreated to his library, as he often did when not wishing to be disturbed. The room was rarely graced by natural light, and it smelled of beeswax and old bindings, despite the carefully controlled climate. Much of the collection that occupied the three walls of floor-to-ceiling shelving had been assembled by his paternal grandfather and then added to by Vanderbilt's father. Although he had enjoyed the run of it in his youth, these days, Vanderbilt's recreational reading rarely strayed from the Bible.

A rare note of melancholy coloured his mood as he ran his eyes over the shelves. Many of the books were valuable first editions and other rarities, but old money rarely troubled itself over such vulgarities. Knowledge, on the other hand, was priceless. Here were the great treatises on philosophy, history, politics, and, of course, theology. If some were penned by godless heathens, who could say Satan was without wisdom? Was that not part of the allure? The devout and righteous had nothing to fear from such works. They could sift through them to find the useful whilst avoiding temptation.

The video call was cued up, but Vanderbilt hesitated He

did not doubt the end justified the means, but dealing with traitors left a taint on the soul that confession struggled to cleanse. He ran his fingers through his hair, iron-grey but still thick as he neared his sixtieth year. Perhaps he had earned a few minutes of indulgence.

He stood, crossed to the shelves behind his chair, and allowed his fingers to play across the spines. *The Republic, The Nicomachean Ethics, Politics, The Prince* – these works had taught him as many don'ts as dos. Moving on, he brushed past *The Art of War* to arrive at *On War*. Von Clausewitz was a strategist who had built on his failures to arrive at victory. Vanderbilt, having been called to appear before a Senate committee to account for a subordinate's failure, knew what humiliation felt like. Continuing round and up brought him to *Fear and Trembling*. Even Abraham, that great father of the Jewish faith, had known doubt. Ah, doubt. The treacherous splinter of the mind's eye. Always trying to work its way deeper and deeper.

He crossed back to his chair and deliberately slumped down, allowing its wings to cast shadows across his face. Morrison answered on the third ring. He looked jumpy, haggard, as any Secretary of Defense faced with the prospect of fighting a war on two fronts might.

'What have you got for me, Lee? How much of a threat does Pulaski's rebellion actually pose?'

'That remains to be seen. Politically, she's pure poison. Gerrard's approval ratings are plummeting and he's getting understandably jumpy with the midterms approaching. He wants Pulaski's nascent rebellion crushed fast, before he loses control of both houses.'

'Indeed. And how is his old friend, the Secretary of Defense, planning to achieve this?'

Morrison permitted himself a smug smile. 'I suggest we deploy your Templars to protect strategic targets. They still enjoy a certain cachet with the public. After we've crushed the rebellion, we'll have them in position to dispose of Gerrard.'

'You seem to be forgetting Gerrard is no fan of myself or the order.'

'True. But as the saying goes, beggars can't be choosers. Faced with having to withdraw our forces from the Middle East and losing all we've gained, or making use of Templar troops, Gerrard will choose what he believes to be the lesser evil.'

Vanderbilt steepled his fingers. He let the moment stretch, building the tension. A tic pulsed below Morrison's right eye. It was followed a short time later by the drumming of his fingers on the desk.

'I believe you're correct,' Vanderbilt said finally. 'Make the recommendation.'

Morrison exhaled loudly. He looked set to remonstrate but thought better of it. 'I take it your men are prepared for what comes next?'

'My men are not your concern. See to it that Gerrard approves their deployment, and all will be well.'

'Just remember our deal.'

'Don't worry,' said the Grand Master. 'I promise you'll receive all that you deserve.'

Vanderbilt stared thoughtfully at the com-unit's now blank screen. Morrison had always been weak and venal, but he was showing signs of unravelling at a far faster rate than anticipated. It would be better to move matters towards their conclusion as quickly as possible, before the secretary's nerve broke.

CHAPTER 9

L ynch swiped off his datapad and placed it on top of the ammunition box that he'd pressed into service as a bedside table. Canvas creaked as he swung his legs off the camp bed and planted them on the floor. At roughly two metres by two and a half, the room reminded him of a cell. Its off-white walls were scarred where shelving had been stripped out to convert it into sleeping quarters. Whether this was purely an act of altruism or a means of keeping him separate from the rank-and-file remained to be seen, but either way, the solitude suited him.

He stretched the cramp out of his muscles, buying another couple of seconds' grace before setting off for the briefing room. His nostrils twitched in response to the recycled air as he made his way down one of the numerous access corridors of the Eagle's Nest. As ever, there seemed to be no shortage of young men and women bustling back and forth about the base's never-ending business. Lynch had tried various greetings during the several weeks he had been there and never received more than a curt nod of acknowledgement. He got one now from the sandy-haired lieutenant posted outside the door of the briefing room as he turned the handle to admit him.

Lynch checked the time on his com-unit as he entered the room; the debrief had been scheduled to start five minutes ago. His hopes of slipping in unobserved were dashed when an aide caught his elbow and steered him to a vacant chair to the right of Captain Jones. He looked across the table and met Pulaski's frosty stare. His attempt at a smile turned into a rictus grin. Brigadier General Drummond, at the head of the table, looked equally grim. As well he might, given the optics of what the media was already referring to as the Wilmington Massacre.

'Fourteen civilian casualties, Captain Jones. Three of them were women and a further two children.' Pulaski fixed him with a withering stare. 'Didn't it occur to you to fire a warning shot?'

'We did. It caused a panic. But those who weren't trying to flee rushed us. I made a judgement call to protect the men under my command.' He shot a venomous glance at Lynch. 'I said it was stupid idea at the time, thinking we could incite a popular uprising. Fifteen of my men paid for it with their lives.'

Lynch bristled. 'If you'd had some goddamn patience, your men might still be alive. I could've talked them round if you'd given me half a chance.'

Drummond slammed his palm on the table. 'Enough! We can all sit here making excuses, trying to push the blame around, and it won't change a thing. The fact remains that after more than a decade of careful planning, we have potentially left ourselves fatally exposed. We need to strike decisively while we still have the advantage.'

'Define decisively,' Pulaski said.

'We need to attack the seat of the RS government in Richmond. Launch a drone strike of our own from the airfield in Pennsylvania.'

'You think it's worth revealing the airfield for this?'

'If not this, then what? All our assets will be at risk as soon as we make them operational. That's a problem we can't avoid. Sometimes you have to grasp the nettle.'

Lynch turned to Pulaski. 'Whoa, let's stop the bus here. You're talking about bombing the Capitol. That's potential collateral of more than a thousand admin and support staff. Just a couple of minutes ago, you were worrying about fourteen. Surely, you don't think anything good will come out of such an attack?'

'Oh, but I do.' Pulaski's smile was cold. 'It will be a declaration of war and intent, the symbolism of which should be obvious. You said it yourself: the RSA has the numbers and the tech, so we will be reliant on guerrilla tactics to degrade the enemy. Now, if you've finished trying to second-guess me, report to Comms HQ. Time you started earning your keep by writing propaganda. See if you can't win those hearts and minds that you keep banging on about.'

'No pressure, eh?'

Pulaski ignored his quip and Lynch excused himself with a brusque grunt. Wilmington rankled because he knew he was right; he could have turned it around if it wasn't for Jones and his trigger-happy twerps. Pulaski's willingness to go to full military escalation made him suspicious. The hawks were definitely in the ascendancy within Free America. It made him nervous.

Lynch turned right on leaving the briefing room, heading away from his living quarters to make good of Pulaski's command. He stopped in front of a battleship-grey security door, fumbled inside his shirt for his swipe card and badged himself in. His eye was immediately drawn to the central column and its surrounding display of holo-screens, stacked four high. Real-time footage from spy-sats flowed across the display, showing the current state of mobilisation within the RSA, with the telemetry of their own forces overlaid. An analyst spared Lynch a quick glance and then went back to crunching the data on his display.

Lynch sidled clockwise, hoping to attract the attention of another one of the techs. The holo-screens in this section were news feeds. The operative was bent over his console and Lynch ignored him as his gaze flitted toward the TV21 logo, his old station in Casablanca. He squinted myopically at the screen and took a step closer. He wasn't mistaken; the black-haired anchor was his former editor, Malik Berkani. None of the feeds had audio, but the tickertape along the bottom of the screen was unequivocal in its condemnation of the attack on Wilmington.

Lynch let out a curse and the man in the chair swivelled round to face him. He did a double take as Russell used his arms to help push himself to his feet. He opened his mouth and then closed it, not knowing what question to ask first.

Russell came to his aid. 'Got in last night. Took a commercial flight to Niagara Falls International. Canadian sympathisers smuggled me across the border.'

Lynch looked Russell up and down. He looked thinner, but his colour was better than the last time Lynch had seen him in Europa City, where they'd been forced to flee to after an RSA assassin had targeted Lynch in Casablanca. There was a stiffness to Russell's right side; the wound from the bullet he had taken during the exfiltration apparently still troubled him, but his grey eyes were clear and focused.

'Starting to feel a little objectified here, Lynch.'

'Sorry. It's good to see a friendly face.'

'You might not feel that way for long.' Russell swept his hand over the displays. 'Been asked to analyse your little trip to Wilmington. Total cluster.'

'Not of my making. Not all of it, anyway. Your man Jones is a bit too keen on the use of lethal force.'

'Eggs are going to get broken, Lynch. You better get used to it. Speaking of which.'

Russell pointed to an adjacent screen, which showed satellite imagery of an airfield. The camera zoomed in on a series of drones as they commenced their taxi along the runway. Scale was hard to judge, but they looked relatively small, with a wingspan of four or so metres set at the rear of a triangular body, along with the prop. As the first one took to the air, Lynch spotted the payload slung underneath.

He counted six in total.

'Latest gen of the Northrup Grumman Bat,' Russell explained. 'Carries a payload of a hundred pounds. Thermobaric in this case – fuel air explosive. It's equivalent to about a third of a ton of TNT.'

Lynch said nothing. The drones had levelled out at less than a hundred feet, flying below radar. They would be visible to satellite, as their own imagery proved, but the RSA would not be expecting an attack from the north across its own landmass. Not from the air, at least.

'Flight time's two and a half hours. Why don't we get a coffee and catch up?'

'Don't you want to monitor them?'

Russell shrugged. 'Birds are in the air. Either they reach target, or they don't. No point wasting time watching a screen.'

'Pulaski wanted me to make a start on some broadcast material.'

'Wouldn't go writing anything till you see the result of this.'

Death and destruction, Lynch thought. But to Russell, it was just scrambled eggs. He allowed Russell to lead him away. The same analyst that had observed his entrance now nodded to him – or, more likely, Russell. For better or worse, these were his new colleagues, and he had better get used to them.

Lynch realised he was pulling ahead of Russell and checked his stride until he caught up.

'Wound still troubling you?'

'Only when I move or breathe. But I'm only doing either of those thanks to you. Doctor reckons another couple of hours and the antibiotics wouldn't have made a difference.'

'Does that mean you're glad they didn't put a bullet in me when I arrived?'

'Way I hear it, it was a close thing.'

'Like I said, Jones is kinda keen with the shooting thing. Pulaski ain't much better, if I'm being honest.'

Russell caught a hold of Lynch's bicep and spun him round to face him. 'You can call them rebels. Or if you want to be even more romantic, freedom fighters. But make no mistake here, Lynch. What we're speaking about is regime change. That's always a bloody and unpleasant business. I thought you had the stomach for that. But if you don't, now's the time to leave.'

Lynch's gaze was unflinching as he pulled his arm free. 'I've got the stomach for plenty, so long as we keep the innocent out of it. Otherwise, we're just the RSA in a different uniform. Maybe that's something *you* ought to think about?'

'Given my line of work, it's far too late to be developing a conscience. But I'm serious – you need to think about what this story means to you. What you think it'll mean to the public. Might be the price is higher than you're willing to pay.'

The atmosphere in the comms room was tense as the drones closed in on their target. Defences had belatedly been scrambled, and a squad of National Guard soldiers was shooting ineffectually at the incoming threat. Drummond glanced at his watch and then back at the drones on the screen.

'Missile launch in five, four, three, two, one!'

The missiles, with their thermobaric payloads, sped away from the drones, homing in on the white stone of the Capitol Building. For now, this one looked very different from the domed ruin Lynch had visited in Washington, with its squat wings spreading on either side of a low, flag bedecked ziggurat.

Movement on the ground caught his eye a moment before the telltale ignition sparks from the ground-based rocket batteries. The defensive rockets arced upwards, glowing like flares, as they sped towards the incoming missiles. He counted four aerial explosions, leaving two missiles in play. Part of him wished they had all been intercepted; he knew once they struck, there could be no going back. Another part balked at the idea of attacking the heart of government. No matter how much he despised it, this was still the country he had been born and raised in. He could tell from their rapt expressions that Pulaski and Drummond felt different about the attack. For them, this was the culmination of years of planning and, in the case of the former, a long festering resentment.

Lynch swore under his breath as the first missile detonated at the edge of the east wing. Glass blew out along the length of the building, jagged shards of which glittered incongruously on the lawn in the late afternoon sun. A cheer went up as Drummond punched the air, heralding a chorus of affirmation from the Free America staffers.

The second missile overshot the Capitol Building. Lynch felt the bile rise up in his throat as it passed over the ornamental gardens and struck the residential buildings beyond. He watched the two- and three-storey homes collapse in on themselves in plumes of smoke and flames. A figure emerged, flames billowing from its clothes, and collapsed to the ground. Lynch wondered how many more innocents had died inside. From the cheers in the room, one would think they had won a major military victory.

'Payload was a little short there, don't you think?' Russell said.

'Missile defence system,' Drummond replied. 'Probably supplied by the Israelis, based on the old Iron Dome system they deployed against attacks by Hamas.'

'Shame our intel didn't warn us about it.'

'Only seventy-five per cent effective.' Drummond shrugged. 'I'd view that as within tolerance.'

'Yeah?' Lynch could hold his silence no longer. He jabbed his finger through the holo-screen, causing the ruined homes to ripple. 'Fifty per cent of which wasn't on target! Have we just killed twenty, thirty, or more civilians?'

'Again, within tolerance.'

Lynch resisted the urge to slug Drummond and turned to Pulaski. 'Is that your reading of it too? Wilmington was unfortunate – this begins to look like damned carelessness!'

'In which case, you better think about how you're going to spin it.' Pulaski smiled coldly. 'Or else, what are you good for?'

The former US senator's words seemed to follow Lynch as he swept from the room, unable to watch the unfolding carnage a second longer. Russell gave him a shrug as he passed by. It might be business as usual for the old Agency spook, but Lynch wasn't ready to cheer on the revolution. Not when it promised to be bloody and uncompromising. He pulled out his hip flask and unscrewed the cap. The liquor burned like acid as he swallowed it down.

CHAPTER 10

Hopkins swiped through the photo gallery, appraising each picture in turn. Smile too cold. Cleavage a little too prominent. Too dowdy. Too frivolous. Over-lit. Under-lit. Her finger paused. The angle didn't flatter her nose, but there was a confidence and resoluteness that couldn't be faked digitally. She made a note to have it touched up and used for her campaign brochure.

Virginia might be a true-blue Southern Democrat state, but there was a risk of voter pushback after the incumbent, Paul Rodgers, was forced to resign following allegations of child abuse. Rumours about his taste for young boys had circulated around the Senate for years, and it had been relatively simple for the private investigator she had hired to obtain photographic evidence. Deposing him in such a manner was a risk, but with Gerrard's backing and the death of Bishop Gibson, her most vocal critic, the electoral calculus appeared to be in her favour. Gibson's spectacular fall from grace involved embezzlement, a murdered sex worker, and a fatal overdose, all of which had Deputy Director Hannah's fingerprints all over it. And unlike Gerrard, Hopkins wouldn't make the mistake of thinking

Hannah served anyone but himself. If you were foolish enough to pick up a serpent, you couldn't complain when it bit you.

She pulled up the proposed campaign itinerary and looked through the stops. As a woman, her polling was higher among the Hispanic and Asian communities; elsewhere, gender bias was clearly evident. She made a note to visit several PTAs. Mothers should be her natural allies, but their values tended to be more conservative. She would hit Gerschwitz for more funding aimed at showing her commitment to spending on community projects. Best not squeeze him too hard, though, or he might opt to take the fallout over his extramarital affair.

The harsh trill of her ringtone cut through her thoughts. Hopkins checked the screen, saw it was Gerrard, and reluctantly accepted the call. The president's livid features filled the screen. She forced a smile.

'What can I do for you, Charles?'

'Don't "Charles" me. Have you seen this shit? They've posted another video.'

The screen cut away to the video. Hopkins recognised the grey-haired woman as Gina Pulaski, the leader of the Free America movement. She repeated her demand that Gerrard step down, warning of dire consequences if he failed to do so.

'I should have ignored you and moved on these fucks straight away. Bunch of harmless cranks, my ass!'

'Now hold on a minute.'

'Hold nothing,' Gerrard interrupted her, only to be interrupted himself by the deafening tone of an air raid siren. It took Hopkins a second to realise she was hearing it from both her com-unit and inside her office.

'What the hell's happening?'

'Those Free America bastards have launched a drone attack!' He called to someone off-screen. 'What's the status of our missile defences?'

Hopkins tuned him out as she heard the incoming whine

of an approaching missile. She wondered if being blown apart would hurt. Electricity was super-fast. Quick enough for signals to travel along nerves to her pain receptors as she was ripped apart. She screwed her eyes shut in response to a nearby explosion, then felt the building shake and heard the tinkle of breaking glass. The expected pain never came. Instead, there was only a ringing in her ears and a warm breeze through the shattered office window.

'Susanna, are you okay?'

Hopkins reached out a trembling hand for her com-unit. 'I think so. Just a little shaken. Blast blew out the windows. What else did they hit?'

'The residential area north of the gardens.' Gerrard's voice was tight. 'There'll be casualties: civilians and the east wing staffers. Goddamn it, how did we miss this? Intel said Pulaski was a nobody, lacking the courage and resources to make good on her rhetoric. If those drones are any indicator, we could be facing a war on two fronts. I want you, Lee and Gene in the Central Office ASAP. We need to reassure the public before panic sets in. And find a way to stop Vanderbilt capitalising on what he'll see as vulnerability. We need to prevent this from turning into a fucking disaster.'

Hopkins nodded and ended the call. Her campaign planning was going to have to wait. If Gerrard was right about the rebels, there was a real danger there might not be a Senate to get elected to.

A wave of nausea gripped her, and she grabbed for the wastebasket. Bile burned her throat as she retched into the basket. Her stomach continued to heave with painful, dry spasms long after it was empty.

Hopkins slumped back in her chair. She pressed the back of her hand to her forehead. It came away damp with perspiration. The buzzing in her ears was drowned out by the cacophony of approaching sirens as first responders raced towards the stricken Capitol Building. She dropped the basket and forced herself to her feet. Her legs felt weak as she gripped the desk for support. She needed to get out of the building.

The corridor was eerily quiet as she walked past the elevator, heading for the fire exit. She was only on the second floor, but the thought of being enclosed filled her with fresh panic. Pausing, she focused on breathing in and out through her nose. Gerrard could bitch all he liked. He wasn't the one a missile had almost dropped on top of.

She moved on, resisting the urge to run as the alarm continued to sound, telling herself there was no smoke or immediate signs of danger. Her heels clattered on the cast plascrete stairs as she descended; the knuckles of her right hand were white as she gripped the handrail. The lights were out on the ground floor, but a luminescent running figure and its attendant arrow pointed to the exit. She slammed the heel of her hand against the push bar and the door swung open.

Hopkins spun round and staggered backwards across the lawn. Her eyes were drawn to the right by the licking flames and curling smoke. Two fire trucks were already in attendance, their crews attaching hoses to a nearby hydrant. Twisted girders reached imploringly from the jumbled plascrete and shattered glass that, only minutes before, had been offices. She counted at least three bodies that, while still recognisably human, were definitely not alive. After almost two years of vidcasts from Israel and Syria, Hopkins thought that she was inured to such horror. But the crackling of the flames and the acrid stench of high explosive made it terrifyingly real. War was no longer some abstract act involving other people in foreign countries. War was happening in her own backyard. And people, good people, were dying.

CHAPTER 11

Cooper had always been close to his little sister. The pair possessed a deep emotional bond that made deceiving one another almost impossible. She could force as many smiles as she wanted and bubble pleasantries, but beneath the bonhomie, he sensed an undercurrent of fear. His fingers tightened on the com-unit. He knew it would eat away at him if he let it go without asking.

'Wanna tell me what's up?'

'Who says anything's up?'

'Someone who's known you all your life. I know when something's wrong. Is it my going back?'

Shania chewed her bottom lip. 'Yes. I mean, no. I just want you home. You've been through so much already. You never say anything, but I can see it in your eyes. I just have to trust you to look after yourself. It's Ma and Pa and the twins I'm worried about. You saw the news, right? The attack on Richmond. Twenty-seven dead. If these Free America rebels can bomb the Capitol, what's to stop them launching a full invasion? This is America – we ought to be safe in our homes.'

'It must be very frightening,' Cooper said, choosing his words carefully. 'But the attack on the Capitol was made for political reasons. Hate to say it, but we were caught with our pants down. There's no way another drone attack will get through. We got intel across the north and Canada.' Cooper lowered his voice. 'Look, I shouldn't be telling you this. But rumour has it that President Gerrard has asked the Templars to be deployed on American soil.'

'So, you'll be staying stateside?'

'It's starting to look that way. One thing I can promise is that I'll do all that I can to protect you. You guys are my world. You know that, right? It's all been for you.'

After a moment's hesitation, Shania nodded. Cooper could sense her doubt, but anything else he said would be just words. Truth was, he didn't know what the attacks by Free America meant for the RSA. Jefferson Lynch's appearance in the first vidcast had inspired hope at first, which was swiftly disabused by the attacks in Wilmington and Richmond. The Lynch he knew would never have condoned attacks on civilians, and Cooper refused to believe he could have changed that much since Jerusalem.

Cooper reluctantly moved on. 'Sorry, sis. Call time is limited. Could you put Ma or Pa on?'

'Don't you remember? They always go to Harps on a Sunday.' Seeing her brother's expression, she added, 'I know they'll be real sorry to have missed you.'

'Damn. I forgot. Why don't you put Dale and Wade on for a bit?'

Cooper heard a muffled shout as Shania called on their brothers. He heard running footsteps and a brief scuffle, then Wade's face filled the screen.

'Hey, Billy Ray. They keeping you busy at the fort?'

'Got me training the latest novitiates. Hard to believe I was ever that green. Guess I must have been, though.'

Wade let out an indignant shout as he was pushed aside, and Dale appeared on screen. While their features were almost indistinguishable to those who did not know them well, with the same broad forehead and green eyes, Dale now wore his brown hair shaved close to the scalp. It gave him a brutish look.

'They still got you wasting your time at Fort Irwin? You need to get yourself back over to Syria and kick some raghead butt.'

Cooper heard Shania gasp. He'd heard far worse in his time, but that wasn't the point. 'I don't know if you think that's funny or acceptable, but it's neither. Pa would tan your hide if he heard you using words like that.' Dale opened his mouth to protest, but Cooper shut him down. 'I'm talking. You're listening. The Caliphate are bad guys. Nobody is denying that. But there's plenty of Muslims who are ordinary people, not so different from you or me. You should always remember that.'

'That ain't what the vid says. Any patriot knows they're a threat to the American way of life. Same as these Free America traitors. Thought I could rely on my brother to give them what they deserve. I just hope the war isn't over before I'm old enough to apply for Templar selection.'

Cooper could tell it wasn't an argument he was going to win on a vid call. He asked Dale to put Shania back on and waited for the sound of running feet to mark the twins' departure. He hated the thought of these poisonous ideas getting a hold on his brother but was powerless to do anything about it. At least Wade appeared more level-headed.

'I wouldn't worry about him too much,' Shania reassured him. 'Probably something he heard in the schoolyard. You know what boys his age are like.'

Trouble was, he did. Fourteen was an age from which prejudices could be carried through puberty with disastrous results. But he didn't want to worry Shania.

'I'm just tired is all. Don't think I've quite recovered from what happened to me in Syria. Look, I'd best be getting on with things. But it was great talking to you, s.s.'

'You too. Take care and stay safe!'

Cooper heard the disappointment in Shania's voice as he killed the connection. There was so much he wanted to tell her, but he didn't know where to begin. And he didn't know if he could trust her not to tell his mother and father. The last thing he wanted was to worry them, because he was worried himself. Doctor Steiner might have given him a clean bill of mental health, but he knew something was wrong. The frequency and duration of his blackouts had increased over the last week. At times, it felt like he was living a double life, with someone else inhabiting his body. And he couldn't shake the suspicion that this other person was up to no good. Perhaps it was no more than the manifestation of a guilt complex, but he didn't want to take the risk.

He scrolled through his contacts to Doctor Steiner and hit dial. Time to make another appointment.

CHAPTER 12

*F*ree *America Interview Transcript #1: Jefferson Lynch in conversation via satellite with Robert Guthrie (Mass.) and Ford Sutherland (Kan).*

Jefferson Lynch: Thank you for agreeing to talk with me this evening. You're two young men on opposite sides of a divided nation. But by asking you to speak about your lives, I hope to show you – and my subscribers – that you have far more in common than you might think. Bob, perhaps you could go first and tell our viewers about yourself and your homelife?

Robert Guthrie: Sure thing. I'm twenty years old and an only child. I live just outside of Charlemont in Franklin County, Massachusetts with my parents. We have a four-hundred-acre farm, given mainly to crops. Soon as I was old enough to go to school, I was old enough to help on the farm in the evenings and at weekends. I was never going to go to college. Always knew once I got my diploma, I'd be working the farm full-time.

JL: That sounds like it's a hard life.

RG: Guess that depends on what you call hard. The hours are long, particularly in the summer at harvest time, but it's good, honest work. Ain't exactly a lot of money in it, but it keeps us fed, clothed and with a roof over our heads. Sure, my truck is fifteen years old, but there ain't a lot of places to go. That's just the reality of life and there ain't no point worrying about it, right?

JL: Thank you. Ford, why don't you tell us about yourself?

Ford Sutherland: Uh, sure. Let's see. I'm also twenty, and I live at home with my folks. Up until two years ago, my older sister lived with us as well. Then she got married. Home is Louisburg, which is in Miami County, Kanas. I graduated high school two years ago, for what it's worth. Corporate is about the only employer now and they want college graduates. Even if I'd wanted to, my family could never have sent me to college. My dad's been unemployed most of his life. Used to get some manual labour jobs back when I was little, but automation has put an end to that. Don't suppose me or my friends will ever work. Leastwise, not unless something changes. What welfare I don't hand over to my folks, I use to keep my car charged and have a few beers. What else are you going to do?

JL: Don't you have any hopes or ambitions?

FS: I got dreams like everybody else. But that's all they are. Maybe I'll meet a girl, but if she's interested in a loser like me, she's probably a loser too. The marriage grant is tempting, and there's plenty who have done it for the money. But I'd have to be pretty certain before I committed to spending the rest of my life with someone. 'Specially if we were to have kids. It's hard to see what kind of future they would have.

JL: How about you, Bob? What's the future got in store for you?

RG: [Long pause] I try not to think too far ahead. Everything's so uncertain. Guess one day my dad will retire and the farm will pass to me – if it's still viable. Gets hotter every year, and the price of irrigation goes up while the harvest sells for much the same. Dad has already re-mortgaged the farm. A year or two of drought and he'll be bankrupt.

Like Ford says, how can you think about marriage or children? Since the Great Flood and the secession, each generation has gotten poorer. Like most folks around me, I take everything a day at a time. Try not to feel too hopeless.

JL: I hear what you're saying. It's a grim life on either side of what used to be the USA. But that goes doubly so for the Religious States. Before you say anything, Ford, I want to give you some figures. The estimated costs of the campaigns in the Middle East to date total 17.3 trillion dollars. Now, a figure that large can seem pretty abstract, so to give it some context, I'll compare it with other government spending for the year 2088. For example, a total of 725 billion was spent on welfare. Health expenditure totalled 2.8 trillion. Federal, state and local governments provided 762 billion for public education. Incidentally, the current federal deficit is 2.5 trillion dollars.

RG: No offence, Mister Lynch, but what's that meant to mean for me? I don't pay taxes to the Religious States.

JL: You're absolutely right. But I want you and Ford to imagine what would happen if the money that was currently being spent fighting wars in the Middle East was instead to be invested in capital projects, re-industrialisation, education and adult training programmes. At present, the RS is a net importer of food, but in a re-unified America, with the additional farmland, it would be far closer to self-sufficient. I'm not saying this is some magic bullet that would fix everything overnight, but it could work. You just have to look at Roosevelt's New Deal to see that. Realistically, it would take several governments to see it through, but your children would finally have a shot at a future you're both currently being robbed of.

FS: But it's our Christian duty to fight the Muslims. If we don't, they'll destroy our way of life. It's a fight for our very survival.

JL: I get you hear that on the news and in church, but if you look long enough, chances are you'll find something in the Bible to support any point of view. Let me see. How about this: 'Get rid of all bitterness,

*rage and anger, brawling and slander, along with every form of malice.
Be kind and compassionate to one another, forgiving each other, just as
in Christ God forgave you.' That's from Ephesians 4. I'm not one for
religion, but even to me, that seems like the sort of message a good
Christian should practice.*

*The fact of the matter is that the American people have been duped
and Islam scapegoated. Don't get me wrong – I certainly don't agree
with the Caliphate, but experience has shown me that we have to find
a way of co-existing peacefully, or both our cultures will perish.
Innocents on both sides are hurting. It's estimated that 749,000 people
have died as a direct result of this war. And that doesn't include deaths
caused by disease, loss of access to food and water, infrastructure, or
other indirect consequences of war. Fighting and killing people because
you don't understand their culture or point of view seems a mighty poor
thing to me. At the end of the day, I hope you and Bob can see that
you're not so different. Two ordinary Joes trying to live their lives the
best they can. Violence is never right – Free America got it wrong in
Wilmington and Richmond. If we want to stop the violence escalating,
ordinary people from both sides are going to have to come together and
discuss what is best for the national interest. That's democracy in a
nutshell.*

*RG: As my father would say, you're a man of high ideals. But ideals
don't get the harvest in or put food on the table. Seems to me Free
America is going to bring war at a time when most folks are already
struggling. Also seems to me that both sides are much the same with
their promises of jam tomorrow, whether it's in this life or the next.*

*FS: Got to agree with Bob on that, Mr Lynch. This Free America of
yours is the one that has the beef. Up till now, folks have pretty much
rubbed along together without too much friction for almost forty years.
Yeah, we got a lot in common. But I daresay that also goes for Europa
City or the Greater Russian Collective.*

Transcript Ends

Lynch paused the video and leaned back in his chair. The interview had not gone entirely to plan. It was salvageable if he cut the ending, but that wasn't the point. Those kids, hicks or not, had got him dead to rights. Free America was the clear aggressor to date – largely because of his arrogance. Pride had made him insist on going to Wilmington, and while he suspected Drummond had always intended to attack Richmond, he had provided the perfect excuse. Then again, had he ever truly believed there could be such a thing as a bloodless revolution? Gerrard wasn't about to quit and Pulaski was obsessed with winning the war she lost forty years previously. He had to somehow try to prevent them from leaving the continent littered with corpses.

Lynch sparked up a cigarette and exhaled in the direction of the extractor fan, which whirred above his head. Allies were thin on the ground, with Russell the only real contender. While the ex-spook might owe Lynch his life, he had been in the business of regime change for the best part of a quarter-century. The only difference was he had finally decided to apply his skills domestically.

He took a long pull at his hip flask, held the bourbon in his mouth, then let it trickle down his throat. Maybe he was looking at this the wrong way. Lynch had come here in search of a story, and if there was one thing that he knew, it was how to find one. Dig deep for the facts, document the corroborating evidence, and get all who were willing to go on the record. He would present the truth of Free America not just to the Religious States but to its own backers as well, and the world would make up its mind. Publish and be damned!

CHAPTER 13

Hannah was a man of average height and build. His features were unremarkable, which had served the former spy well when he wished to go unobserved. But now he had perfected an arctic coldness in his eyes and a disdainful curl of his lip. The deputy director had arrived unannounced at Steiner's office and dismissed his two o'clock appointment. They might have been in the doctor's office, on his home turf, but there was no doubt as to who the master was. Steiner licked his dry lips.

'You would like an update on the patient?'

Hannah said nothing, compelling the doctor to fill the silence.

'Data from the neuro-link shows some resistance on the subject's part, but when asserted, control is absolute. The resultant blackouts are causing the subject concern, but I have convinced him they are a result of PTSD, which I continue to *treat* with regular sessions.'

'Yes,' Hannah finally spoke. 'I've read the transcripts. But will he perform as required? I could easily find some mutt to pull a trigger. For maximum effect, this has to be personal. The public needs to see Cooper with blood on his hands. There must be no doubt or confusion as to who struck the fatal blow.'

'On balance of probability, yes.' Steiner paused, but professionalism overcame self-preservation. 'Nothing, however, is a hundred per cent certain.'

'That, my good doctor, is the wrong answer. I strongly advise you to find certainty. Failure to do so, need I remind you, will not bode well for you personally or professionally.'

Hannah stood and smoothed the creases from his suit. He subjected Steiner to a final baleful stare. 'I'll see myself out.'

Cooper examined himself in the mirror. The sharp crease of his trousers was perfectly centred along the length of his legs, the toecaps of his boots were buffed to a high sheen, and his navy tunic was cinched at the waist with a white belt. It was the first time he had worn his dress uniform since completing selection and taking his vows as a Templar. He had forgotten how much the stiff collar chaffed his throat and the scratchy feel of the trousers. But today they were being visited by a VIP: Grand Master Thaddeus Vanderbilt himself.

He turned his head left and right, angling it slightly to examine it better. His hair had grown back during his six weeks' R&R, but that morning, he'd had it cut high and tight. The back and sides were shaved to the scalp. He pulled on his kid gloves, interlacing his fingers to ensure they fitted right down to the knuckles, and retrieved his peaked cap from the bed. A Templar good and true.

Cooper checked his watch. They were to assemble outside the chapel in fifteen minutes, forming an honour guard. Vanderbilt would then proceed to the chapel, where, after a short blessing, he would address the men. It was a poorly kept secret that they were to deploy as rapid response units in the event of any further incursions by Free America. The attack on the Capitol had clearly rattled President Gerrard.

Cooper raised his hand and rubbed behind his right ear in response to the now familiar nagging ache. He kept meaning to ask Doctor Steiner about it, but somehow, the topic always slipped his mind during their sessions. A falling sensation in his stomach reminded him of the moment when a car hit a bump or crested a hill too fast and briefly parted company with the road. The feeling passed and he lowered his hand, staring at it in surprise. He let his hand drop to his side and walked around to the metal locker at the foot of his bed. The hinges creaked as he pulled back the lid. He sifted through the camouflage clothing until his hand wrapped around the MTP MOLLE sheath. The Velcro rasped as he undid the fastening strap and unsheathed the fighting knife. Light glinted from the polished blade, which was double-edged and wasp-waisted. He sheathed the knife and slid it into the small of his back, settled his tunic over the top, and checked his reflection for any telltale bulges.

Cooper took one last look at himself in the mirror, flicked some imaginary lint from the breast of his tunic, did an about-face, and marched to the door of the dorm. He angled his head slightly, shielding his eyes from the sun with the peak of his cap. The blacktop was lined with smartly dressed figures; the novitiates were differentiated from their sworn-in brethren by their white tunics. Navy tunics were few and far between, but Jackson's dark skin and squat figure would still have been unmistakeable. Cooper made a beeline towards him. The sergeant nodded curtly, indicating that today was all about the ceremony.

Jackson ordered the men to form up in two lines on either side of the road, with himself and Cooper nearest the chapel's west door. Cooper fixed his eyes on a point six inches above Jackson's head as the procession approached. Vanderbilt walked at its head, carrying a cross; the baucent, the Templar battle flag, hung from its arm. At fifty-six, his body remained corded with muscle and his back ramrod-straight, the product of an ascetic life of fasting and exercise.

His adjutant, Lachlan, followed him, holding a large, leather-bound bible held to his chest. It was that book on which Cooper had taken his vows on completing his selection.

The adjutant was followed by a huge bear of a man, standing an easy six-foot-six. His arms were bent at ninety degrees and his hands gripped the ornate scabbard of a sword. While the role of sword bearer was ceremonial, the sword was anything but; its wielder was ready to defend the Grand Master with his life. Chaplain-Commander Du Pont brought up the rear of the procession, carrying a silver chalice. He wore an embroidered chasuble over his alb, as he was to officiate at the service.

With the procession inside the chapel, Jackson dismissed the honour guard. The pair at the end of the line turned to face the chapel and started to march towards it, with each subsequent pair falling in behind as they passed. As the last pair filed past, Cooper and Jackson turned in behind them. Each took hold of one of the heavy wooden doors and pulled it closed. There being no pews, they knelt behind their brethren on the stone floor.

Du Pont had already taken up his position at the lectern, flanked by the chapel's two great pillars. Vanderbilt knelt on the dais behind with Colonel Willard to his right. Both men bowed their heads as Du Pont commenced the opening prayer. Cooper, feeling the cold metal of the dagger's hilt pressing against the small of his back, scanned the kneeling audience and located the sword bearer in the front row with Lachlan beside him. Cooper breathed in and lowered his head. Patience.

The chaplain-commander finished the prayer and moved aside as Vanderbilt stepped up to the lectern. His knuckles bulged as he gripped either side of its flimsy wooden top. Cooper half expected it to snap like matchwood, but Vanderbilt's voice was calm and authoritative when he spoke.

'Brothers, we are gathered here at an unprecedented moment in history. Our long campaign in the Middle East has borne fruit, first with the liberation of Israel and then with our advances in Jordan and Syria. And yet, at a time when we have never been closer to achieving our goal of destroying the Islamic Caliphate, we have been forced to withdraw from our holy mission. But make no mistake about it – the enemy we face on our own soil is every bit as godless. These so-called Free Americans, these old republicans, are atheists, apostates and idolators. As such, it is our sworn duty to smite them with His holy wrath and protect the foundations of this great Christian nation of ours.

'Effective immediately, all Templars are to be placed on operational alert with rotating duty squads ready to deploy at immediate notice. Colonel Willard will hand out your assignments at a briefing following this service. I know you will be every bit as unflinching and assiduous in fulfilling this duty as you have been in our war against the Caliphate. God willing, we will defeat our foes swiftly and return to our true mission: the complete destruction of the Caliphate.'

Vanderbilt stepped back from the lectern and allowed Du Pont to resume his place. The chaplain-commander waited for him to kneel before addressing the congregation.

'Thank you, Grand Master, for reminding the brethren of their holy duty. Many of our brothers have made the ultimate sacrifice defending Christianity from the Islamist threat.' Du Pont turned and pointed to the wall below the rose window. There, three bronze plaques bore the names of those Templars who had been killed on active duty. A fourth plaque had been added at the end, its surface concealed by a black cloth. 'Today, we honour those who have made the ultimate sacrifice during the Fourth Crusade.'

Willard and Vanderbilt rose and walked over to the plaque. They reached out to take their respective drawstrings and pulled, revealing the names of the fallen. Cooper ran through the roll of honour in his head: Arturo Garcia; Kai Schreiber, the crazy padre who had blown himself up in a suicide bomb attack; Dwight Mackinlay, the closest thing he'd had to a friend in the Order; Jan Pedersen; and Rafael Martinez.

One name was conspicuous by its absence: Willard's predecessor, Colonel Martin Tyler. Officially, Tyler had committed suicide after Jefferson Lynch had broadcast evidence of him ordering the destruction of a refugee column to cover up an accidental attack on one of the busses by Cooper and Mackinlay. But Cooper knew it was Sergeant Jackson who had fired the fatal shot when Tyler looked set to shoot Cooper, who was in turn protecting Lynch. Cooper didn't flatter himself that Jackson had acted for his benefit. He had long suspected the real cause of the assassination was rooted in internal politics.

Du Pont commenced a prayer for the fallen, but Cooper's attention remained fixed upon Vanderbilt. Like in a dream, he felt himself falling, but instead of jolting to wakefulness, Cooper found himself occupying a space outside his body. He heard a voice in his head, one he could not be certain was his own. The Grand Master was the cause of all those names on the wall, exhorting his sworn brothers to lay down their lives in the name of Jesus Christ. Here he was inciting fresh division and violence on American soil, after which they would be expected to return to the Middle East and finish what they had begun. Vanderbilt was the alpha and omega, the head of the snake. What was one more death on Cooper's conscience, particularly if it saved thousands of lives? He should draw his knife and strike him down.

The prayer concluded, Du Pont uttered a final blessing and then the men were dismissed. Cooper started as Jackson tapped him on the shoulder. The sergeant pointed to the chapel door, reminding Cooper of his duty. They pulled open the doors and took up their respective stations outside. The men left in pairs as they had entered. The sword bearer and Lachlan led the exodus; the former now carried the baucent in addition to his blade. They strode purposely towards a waiting hopper, its engines already cycling.

Lachlan boarded. The sword bearer handed him the battle flag and then the bible, then took up his post to the left of the cabin door.

Cooper counted the others out; some made for the barracks while others cut diagonally towards the mess hall. Now only Vanderbilt, Willard and Du Pont remained in the chapel. They stood in a tight knot in front of the lectern, heads bent conspiratorially, apparently in no rush to exit.

Jackson broke the silence. 'I hear you've been seeing Doctor Steiner. Anything I should know?'

'With all due respect, it's not your concern.'

'No? Have you forgotten your vows so quickly? You have a duty to your brothers to be sound in body and soul. Not to jeopardise them by being unfit. We could be back in combat at any moment. I need to know I can rely on you.'

Cooper counselled himself to be calm, to avoid jeopardising the mission. He took a couple of steps back from the sergeant and smiled. 'I get that you have a duty to the men, but I won't let you down. I've worked hard with Doctor Steiner – cleared my head – and I'm ready to do my duty. At home or abroad.'

Vanderbilt broke off his conversation with an admonishing wag of his finger in Du Pont's direction. Willard fell into step with him as they left the chaplain-commander to tidy the chapel. Cooper felt a surge of adrenaline as they approached. His position left him too little room for manoeuvre and Jackson was an added complication. Vanderbilt acknowledged their service with a nod that also served as a dismissal. Cooper let them get twenty metres in front before starting after them.

'Hey,' Jackson said. 'Where are you going?'

'There's something I need to ask the colonel. Why don't you get me a cup of coffee and I'll see you in the mess? We'll talk things through. Hopefully put your mind at ease.'

Jackson hesitated, but he had no reason to detain Cooper. 'Sure.'

Vanderbilt was at the hopper door. Willard stood beside

him in the downdraft, holding his cap on with one hand. That distraction was good. Cooper slipped his hand under his tunic and released the strap from the hilt of the knife.

CHAPTER 14

C ooper pulled down the chin strap on his cap as he approached the hopper. Willard's eyes narrowed as he saw him. He possibly suspected Cooper of trying to circumnavigate the chain of command by asking Vanderbilt directly about his request to leave the Order. The voice in his head told him to ignore Willard unless he intervened. Focus on the primary target. Complete the mission at all costs.

Vanderbilt stepped back from the hopper, moving away from the downdraft. He looked Cooper up and down. 'Templar-Private Cooper, isn't it? You fought under Colonel Tyler in Jerusalem.'

Images flashed through Cooper's mind at the mention of Tyler. He saw the colonel striding through the chaos of the landing on Palmachim Beach – first boots on the ground at the start of the new crusade. The resignation in his eyes when he was forced to hand Commander al-Hashimi to a mob of freed political prisoners in Jerusalem to prevent a riot. His implacable fury as he ordered Cooper to step aside to allow him to shoot Lynch. And the final look of betrayal as Jackson forced his own pistol to his head and pulled the trigger.

'Is there something I can do for you, son?'

Vanderbilt's voice jolted Cooper back to the present. He saw the Grand Master with Willard standing at his shoulder, the waiting hopper ready for dust off. The treacherous dagger hilt pressed against his spine. The ground seemed to fall away from him, and for a moment he thought he would fall, but he locked his knees and forced himself back to attention. Another wave of panic washed over him as he encountered vacant space where his memory should be. Last thing he remembered was getting dressed for the remembrance service at the chapel. After that was nothing but static.

'The Grand Master asked you a question,' Willard barked.

Cooper stumbled over his words as he tried to formulate a reply. 'Er … just wanted to … um … yeah, to thank you for the rousing speech, sir. Tell you that I'm ready to take the fight to the rebels.'

'As are all the men under my command.'

'Of course, sir.'

'If there's nothing else…'

Cooper shook his head, desperate to end the interview and escape to safety. Vanderbilt nodded to Willard and turned on his heel. Cooper didn't need to turn around to know the colonel's eyes were boring into the back of his skull. He felt a curious sense of relief as he watched Vanderbilt board the hopper. The side fuselage door slid shut and the engines cycled up to full lift, scattering dust and grit.

'Something troubling you, Templar-Private Cooper?'

'Yes – I mean, no, sir. Reckon I'm a little tired, is all.'

'Then I suggest you get some food and an early night.'

Willard's tone made it clear his words were not a suggestion, so Cooper confirmed he would do just that. He fought to keep both panic and fear in check as he walked away. The unyielding metal of the dagger against his back was a constant reminder that everything was far from all right. Was it possible that Steiner had missed something? Cooper thought it unlikely, which made him wonder if the doctor had a vested interest in Vanderbilt's elimination. But Steiner had never struck him as a brave man, which meant the order had to have originated elsewhere. Perhaps with the president himself?

The thought stopped Cooper in his tracks. If the conspiracy actually existed outside of his head, and it went that high, he would be powerless to prevent it. A second, more pernicious thought followed: did he want to stop it? He had taken a solemn oath binding him to the Order and his sworn brothers, but after everything he had seen, first in the Middle East and now at home, he had to ask himself what kind of God could endorse suffering on such a large scale. Perhaps the Templars' time had come. Only then he had to wonder as to his own fate.

He moved off, determined not to display further flaky behaviour. Jackson was waiting for him in the mess. Maybe he should come clean to him? But what proof did he have? Steiner had already recorded his blackouts and lost time, ascribing them to PTSD. He would only confirm Jackson's suspicion that he was unfit for duty. They would find him a padded cell next to Goodman in the secure wing, and he would never get home to his family. That wasn't an option.

Cooper took a deep breath and centred himself. Fifteen minutes spent acting normal over a hot cup of Joe. He could do that. Where he went from there was the big question — which he did not yet have an answer to.

CHAPTER 15

The footage was hi-res but shaky, unable to compensate for the rapid movements of the soldier wearing the camera on his helmet. It panned rapidly from side to side, catching the men flanking him. Lynch zoomed in and paused, picking up the red cross pattée on their uniforms. Templars. He hit play again and the camera panned round to pick up a line of five kneeling youths. Their olive complexions and dark hair pointed towards Arab ethnicity. It was impossible to say with absolute certainty, but none of them looked older than thirteen. The white adobe building in the background was common to Lebanon, Syria, or Jordan. But the precise location was irrelevant next to what was about to unfold.

The soldier drew his sidearm and pointed it at one of the kneeling children. His arm moved back and forth, taking aim at each one in quick succession. The video had no audio, but Lynch could almost hear the bastard counting eeny, meeny, miny, moe. He imagined the sobbing, the cries for mercy that must have accompanied the tears he saw running down the boys' faces. The roving pistol finally stopped, aimed once more at its original target. The camera pulled in until the boy's face filled the screen. A fuzzy down was now visible on his cheeks. A neat hole appeared in the centre of his forehead and his head snapped back out of shot, leaving behind a trail of crimson. The boy to his left tried to get to his feet and was shot in the chest. His companion at the start of the line managed to turn and run. He made it less than dozen strides before a bullet caught him in the back of the head. The remaining two sat meekly awaiting their execution.

Lynch had seen enough. He hit pause, straightened his back, and stretched out his arms. Eagle's Nest had been on lockdown since the attack on Richmond and he had been tasked with compiling a list of Templar war crimes to present the RSA as a rogue state in an attempt to justify Pulaski's invasion. While it took little effort to source such clips, he doubted it would serve Pulaski's cause in the way she wanted.

The CEOs of the Europa City manufactories and the African Tech Corps didn't care what happened to little Abu, Kaled, or Faisal as long as their share price remained high. The RSA had been operating on a war economy almost since its inception and the corporations were strongly motivated to ensure it continued to do so. Highlighting abuses of RSA citizens might prove more effective. Unconscious bias tended to ensure people were more sympathetic to those they perceived as sharing physical and social traits with. But to do so, he would have to focus on the gender divide between its citizens, at which point they would simply point to the Caliphate and say their female citizens were free by comparison.

Lynch scrubbed his face with his hands, feeling the rasp of stubble. The real problem wasn't a lack of compassion or empathy, but that his heart wasn't in the work. He'd witnessed Templar war crimes first-hand and broadcast them to the world. This wasn't news, and it sure as hell wasn't the story he'd come here for. He had a nose for a story, and right now it was telling him there was something rotten in the state of Free America. For every briefing he was invited to, three more were held behind closed doors. That, in Lynch's opinion, equated to a lot of secrets for an organisation with nothing to hide.

Then there was Doctor Bendix and his mysterious trials. Bendix knew how to keep a secret. Fortunately for Lynch, the doctor's lab assistant, Ramesh, wasn't so careful. An evening's drinking had seen him offer up a name, Project Phoenix, and confirmation that it involved some form of nanotech. Anything they were shielding that closely was neither legal nor safe. But before he could snoop around, he needed to get Pulaski off his back by completing the task at hand.

Lynch leaned back in his chair and clasped his hands behind his head. As a goddamned certified journalistic genius, knocking out a few lines of copy should be easy. Time to go back to basics: the golden rule of marketing was making them ask *What's in it for me?* He had tried and largely failed in his earlier interview to show that a reunited America focused on regeneration would usher in a new age of prosperity. The trouble was that the vast majority of its inhabitants were economically illiterate. Contrary to popular belief, the country's finances could not be equated to a credit card. A debt-GDP ratio greater than one hundred per cent, while undesirable, was not necessarily the herald of a financial apocalypse. Those committed to a low-tax small state were quick to decry increases in public spending as unfairly burdening future generations with paying off the debt. But many would accept it as a burden worth bearing as long as there was a concomitant rise in living standards.

Lynch swiped open the keyboard on his workstation and typed: "WIIFM? A better life for me and my children.' All he needed now was some easily grasped allegory to illustrate it and then he could concentrate on what really mattered.

Lynch had received an impromptu summons to the briefing room. Instinct told him it boded ill. His unease intensified at finding Pulaski, Brigadier General Drummond and Russell already assembled by the speaker's podium. Pulaski's expression was inscrutable as Lynch pulled the door closed behind himself. He wondered if the former New York senator was already regretting giving him a seat at the table. Tough. He was here for the duration.

He found himself a place among the waiting staffers and strategists, next to a slightly overweight woman with mousy hair. Lynch tried to remember her name. Dani? Danielle? She worked as a data analyst, tracking RS troop movements and calculating their likely response times. Lynch had tuned out within thirty seconds of being introduced to her when she had started talking about metrics. But he was under no illusion as to her perceived value to the revolution compared with his own.

Drummond came to the centre of the floor. He stood ramrod-straight, staring out at the assembled staffers until he was certain their attention was focused solely on him. A holo-display fizzed to life, detailing assets and targets as he commenced the briefing.

'We are currently proceeding with the activation of sleeper units in what will be a series of coordinated asymmetrical attacks across multiple states, including cyber-attacks, aimed at critical national infrastructure. Shipping convoys will be targeted simultaneously to prevent vital materials from landing at RS ports. By disrupting energy, transport and food supplies, RS forces will be tied up dealing with the ensuing civil chaos, opening them up to our main military assault. Landing will be accomplished via air assaults from suborbital attack craft, where the populace will already be close to breaking point as a result of the loss of food, energy and fuel.'

Lynch shook his head. 'I've seen those tactics played out across the Middle East. I can tell you that we won't win the peace if RS civilians – Americans just like us, in case you've forgotten – are left harbouring grudges.'

'It was a failure to take tough action against the zealots

forty years ago that led to the breakup of America,' Pulaski said. 'The will to power was lacking then, but it won't be this time. Sometimes, in order to build anew, you have to tear everything down.'

Faced with Pulaski's implacability, Lynch appealed to Russell. 'C'mon, Hank. You of all people ought to know this kind of shit never ends well.'

'Difference is the goat herders and camel jockeys never had democracy. Not like America. But if it makes you feel any better, civilians won't be targeted directly. We're not barbarians. The key to this strategy is leverage. Their loyalty to Gerrard will fail pretty quick once the shelves are bare and the lights are out.'

'And then what? Our troops hand out chocolate, chewing gum and nylons in the midst of a ticker-tape parade? All hail America's brave liberators!'

'Enough with the shit,' snapped Drummond. 'If you've nothing better to offer than sarcasm, I suggest you get back to making your little videos and leave the strategy to the thinkers. We've a war to win, and your negativity isn't contributing.'

Lynch shook his head. A lifetime on the edge had left him ill equipped for being the adult in the room. And yet here he was, apparently the sole voice of reason. He'd laugh if it wasn't so fucked up. Jefferson Lynch, resurrector of the American dream. And all of it in the name of the people. He flicked his eyes Heavenward. While he wasn't totally opposed to prayer, he was a firm believer in rowing away from the rocks.

CHAPTER 16

Steiner shifted nervously in his chair and tapped on his desk light, no doubt hoping to deflect his unwelcome visitor's attention. Hannah, unfazed, narrowed his eyes to slits.

'Why is Vanderbilt still alive?'

'It's very difficult to override a subject's morality, especially when trying to overwrite previous programming. I said as much during our last meeting. Nothing can be guaranteed with absolute certainty.'

'The Templars are supposed to be stone killers. Assassination shouldn't be much of a stretch for one.'

Steiner risked a smile. 'Cooper is something of an aberration. He was able to pass the selection process without developing the usual zealotry. And he's genuinely traumatised by his combat experiences.'

'I'm not interested in excuses.' Hannah placed his palms flat on the Steiner's desk and pushed himself to his feet. 'And I have no time for failure. I warned you of the consequences.'

'Please.' Steiner caught himself stretching out a supplicating hand and snatched it back. 'I just need a little more time. Cooper can't hold out against the programming for much longer.'

'Time is a luxury neither of us has. Goodbye.'

Steiner's protests fell on deaf ears as Hannah swept from the room. He also had no time for loose ends, of which the good doctor had most certainly become one.

Albright was standing in the waiting room outside, dressed in white SOC coveralls and blue plastic overshoes. It was after hours, but he had drawn the blinds anyway. He looked at Hannah for confirmation.

'Do it.'

Albright snapped on a pair of nitrile gloves and proceeded towards Steiner's office. Hannah took out his com-unit and checked his messages. Steiner had been doomed as soon as he had agreed to alter the programming Cooper had undergone while held captive by Marshal Ismail. His original target had been President Gerrard, but Steiner used an implanted neuro-link to direct him at Grand Master Vanderbilt instead. Cooper's resilience was a setback but nothing he couldn't overcome. There was more than one way to skin a cat.

Albright emerged from Steiner's consulting room, disassembling a needle-gun. The phial inside had contained potassium chloride, inducing cardiac arrest. Albright nodded to confirm the job was done and started to strip off his coveralls.

Hannah tapped his lips with the edge of his com-unit. While the optics of a mentally unstable vet killing Vanderbilt were better, he could no longer afford the luxury of waiting.

'I want the Grand Master taken care of in similar fashion. Top priority.'

Albright nodded again. There was something altogether dead about the man, but he could be relied on to get results. With nothing more to be said, Hannah turned on his heel and left. He was late for his next appointment, and much as he'd like to delegate, there were some matters he couldn't trust to others. None more so than leaving the running of the country to its elected officials.

CHAPTER 17

It was two o'clock in the morning and tiredness crept in as the night shift started to drag. Parker stifled a yawn and looked around the network management centre control room. There was only one other control engineer on duty; the other workstations were empty. Tre tapped the face of his watch and Parker shook his head. He would go another hour before taking his break. He had worked for the Electric Reliability Council of Texas for a little over five years, and even with the alternating two-week blocks of day and night shifts, it was the best job he'd ever had. The nights did drag, though. At least during the day, he was kept busy with switching as the electricity grid was reconfigured in response to changing demand and planned outages. Sometimes the monotony almost made him wish for a fault.

Parker tapped the centre screen of the bank of monitors that lined his desk and a graphical display of the electricity transmission network appeared. He used his fingers to zoom in, navigating down to the detail page of Hamilton substation. The power readings showed it was currently exporting electricity. He checked the event logs. The last activity was a little after ten pm, when the transformers tapped down in response to the reduced energy demand as people turned in for the night. He yawned openly this time. Shift end couldn't come fast enough.

'Fuck. No, no, no!'

Parker looked across the control room and saw Tre frantically tapping at his screen. Then his own screen filled up with alarms. Swiping back to the Hamilton overview, he watched the feeder circuit breakers open spontaneously. The power readings dropped to zero.

'Shit, this can't be happening. Come on, damn it!'

Parker's finger stabbed repeatedly at the screen as he tried to open a control window and select a breaker to reclose it. He was locked out. He zoomed out and watched helplessly as another substation went black. Malware cascaded through the system. Generation was being islanded. Soon the entire power grid would collapse. The lights went out and then flickered back to life as the backup generator kicked in.

Tre pushed back his chair and stood with his hands raised helplessly. 'What the fuck are we going to do?'

'We're not going to panic. Okay?'

Parker hoped he sounded more confident than he felt. This was a major cyber-security breach. How they had got through the firewalls and past the intrusion detection software was a question for another day. He took a deep breath. They had been trained for such an eventuality and drilled relentlessly on it. Time to follow the black start protocol. He picked up the desk phone; there was no dial tone. He tried the next desk along and motioned Tre to do the same. Nothing. He tried an internal call to the customer service centre and found it dead as well. Most likely a Denial-of-Service attack on the telephone exchange. A cyber-attack this sophisticated had to be the work of a hostile state. How much worse could it get? In answer to his question, the monitor displays around the control room went blank.

He grabbed the lanyard with his ID card from the desk and hurried across the room. Tre caught up with him as he swiped open the door to the server room. The hairs rose on his arms in response to the chilled air inside. His eyes flitted between the main and backup racks, taking in the red warning lights. Not good. Not good at all.

'Tre, check the backup servers.'

Parker opened the door of the main comms rack, pulled out a sliding shelf, and folded open the monitor to reveal a keyboard. He ran his finger across the touch pad, but the screen remained obstinately blank.

'Wiped. They must have run a kill disk program.'

Tre shook his head; the backup was gone as well. The whole system would have to be rebuilt from scratch In the meantime, most of the state was off supply. There was only so long hospitals and com-unit masts could run off emergency generators and battery supplies. They would just have to do this the old-fashioned way.

Parker went back to his desk and pulled out the file with the hard copy of the black start procedure. The sequence generation would need to be restored to safely re-energise the power grid. His com-unit at least showed full signal. Finally, a break. He thumbed through a hardcopy of the on-call rota and looked up the appropriate region for the first site.

'Okay, let's start calling the standby engineers. They're going to have to go round the sites and manually bang the breakers back in.'

Patrick Donaghy finished lacing his work boots and stood up. His wife rolled over to his side of the bed and said something indistinguishable in her sleep. Sharon had taken a couple of Ambien before turning in and had barely stirred when his com-unit went off. He wondered if he should leave a note. She knew he was on standby, and the blackout ought to be a clue, but from what the control engineer had told him he would be out most of the day. He bent down and kissed Sharon on the forehead. The sooner he got started, the quicker people would be back on supply.

The headlights of his truck lit up the drive as he turned over the engine. He reversed onto the main road and spun the front around, splashing light across the darkness. It was a total blackout; there were no house lights, no streetlights, and no stoplights. He started to pick up speed. The substation was on the outskirts of town, near the western shore of Lake Wichita. About ten minutes away at his present speed.

The threat of a bad actor compromising the power grid had receded somewhat following the Great Flood, with Russia and China's capability every bit as crippled as their own. Despite the decades of conflict, no hard evidence had emerged to suggest the Caliphate possessed the skills and knowledge to pose a serious threat. But the darkened streets and houses that surrounded Donaghy as he drove through the suburbs appeared to disprove that assumption.

He heard the *whoop-whoop* of the siren and saw the flash of blue lights in his rear-view mirror. Donaghy cussed quietly and pulled the truck into the side of the road. He turned off the engine and lowered his window as the officer approached, right hand on his hip above his gun. Donaghy placed his hands on the steering wheel where they could be seen. He squinted and turned his head as the cop shone his flashlight into the cab.

'Is there a problem, Officer?'

'You tell me. It's two forty-five in the morning, we're in the middle of a blackout, and you're doing fifty-five in a thirty zone.'

'I work for ERCOT. I'm on a call out to Wichita Falls substation to see if I can do something about this blackout. Over ninety per cent of the state is off supply. With the roads being empty, I guess I got a little carried away there. Sorry.'

'Okay, let's see some ID. Nice and slow.'

Donaghy took his right hand off the steering wheel and held it up before reaching into his jacket pocket. He took out his wallet and flipped it open to display his driver's license. The cop took it off him and looked at him and then the photo. He spoke into the radio clipped to his lapel, and Donaghy caught his name and address. There was a squelch of static and whatever reply came back in his earpiece appeared to satisfy his interrogator.

'Do you have your ERCOT ID?'

Donaghy fished out the lanyard from inside his coat and angled it toward the beam of the flashlight. He got a nod of acceptance and let the pass fall back against his chest.

'Any other time, I'd write you a ticket. But I reckon we've both got better things to do tonight.' He held up an admonishing finger. 'But stick to the speed limit. Understood?'

'Absolutely, Officer. And thank you.'

'You want to thank me? Get the lights back on. Only a matter of time before every gangbanger and crazy realises that all the alarm systems are dead as well. That's when the looting will start.'

Donaghy started the truck, put it in drive, and eased his foot down on the accelerator. He kept it at twenty-five miles per hour all the way down the street. Perhaps the cop had genuinely done him a solid, or maybe he'd radioed a colleague further down the road to see if he could catch him again and throw the book at him. If so, he was in for a disappointment. The state of Texas could sit in the dark for an extra five minutes.

The truck's headlights picked out the ERCOT branding on another truck parked outside the substation gates. The driver's door swung open, and a lanky figure stepped down, Hi-Viz vest fluorescing in the light. The figure waved before turning around and retrieving his hard hat from the cab. Donaghy turned his own truck to focus its high beams on the substation gates, then grabbed his hard hat.

He checked the sensor on the gates in case the electric fence was somehow still armed, then fished in his trouser pocket for his keys. He recognised the other engineer as

Andrew Fleming, a member of the SCADA team.

'Hey, Andy. Guess no one told you there isn't a control room for your kit to talk back to?'

'Making sure the RTUs and the comms haven't been compromised for when they get the Disaster Backup online. This is a proper cluster, right?'

Donaghy shrugged as he unlocked the padlock on the gate and slid back the retaining bar. He pushed open the gate and swung it back. Fleming did the same with the other side.

'On you go, Pat. I'll get the gates behind us.'

Donaghy gave Fleming the thumbs up and climbed back into his truck. He drove slowly along the access road and parked in front of the control building. The switchyard was protected by a second fence, the gate of which he unlocked and closed behind him. He unclipped his flashlight and ran the beam down a tower and onto the cable sealing ends, then back up to the busbars. Satisfied, he followed the circuit through, checking the earth switches were open, the isolators were closed, and that no one had tampered with the earthing mat. It took him twenty minutes to inspect the rest of the circuits, confirming the plant position and its condition.

Fleming was waiting for him in the control building, sitting in front of the HMI, a local version of the network management centre that allowed control of the substation plant and equipment. Donaghy could see from the overview page that all the site circuit breakers were open.

'You want to scoot over and let me in, Andy?'

'Afraid I can't do that.'

'Say what?'

Fleming swivelled the chair around, allowing Donaghy to see the squat pistol in his hand. 'Nothing personal, but I can't let you re-energise the site.' He raised the gun. 'I don't want to shoot you, but I will if I have to. Make no mistake about that.'

'Why? Why the hell would you do this? You some sort

of Caliphate sympathiser?'

Fleming snorted. 'Give me some credit, will ya? I'm doing this because I believe in a better America. It's time to end the division that has blighted our country for so long. Time for a re-united America to take its place on the world stage again.'

'Those whack jobs from the East?' Donaghy shook his head. 'Guess you really have been drinking the Kool-Aid.'

'That's enough of the mouth. Sit your ass on the seat opposite and keep your hands where I can see them.

'And then what?'

'Then we wait.'

Laura Byers checked the readout on the screen. Brain activity was negligeable, as it had been for the past five days, ever since Mark Daniels ran a stoplight in his car and came off worse in a collision with a freight truck. The beep of the heart monitor formed a counterpoint to the hum of the ventilator. His tearful mother had already given permission for life support to be turned off; they were simply waiting to see if there were matches for any of his organs. Laura hoped so. At least then some good would come out of this tragedy. Sometimes eighteen years was a lifetime.

She moved on. Presently, only one other bed was occupied in the intensive care unit. Pamela Downey, thirty-two, suffered from forty per cent full-thickness burns following a house fire. Her insurance didn't cover nano-therapy, so here she was, taking her chances with skin grafts and infection, body shrouded in a sterile tent.

Byers moved a little closer to check the readings on the heart monitor. The ward – and the rest of Mercy Heights General – was running on emergency lighting. The backup generator was devoted to life support and the surgeon-bots in the operating theatre. Five years ago, the low lighting wouldn't have made a difference, but now she struggled to read some of the displays. Hard to believe she would be fifty in a little over three years' time. Then again, sometimes she found it had to believe she was a mother to three teenage children. She hoped the power would be back on before they woke up. If not, Jack would know what to do. Her husband was nothing if not a practical man.

She wiped her forehead with the back of her hand and plucked at the front of her scrubs. Air-con was another system deemed non-essential. She checked her watch and decided she could fit in a break. Wasn't like either of her charges was going anywhere.

The nurses' station was at the end of the corridor, positioned to provide a view of the adjacent ward. Byers stopped at the water cooler, filled a cup, drank it, then refilled it. She carried it over to the desk and eased herself into chair in front of the workstation. Five minutes, then she would log in and check the weekly replenishment order.

The rumble sounded like thunder, but thunder didn't make buildings shake. Byers pushed her keyboard to the side. Water slopped out of her plastic cup, ran to the edge of the desk, and then dripped to the floor. She tore a couple sheets from the blue roll next to the monitor and mopped up the water. As she was dropping the soggy paper into the wastebasket, she noticed the power indication on the workstation was dead. She tapped the keyboard, and the monitor remained dark. She tried the desk fan and discovered it to be dead as well. The backup generator must have failed, cutting all essential services within the hospital.

Byers pushed back her chair and leapt to her feet. She tried to ignore the cold knot of dread in her stomach as she ran towards the ICU, but the silence told her all she needed to know. No beeps, pings, or whirring hums. The silence of the grave.

She positioned herself at the side of Mark Daniels's bed and willed him to breathe on his own in defiance of her medical knowledge and experience. The hoped-for miracle was not forthcoming. She checked her watch and noted the time of death. Across from her, Pamela Downey moaned in her sleep in the absence of the automated delivery of sedatives and painkillers. At least they could be delivered manually. In the meantime, she needed to find out what had happened to the power.

The elevators were out, so she used the fire escape. The rubber soles of her trainers squeaked against the p ascrete stairs as she descended three storeys to the ground floor. She pushed open the door to a scene of chaos. Broken glass and overturned chairs littered the floor of the A&E waiting room.

She spotted Chad from hospital security sitting in one of the few upright chairs. His cap was missing, and his uniform was covered in dust. He pressed a wodge of tissues against his temple while staring at the com-unit in his other hand.

Byers' training took over. 'Mind if I have a look at that, Chad?'

The security guard pulled the tissue away revealing a laceration running from his hairline to the top of his ear. His thumb continued to scroll through the newsfeed on his com-unit.

'What happened?'

'Generator blew up. Think it was sabotage.'

Byers' fingers froze at the edge of the wound. 'What the actual fuck?'

Chad angled the com-unit's screen towards her. 'It's all over the news. Most of the country is blacked out. Not just power. Gas, water, hydrogen plants – it's all been attacked. People are blocking the police and emergency services. Goddamn terrorists on American soil.'

'The Caliphate?'

'No, these Free America nutjobs. Says it's the precursor to an invasion. Reckon a thousand innocent souls have been taken already.'

Byers thought of Mark Daniels. 'Make that a thousand and one.'

CHAPTER 18

Cooper fastened the chin strap on his helmet, then sprinted towards the SB Defiant XV attack helicopter. Jackson and Adler were already onboard; the latter was running through checks on the port side swivel mounted M60 machine gun. The main rotors spun up as he reached the copter and clambered inside. Jackson looked up from where he was monitoring coms and gave him the thumbs up. Cooper clipped on his lanyard and commenced his own pre-checks on the starboard M60. The copter lifted into the air to form the rear point of a four-aircraft diamond formation.

'Locked and loaded,' Adler's voice crackled in Cooper's earpiece.

He checked his throat mic and confirmed his own status. Five minutes from receiving the order to scramble to being airborne and ready for combat. That ought to please even Willard.

Cyber-attacks on critical national infrastructure had taken place state-wide in conjunction with physical acts of sabotage by Free America fifth columnists. With members of the police and National Guard turning on their own colleagues, it was clear that this was an attack that had been long in the planning. And equally clear was that the security services had dropped the ball, which the Templars were now expected to recover.

Willard's voice sounded over the comms as he confirmed their target was a substation on the outskirts of Palm Springs. Rebels had blockaded the gate, preventing access by the utility engineers sent to restore power. They were to clear the barrier. Jackson acknowledged receipt of the order and their Defiant peeled away from the formation. Remaining flight time was forty minutes.

Cooper seated himself back in the cabin and ran through his weapons' checks. His tactical knife was slung upside down from his left shoulder, its spring-loaded sheath activated by pressure. He pulled the SIG Sauer M19 from the holster on his hip and racked back the slide to chamber a round. His final piece of kit was an M8 carbine, fitted with an under barrel M203A4 40mm grenade launcher and an Aimpoint Pro Red Dot sight. He extracted the magazine, checked the rounds were correctly loaded, and clicked it back in place. ETA thirty-seven minutes.

The copter banked to the West, following the powerlines as they stretched between the pylons. Dawn was still an hour away. Cooper viewed the landscape through the ghostly green of his night-vision goggles, taking in the deserted freeway and darkened houses. The world really had been turned off at the flick of a switch.

They were following the road now, the powerlines running parallel as they approached the target zone. Beams of light pierced the darkness, shinning out from headlights of a pickup truck and an ancient station wagon, which were parked side-by-side to barricade the substation gates. A second truck belonging to the utility company was parked a hundred metres along the access road. A crewman leaned against the open driver's door. A blueish flame sparked briefly to life, then was replaced by the glowing red tip of a cigarette.

Jackson toggled on the speaker and picked up the

microphone. 'This is Sergeant Jackson of the First Templar Division's Combat Aviation Brigade. You are illegally blocking access to critical national infrastructure. You have thirty seconds to move your vehicles to a safe distance, or we are authorised to use lethal force.'

A muzzle flash preceded the rattle of bullets off the copter's fuselage. Cooper swung the M60 round and returned fire, aiming for the figure now highlighted on the bed of the pickup truck. The silhouetted man threw his arms up and fell backwards. Adler raked the truck from the opposite side as the Defiant banked away, shattering glass, bursting tyres and putting out the off-side headlight. A bullet whistled past Cooper's arm as someone returned fire from the station wagon. Cooper's retaliating burst went wide and then they were out of range.

'Time for a round of hellfire, Sarge?' Adler asked.

Jack pointed to a bulky shape next to the fence line on the Defiant's tactical display. 'That's the main tank of one of the substation transformers. Contains over three thousand litres of oil. So we won't be launching any missiles. Going to finish our turn, rappel to the ground, make sure the utility work crew keeps out of the way, then clear out this traitorous scum.'

Cooper unclipped his lanyard and fastened one end of a rope in its place, then threw the other end out of the copter. He stepped into his rappelling harness and buckled it about his waist, clipping the descender around the rope. Jackson gave him the thumbs up, and Cooper turned about and stepped backwards from the copter. He felt the friction of the rope through his gloves as he descended, dropping in two metre stages to the ground below.

Cooper hit the quick release on the descender and brought his carbine to bear as he took up position crouching some fifty metres from the road. He hit the magnification on his goggles and scanned the barricade. Someone else had taken up residence on the bed of the pickup, resting a long gun on the roof of the cab. The driver's door of the station wagon and the passenger door of the pickup were open, offering the illusion of protection to those sheltering behind them. With the substation gates only a couple of metres to the rear of the vehicles, they had effectively boxed themselves in. With no discernible exit strategy, they would fight to the death.

Jackson came up on Cooper's left side, and he gave the sergeant a quick sitrep. The lights of the blockading vehicles were running off to the left of the road, allowing them to approach unobserved from the scrubland on the right. Cooper, taking point, set off again. After twenty metres, he picked up the outline of an abandoned vehicle. The outline resolved itself into the shape of a police cruiser with the front end facing away from the road. A silhouetted head and shoulders were visible against the glass of the driver's door. A trap?

Cooper took out a scanner and ran it over the car. There were no traces of explosives or accelerants. Also clear for trip wires and pressure pads. Infrared showed only residual body heat; the occupant had been dead for at least an hour. He whispered into his mic for Adler to cover him and pulled open the door. The deceased's head lolled to the side as the seat belt took up the weight of the body. A neat hole in the officer's right temple identified the entry wound. The powder burn around it indicated he had been shot point-blank from the passenger side.

'Looks like his partner shot him.'

'Stay sharp,' Jackson replied. 'Trust no one.'

The moved off again, Adler now taking point as they curved back towards the road to intercept the utility truck. Desert Community Energy had supplied their radio frequency, and Jackson switched to it.

'This is Sergeant Jackson, Templar First Division. We can see your vehicle. Please confirm your name.'

'Brad Walton, DCE Senior Authorised Person. I've got Aaron Peters from our maintenance crew in the truck with me. We tried to access the site ninety minutes ago and were turned back.'

'Okay, Brad, we're here to help with that. We're about to engage with the hostiles. For your own safety, I need you and your colleague to stay in your truck. Do not leave it or approach the substation until I give you the all-clear.'

'Understood.'

Cooper hoped that he did. If anything happened to the DCE engineers, he didn't have a clue how to switch the electricity back on.

Jackson halted them ten metres out at the periphery of the cones cast by the headlights. Cooper raised his M8 and squinted through the scope. Tango One was visible through the glass of the pickup door, Tango Two through the windscreen, Tango Three above the truck's cab, and Tango Four behind the door of the station wagon.

Jackson signed he would take One and Two, Cooper Three and Adler Four. Jackson's voice sounded in Cooper's earpiece as he sighted on his target.

'On my mark … mark!'

The first three shots sounded almost simultaneously, with Jackson's second shot an instant behind. Cooper was up at a run before his target hit the ground. Adler was close behind, with the Sarge covering them. Tango One was visible on the ground, lying face-down on the road. Cooper pumped another round into him as he swung around the passenger door. He pivoted in response to a groan and saw the driver inside the cab, clutching a gut wound. His M8 barked again, splattering blood and brain matter across the window.

Tango Three was draped across the side of the pickup, lifeless eyes staring into space, Cooper having shot him through the heart. He was dressed in the uniform of a California Highway Patrol officer. If Free America had penetrated the police, there was no telling how far their influence reached. He pushed the body back onto the bed of the pickup.

Cooper shouted, 'Clear!' and slung his carbine over his

shoulder. He climbed into the cab and grabbed the dead driver under the arms. He hauled him clear of the truck and hefted the body up to join the dead CHP officer.

The windscreen had crazed into a spider's web of cracks around the bullet hole and Cooper used the stock of his carbine to smash it outwards. The ignition fob was sitting in the cup holder between the seats. The engine juddered to life as Cooper pressed the starter. Jackson waved him forward and he put it in drive. The pickup bumped and shuddered on its flat tyres. Cooper let it jolt and bounce for a dozen metres before drawing it off the road. Adler passed him driving the station wagon as he walked back to the gates.

Jackson called the DCE crew. The utility truck rolled forward, slowing noticeably as it passed the two shot-up vehicles on either side of the road. The truck stopped and Peters jumped out.

Jackson held out his hand for his PAC access card and keys. The maintenance engineer surrendered them, and the sergeant handed them to Cooper.

'I want you and Adler to secure the area. Make sure our friends over there haven't left any surprises. You get me?'

Cooper disarmed the electric fence and opened the gates, securing them at either side of the road. He synched the motion detector on his wrist to his HUD, overlaying it with infrared. It showed clear as he set off down the access track. Adler watched his six. Nothing stirred as they approached the control building, its roofline visible in the first light of dawn. He signalled to Adler, and they split apart, heading left and right. They followed each path along the building to either side, checking each door as they went until they met again at the rear.

'All clear, Sarge,' Cooper spoke into his radio.

'Fall back to the gate. I'll come in with the crew.'

Stone chippings crunched underfoot as Cooper stepped off the road to let the truck go past. Now that dawn was coming, he could see that the switchyard was covered with them. Weeds poked through at random intervals, densest around the fence line. The legs of the towers were covered in barbed wire. He found himself moving into the centre of the road to be as far from the structures as possible.

Cooper flinched as a dull bang sounded from the switchyard. Two more sounded in quick succession and the hairs on the back of his neck lifted as he heard the crackle of electricity. Along the access road streetlights fluoresced to life. Looking towards town, lights blinked on like so many dancing fireflies. Cooper smiled. They'd done it with minimum resistance.

Cooper heard the roar of the incoming suborbital attack craft before he saw it streaking across the sky. He saw the telltale smoke of a missile launch, the projectile streaking past the substation, with the suborbital trailing in its wake. He squinted, trying to determine the target, then quickly turned his head to the sudden fireball as it took out the hovering Defiant, leaving them stranded.

The suborbital dusted down fifty metres from the substation. Its rear ramp dropped, and a dozen combat troops rushed forward. Cooper swung the gates to and snapped the padlock closed.

He activated his throat mic. 'Sarge, we've got company!'

CHAPTER 19

Lynch watched the Defiant transform into a ball of flaming debris. He gripped the restraint webbing across his chest as the suborbital banked sharply into its descent. In addition to himself and the pilot, the hold carried ten commandos, led by Captain Jones. Their mission was to destroy the substation.

Lynch closed his eyes as the ground loomed up. The angle of descent was close to sixty degrees. His stomach leaped as the fast attack craft levelled out, almost standing on its tail before dropping the last couple of feet to the ground. He kept his eyes shut until the landing gear shocks had stopped bouncing, by which time the rear ramp was down and Jones' commando unit was lining up to disembark.

He followed them out as they fanned across the road. He might not agree with Drummond's scorched earth policy, but there was no denying the proficiency or speed with which it had been implemented.

'Time to make yourself useful, Lynch.'

Lynch synched his implant to his camera drones in response to Jones' command. The bat-like drones flitted into the air from the docking station on his hip. The crudely painted names Truth and Justice were visible across their wings. He directed them along the access road towards the gate, viewing the live camera feed on his HUD. Infrared showed no signs of life in either the pickup truck or the station wagon. Depending on the outcome of the war, they would either be remembered as traitors or heroes of the revolution.

'Gah!'

Lynch screwed his eyes shut and turned his head away as the substation floodlights flared to life, illuminating the area like some alien mothership. He blinked away the afterimage as the feed from the drones automatically compensated. A single figure was visible behind the substation gates, wearing a helmet, tactical vest and unform covert-ops black. Two similar figures, weapons at the ready, were advancing towards him from the substation control building. Something about the way the soldier at the gate held himself seemed familiar and Lynch zoomed in. The red cross pattée stood out first. It was a sign of the RSA's desperation that it was willing to deploy Templars domestically. Most of the soldier's face was hidden beneath his helmet and goggles, but Lynch felt a shudder of recognition as he turned his head and presented his profile to the camera. He needed to be sure, so he zoomed in on the name tape on his left breast: Cooper.

'You stupid, stupid bastard,' Lynch muttered under his breath.

He panned the drones around, moving into focus on the other two Templars as they reached the gate. The muscular figure with the sergeant stripes was also instantly recognisable to him as Tyrone Jackson. While they had never been friends, he owed him and respected him. The third, Adler, he only had vague recollections of. Part of the same intake as Cooper, he had been assigned to the Tel Aviv landing, while Lynch had been embedded as war correspondent for the forces at Palmachim Beach. The survivors came together for the siege of Jerusalem, followed by the final, fateful assault.

Jones snapped his fingers in front of Lynch's HUD. 'Hey! Want to share with the rest of us?'

'Three soldiers – Templars. Watching the gates. Looks like they've got grenade launchers in addition to the standard small arms.'

'Then we go for a missile strike. No point wasting lives trying to take those fanatics out.'

'Wait! Got a couple of others approaching.' Lynch zoomed in again. 'Civies. Look like DCE engineers. Guess they're the ones who restored the power.'

'And your point is?'

'We're meant to be filming this attack for propaganda purposes. Won't look good if we're seen indiscriminately killing civilians. Those guys there are just the sort you'll want to build your new America.'

'Tell you what. We'll just ask them nicely to open the gates and surrender, shall we?'

Lynch hesitated, but he knew Jones neither liked nor trusted him, so his confession was unlikely to damage his standing any further.

'I know the sergeant and one of the other Templars. I was with their unit during the Israel campaign. I can end this peacefully.'

'Yeah? Your oratory skills weren't much help in Wilmington.'

Lynch wanted to tell him to go fuck himself. That it was his trigger-happy twerps that started it all. But trying to save Cooper and Jackson was more important than getting into a pissing contest, so he swallowed his indignation.

'What have you got to lose? If they won't listen, you can call in the strike. But if they do? Well, we've got Templars, the most devout and fanatical of the Religious States' soldiers, surrendering without a shot been fired. Reckon that's worth something to Pulaski, don't you?'

'Fuck it.' Jones spat on the ground. 'Five minutes. Then these "friends" of yours are toast.'

Lynch started towards the gate before Jones could change his mind. He heard the commando unit following behind. They might be making a show of force, but he was all about the peace. He raised his hands as he stepped into the pool of light emanating from the substation. In the glare of the floodlights, he would be little more than a silhouette. Best make himself known.

'Hey, Coop! I thought you were getting out of this shitshow?'

'Lynch?' Cooper squinted into the light. 'Fuck, it really is you.'

Jackson silenced Cooper with a look. 'I'd say it was good to see you again, Lynch, but I'd be lying. No offence, but I'm not interested in talking to the monkey. Who's in command here?'

Jones stepped forward and raised his rifle. 'That would be me, Captain Jones. And before we get off on the wrong foot let me make it clear that this isn't a negotiation. You're outnumbered and outgunned. A single strike from the suborbital will take out you and your men. But we're not monsters. Lay down your weapons and I'll let you walk away. Better still, why not join the righteousness of our cause? A new America is possible. A better America.'

'It's a shame you think that,' Jackson said scornfully, 'because I'm willing to die for the current America. As are my men.'

'That would be a pity,' Lynch interrupted, 'given you saved my life. Probably more than once, if I'm honest. Look, I respect your sense of duty. But ask yourself if this is really the hill you want to die on? Wouldn't it be better to live to fight another day?'

'Everyone dies eventually.'

'True. But not everyone dies senselessly. You might have your duty, but what about the civilians? How about letting them leave the station as a sign of good faith?'

'And give you a couple of hostages? I don't think so.'

'Hey!' a tall man wearing DCE coveralls objected. 'Don't

we get a say in this?'

Jackson shifted his grip on his carbine. 'Reckon you and your colleague ought to make your way back to the control building.'

Jones waved an impatient hand. 'Enough of the racking. The time for debate is over. If your Templar friend here won't order his men to stand down, they can die where they stand.'

Lynch turned to Cooper. 'Goddamnit, kid, you told me in Jerusalem you were done with this shit. If you truly want out, this is your chance. I doubt you'll get another.'

Cooper looked away, either unwilling or unable to make eye contact. Lynch opened his mouth to repeat his appeal but was cut off by an angry shout.

'Don't listen to this heathen scum.' Adler turned to Jackson. 'Whatever your play, Sarge, I'll back it all the way.'

Jones opened a comms channel to the suborbital. 'Trojan Two, this is Apollo. You are clear to commence attack run.'

'Wait.' Jackson's voice was strangled. 'I agree to your terms.'

Jones called off the attack as the Templars laid down their weapons. Lynch could see how much it was costing the sergeant to comply. Adler, by contrast, looked mutinous, while Cooper continued to avoid eye contact.

Jackson unlocked the gates and stepped back as the Free America commandos pushed them open. Lynch followed them through and stayed with the six-man guard detail while Jones led the remaining three to destroy the transformers. They moved quickly, pressing blocks of C4 against the main tanks of the transformers and inserting wireless detonators. Lynch wondered how thick the battleship-grey steel was. But they'd presumably done their homework.

Jones led the demolition party back to the gates. Together, they escorted the Templars and the utility engineers back along the access road and beyond the shot-up vehicles. He opened one of the pouches on his vest, took out a radio detonator and extended the aerial. His thumb pressed down on the trigger.

Even at a distance of a hundred and fifty meters, Lynch felt the tremor in his shins as the C4 exploded. The lights around the station went out and were replaced by yellow and red flames as thousands of gallons of oil ignited, sending a pall of greasy black smoke mushrooming into the sky. Lynch's nose twitched in response to the acrid smell and he took a step back.

Mission complete, Jones called in the suborbital; this was only the first of the night's targets. The craft dusted down and lowered the rear ramp, ready for boarding.

'Looks like this is it, kid. That's twice you've turned me down. I hope you know what you're doing.'

Cooper stared down at his wrists, now bound together with flex cuffs. Something seemed to change in him and he stood up straight. 'Ah, shit. Hold up there. I'm sure I'll live to regret it, but I'm in. Providing you'll still have me?'

Lynch grinned. 'Knew you had it in you, kid.'

Jackson looked as though he'd been stabbed. 'I know you've had doubts lately, been struggling with your faith. Few men wouldn't after what you've been through. But are you really going to abandon your vows after all we've been through together? Breaking that holy trust is a sin there's no coming back from.'

'I'm sorry, I really am, but I don't see any enemies of the church here, only fellow Americans. Our country is broken, and this war is wrong. I'm not sure how to fix either, but this seems a whole lot better than fighting for Gerrard and his cronies. That's as best as I can explain it. I guess you either understand or you don't. All I know for certain is I can't go on the way I have for any longer.'

'Dirty apostate scum!'

Cooper turned and deflected Adler's blow with his forearm. He danced back out of range as he took another wild swing. Then two of Jones' commandos wrestled Adler to the ground and sat on him, and it was over.

Cooper made to go towards Adler and found his way blocked by a third commando. The message was clear: he was either with them or against them. He walked towards the suborbital instead, guns pointing at his back.

CHAPTER 20

Hopkins felt her teeth grind and forced herself to relax. The tension in the Panopticon's briefing room always got to her. Although *bunker* would be a more accurate description, given it was situated five storeys belowground and encased in a thick layer of steel-reinforced plascrete, from which the white marble finger of the Watchtower rose. That tower, to the Central Office, symbolised the power of the Religious States of America. That power was crumbling before her very eyes now, as evidenced by the expressions of the Secretary of Defense, Vice President Kordowski and President Gerrard, the latter of whom had called a crisis meeting.

Gerrard swiped his hand through the holo-display, creating a fuzz of pixels. 'Reports are coming in across the country of cyber-attacks and physical assaults launched by Free America rebels, who have been joined in many cases by fifth columnists. Substations have been blown up and reactors put offline, paralysing the electricity grid. Water treatment plants have also been targeted, as have air traffic control and the smart freeways. The country is in uproar and the media is demanding answers and reassurances. Last time I checked, Susanna, it was your job to provide that assurance. Where are we with a press release?'

'That rather depends on whether you want to put out fluff that nobody will believe or something with a bit more substance.' Hopkins paused, but she had committed herself too far to pull out. 'The people aren't as stupid as you seem to believe. They know we're on the back foot here, so we need to be seen actively doing something to combat the attacks.'

'Okay…' Gerrard's expression indicated things were far from all right. 'In that case, what are the options?'

Kordowski shrugged. 'We've already mobilised the National Guard and state troopers. But with power still out in many towns and cities, law enforcement is tied up dealing with rioters and looters. We've no choice but to declare a state of national emergency and implement martial law. More than that, we need to pull back troops from Syria and Jordan, even if it means conceding those countries once again to the Caliphate.'

'Unacceptable.' Gerrard scrubbed his face with his hands. 'We can't afford the kind of voter backlash even short-term losses would cause. Give me something else.'

'Chuck,' Kordowski said, 'if the rebels battle through, no one sitting at this table will need to worry about the next election.'

Morrison chimed in, 'Truth is, we're wasting a valuable resource using the Templars as firefighters. We should recall them to Richmond to protect Congress. Just because their last attack failed doesn't mean Free America won't try again.'

Gerrard looked uncertain, but fresh damage reports continued to scroll up the holo-display. 'Damn it. Give the order to withdraw the troops from the Middle Eastern theatre. But I want a *peacekeeping* force left behind.' He looked over at Hopkins. 'Draft a press release to that effect and mention the deployment of the Templars to protect the heart of government. That ought to reassure the people.'

Hopkins nodded, but Gerrard looked worryingly

unstable to her, struggling to make the difficult choices. If he cracked, she didn't have much faith in Kordowski to take over. Probably time to start planning her own contingency.

Deputy Director Hannah answered on the third ring. He greeted her by name, the drawn-out syllables both questioning and accusatory.

'Don't worry. It's a secure line.'

'Then I assume this is not a social call.'

'Like that was ever going to happen.'

'Indeed. Much as it's a pleasure to see your glowering face, perhaps we can cut to the chase?'

'It can't have escaped your notice that Charles is starting to unravel. It's one thing to fight a war thousands of miles away, but it's very different when it's on your doorstep and your actual voters are dying.'

'Yes, the consequences of your decisions are certainly felt more quickly and acutely. But I'm not sure how you think I can help with that.'

'You're really going to make me spell it out, aren't you? Probably so you've got me on tape. Well, damn it, is Charles the right man to lead us in these new circumstances?'

'If not him, then who? Would you trust Kordowski to run a bath, let alone the country? Even assuming we had a suitable candidate, how is the succession to be arranged? Having one president assassinated is unfortunate, but two looks like damned carelessness. Or perhaps I should just dissolve the Senate and appoint you? After all, you clearly believe you're best qualified for the job. Although, if I'm being honest, I preferred your previous strategy of using Tyler as your proxy.'

'You knew about me and Martin?'

'That you were fucking a Templar colonel in the hope of moulding him for political office?' Hannah smiled coldly. 'Kind of my job. For what it's worth, it would never have worked. Tyler was too volatile, too full of rage, and incapable of seeing the big picture. His demographic was predominantly the uneducated white male. Oh, he was handsome enough to quicken the pulse of the soccer moms, but that wouldn't have been enough. Not nearly. Not without the Blacks and the Latinos.'

'I was kind of counting on the liberation of Jerusalem to sway them.'

'The problem with that, particularly from a Roman Catholic perspective, is that we drove out the Caliphate only to hand the country back to the Jews. They still tend to get a little touchy about the whole crucifixion business.'

'Careful now. Sounds like you're mocking the suffering of our Lord and saviour.'

'Says the fornicator.'

'Are we playing "my sin is greater than yours?"'

Hannah sighed. 'No, I'm just trying to give you the lay of the land. We – and I include myself in this – made our choice with Gerrard. For good or ill, under the Twenty-fifth Amendment, he is our legal president and de facto commander-in-chief of our armed forces. It's going to take more than the odd wobble to invoke Section Four for his removal. And, as I've already said, all that gives us is President Kordowski.'

'In other words, suck it up.'

'Your phrase, not mine. If you're feeling vulnerable here, remember what old Ben Franklin said about hanging together, or surely hanging separately.'

'You spend a lot of time referring to the old republic.'

'You don't throw the baby out with the bathwater. Now, if we're done here, I need to get back to monitoring Free America activity. I'm sure you don't want to see them in Richmond any more than I do.'

'You really are a dick.'

'Been called a lot worse by more important people than you, Susanna.'

Hopkins launched her com-unit across the office. It hit the wall with a satisfying crack and rebounded to bounce off the desk, then came to rest on the carpet. She took a deep breath and crossed the floor to retrieve her com-unit. Her distorted features stared back at her from the crazed screen. She hoped it wasn't a sign that she was going to pieces.

CHAPTER 21

The interview room was painted grey, including the floor and ceiling. It contained a table and two chairs on opposite sides of the scarred Formica top, all of which were bolted securely to the floor. A mirror covered the top half of the adjacent wall, reflecting Cooper's image back at him while members of the Free America movement observed him through the one-way glass. Chains rattled as he lifted his right arm to scratch his brow; the other end of the handcuffs was fastened to an eye bolt on the table.

A black line appeared in the wall as the door, which had no handle on the inside, swung open to admit Hank Russell. His interrogator approached and sat opposite, leaning back in his chair, keeping a safe distance between himself and the man he knew to be a highly trained killer. He got straight to business.

'You want to run me through the events that led up to your decision to defect?'

'I've already run through it five times.'

'Then I guess it won't hurt to go through it one more time. Will it?'

'Where's Lynch? I want to speak to him. He can sort this out.'

'That's not possible right now, so you might as well talk to me. Maybe you've remembered something you forgot last time. Maybe there are things you didn't think were important. Doesn't matter. I want you to go through everything in your head. No matter how inconsequential you believe it to be. Do that and we'll see what happens next.'

Seeing no other option, Cooper began again. 'If I had doubts before, I guess they were all minor. It was the bus and the cover-up that changed everything. We'd secured the landing at Palmachim Beach and were travelling inland on Route Four-Three-One following the liberation of Rishon LeZion when we encountered a refugee convoy blocking the road. Normally, we would have gone around, but the walls of a canyon prevented that. The obstruction was a bus with a flat tyre. Two men were trying to change it. We told them to forget it and push the bus to the side of the road to let us past. I guess they didn't speak much English, and we sure as shit didn't speak Arabic, so things got kinda heated, especially when the pregnant wife left the bus. Then Mac got spooked, thought it was a trap.'

'That would be Templar-Private Dwayne Mackinlay, who is listed as killed in action during the siege of Jerusalem?'

'Yeah, Mac. Anyway, one of the men turned round, probably didn't think about the tyre iron in his hand, and Mac just opened fire. My training kicked in, you know, reflex reaction, so I started spraying the bus too. We kept going, despite Sergeant Jackson's order to cease fire, until our mags were empty. Killed the entire family – pregnant woman, children, the lot. A mistake. A hellish, stupid, pointless tragedy. Believe me when I say it haunts me to this day. But what happened next was a hundred times worse.'

'The airstrike?'

'That's right. The one that Lynch broadcast the recording of Colonel Tyler calling in. He had that entire convoy destroyed just to cover up me and Mac's fuck up.

Where'd you even begin with shit like that? Mac shrugged it off, but it kept eating at me, feeding my doubts. Somehow, I made it through to the end. Mac, like you said, wasn't so lucky. Caught a bullet during the final push to take Jerusalem. Anyway, the caliph was dead, the remaining Caliphate troops were retreating, and Israel had been returned to the Jewish people. Colonel Tyler was a war hero, and Lynch was due to flyback stateside, where he was assigned to the Panopticon press corps – his reward for churning out propaganda during the campaign.

'That should have been a happy ending for them both, but Lynch couldn't let it go. Must have burned him something terrible to see Tyler get rewarded for all the death and destruction he'd caused. And all the while, he was forced to sacrifice his journalistic principles to avoid them throwing his ass in prison for drug smuggling. But Lynch, whatever else you say about him, is no dummy. He's spent his downtime hacking the Black ICE that prevents him making unauthorised broadcasts. Put Tyler firmly in the frame for ordering the destruction of the refugee convoy. There was no way the government could spin that as anything other than a war crime.

'Tyler, as you can imagine, completely lost his shit. Decided it was Lynch's word against his own, and if Lynch wasn't around to tell his side of the story… I'd like to think it was more than my guilty conscience, but whatever it was, I couldn't let Tyler shoot him like some rabid dog. I got between him and the colonel and pointed my weapon at my CO. Honestly thought Tyler was going to pop me and then Lynch. But that's when it got weird. Sergeant Jackson stepped up behind Tyler, forced the colonel's own pistol to his head and made him shoot himself. Now, he and Tyler fought a lot of campaigns together. Always came across as pretty tight. Plus, there was no love lost between him and Lynch. And I wouldn't have said he was any closer to me than any of the other men he commanded. So, you gotta figure something else was happening in the background.'

'You suspect some kind of internal politics within the Templar order?'

'Something like that.'

'So, what happened next?'

'Lynch decided he'd be better taking his chances on his own than heading back stateside. We let him take a JLTV and then reported Tyler's apparent suicide. Given the damage done by Lynch's broadcast, it was an easy enough sell. A disgraced officer took his own life rather than face trial for war crimes. Me? I was done. Told them I wanted to cash out at the end of my tour.'

Russell raised his brow. 'And yet, here you are.'

'Don't I know it!' Cooper snapped. 'All leave was cancelled after President Hamilton's assassination and my request put on hold. Suddenly, we were launching a fresh offensive in Syria, pushing the Caliphate back while it was still reeling from the death of the caliph.'

'Being a bit modest there, Cooper. You did a bit more than that. You and Sergeant Jackson were part of the strike force that assassinated Omar El Zayyoud, leader of the Armed Islamic Group of Jordan. The so-called mastermind of Hamilton's assassination.'

'Are you saying he was innocent?'

'Innocent is a relative term. It's undeniable that, despite your apparent doubts and loss of faith, you remained in the vanguard of the attack on Syria.'

Cooper tapped the red cross pattée on his tunic. 'Kind of goes with the territory. The more I wanted out, the further they dragged me in. The further we progressed, the more desperate they became, and suddenly we were killing child soldiers. Doesn't matter a damn that if we didn't kill them, they would have killed us. I still see their faces when I close my eyes. Perverse as it sounds, what happened next was kind of a blessing.'

'You're referring to yourself and Corporal Peter Goodman being captured by Marshal Abu Salman Ismail?'

'Yeah. If I'd continued in combat, I think I might have

snapped completely. Couldn't square away what I was doing every day with what I felt in my head. Course, like everyone else in this damn war, Ismail had an agenda. Spent his time lecturing us on Islam and the historic achievements of its followers. He wanted to convert the fanatical Templars to his cause. We played along, getting strong and healthy, until we were ready to escape. But Ismail was watching us and expected it all along. We were put out in cages awaiting public execution, unless President Gerrard agreed to an exchange of prisoners. Gerrard knew he couldn't do that, but he also knew how bad the optics would be if he allowed us to be publicly executed. So, he sent in a special-ops team to extract us. It went pretty much as planned, right up until Goodman tried to kill their commander, Major Stanley. Turns out Marshal Ismail was doing a bit more than simply lecturing us – neuro programming, brainwashing, whatever you want to call it.'

'But not on you?'

'Not according to the shrink. But like I said, nobody in this war is without an agenda. The important thing is I'm finally back stateside with my family. Everything I've done in this war has been for them. Right now, God only knows what they think of me, or what will become of them. But I couldn't go on. Not any longer. I was adrift. Conflicted. Didn't know who to turn to or where to turn. But when I heard Lynch talk of a better America, one with equal opportunities for all, I figured that might be something worth fighting for. Something I could finally believe in. Crazy as that may sound.'

'It's certainly a pretty story.' Russell leaned back and steepled his fingers. 'But the problem I have is the Templars are zealots. I find it difficult to believe you'd betray your sworn brothers. Seems more likely you're here as a spy, using your previous relationship with Lynch as a cover.'

Cooper threw up his hands; the right one caught as the cuff reached the extent of the chain. 'Well, I'm afraid I don't have any other story to tell. Maybe you should talk to

Lynch? After all, he said I should throw in with you. From where I'm sitting, my knowledge of Templar strengths and tactics would be an advantage to you. But if you don't want to use it, that's your loss.'

The door swung open again and Lynch barrelled into the interrogation room. 'Cut the shit, Russell. I can vouch for the kid.'

Russell snorted. 'And what happens when he gets near Pulaski and decides to snap her neck before anyone can do anything about it?'

'Guess you'll get to say, "I told you so."'

'Not helping,' Russell retorted.

'If you don't want my help and won't trust me, fine. Kick me loose and let me take my chances.'

'See? What did I say? He's just looking for an opportunity to spy.'

'He's no goddamn spy,' Lynch snarled.

'Only got his and your word for that. He stays here until I discuss it with Pulaski.' Russell paused at the door. 'Are you coming?'

'Reckon I'll stay here.'

'Suit yourself. But if you get taken prisoner, I won't be rushing to the rescue.'

The door slammed. Lynch looked away as he scratched behind his ear. 'Sorry about that. Might not seem that way, but Russell is actually an okay guy.'

'It's fine. I needed that push to finally get out.'

The door opened again and a grey-haired woman appeared, flanked by a pair of armed guards. She looked Cooper up and down, taking his measure.

'So, this is one of the infamous Templars? Got to say, he doesn't look that remarkable. But maybe that will be a positive.' She pointed at Lynch. 'Seems to me we have a golden propaganda opportunity here. Get him prepped and in front of a camera inside the hour.'

Cooper watched Lynch from the side of his eye as he lit a fresh cigarette from the stub of the one that he had just smoked. He exhaled slowly, blowing the smoke towards the ceiling. Lynch had briefed Cooper on the questions he was going to ask, with the focus inevitably being on his decision to defect. Yet another rehash of everything he had told Russell and, more importantly, the continued concealment of what he had withheld: his desire to kill Vanderbilt. It was like an itch he couldn't scratch. No, it was more nebulous than that, a subconscious desire that surfaced without warning but then disappeared as soon as he tried to analyse it. A product of trauma, insanity, or something more malignant? Yes! That's what it felt like: cells mutating and growing, destroying healthy tissue. Could it be excised, or had it already metastasised? He needed help. Lynch would know what to do. Cooper opened his mouth and then closed it again.

'Nervous, kid?' Lynch asked.

'I guess. If I say the wrong thing, Russell will lock me up and throw away the key.'

'Just stick with what we discussed – it comes from the heart. It will humanise you in the eyes of the viewers.'

'Is that opposed to coming across like a deranged zealot?'

'The first lesson of media is that public perception is everything. The modern Templar order exists as a counterpoint to the Muslim bogeyman. The public expects an Old Testament prophet raining down fire on his enemies. You need to show that beneath the uniform, you're just another young American. Perverse and contrary as it seems, the goal of the civil war is unity.'

'Because killing always brings folks together.'

'Never said it was easy. But what's the alternative? We fight until the country is a smoking ruin and the roaches take over. Gotta be more hope than that.'

Cooper massaged his temples with his fingers. If he wasn't nervous before, he certainly was now. If the journalist wasn't good for words of comfort, he was definitely good for one thing. He thrust out his hand.

'Give us a drink, will you?'

Lynch arched an eyebrow, then fished his hipflask from his gillet and handed it over. He watched, hawk-like, as Cooper unscrewed the cap and took a long drink, his Adam's apple bobbing up and down.

'Didn't think you were much of a drinker.'

'I'm not. But I'm sure it will help that authenticity you're after.'

Lynch took the flask back. 'I'll drink to that!'

CHAPTER 22

Vanderbilt kept his expression neutral as he ended the video call. He settled back in his chair and looked across the polished expanse of the conference table to where a life-size wooden crucifix hung on the wall. The crown of thorns and nail heads were gilded, the stigmata picked out in red, the loin cloth lambskin-white. But it was the eyes of his Lord and saviour that held him, for they seemed to pierce his soul, just as the thorns pierced the Nazarene's flesh. A warning to embrace humility in the face of triumph. He thought of the mocking inscription the Romans had placed on the cross: *Iesus Nazarenus Rex Iudaeorum*. Jesus of Nazareth, King of the Jews. Vanderbilt didn't wish to be king, or even president. But he recognised his God-given duty to lead.

His com-unit beeped and he swiped it open to reveal confirmation of the executive order he had just received from President Gerrard. It recalled all available Templars to Richmond to protect Congress. Everything was falling into place as he had planned. Soon, he would have five hundred Templars ready to seize control of Congress and arrest the president and his staff. And all because of Morrison's vanity. He looked forward to seeing the look on his face when the

Secretary of Defense realised he wasn't to be installed as president.

That fat, pompous fool of a bishop, Connors, would also get a rude awakening when Vanderbilt became the joint head of Church and State in the new theocracy he envisaged. One way or another, the people would be led back to God and the sinners duly punished. God would see it was duty and not hubris that drove him. He strove not for the purple or the laurel wreaths of victory, nor would he shrink from them if they were thrust upon him. As such, he must attend to temporal matters.

Vanderbilt initiated an encrypted call to Colonel Willard. The face that appeared on the screen seemed distracted.

'Something troubling you, Colonel?'

'We are betrayed by one of our own, Grand Master. Templar-Private Cooper has ... joined the Free America rebels. As his commanding officer and spiritual superior, I take full responsibility and will submit to whatever punishment you see fit to deliver.'

'You are too harsh on yourself.' Vanderbilt paused, as though weighing his next words carefully. 'The fault lies with many, me included. While it's unfortunate our brother has fallen, you may rest assured that there will be a reckoning for all apostates, starting with Gerrard and his administration. The day of judgement is at hand. Now, more than ever, you and your men must be steadfast in your faith and respect the chain of command. A New World Order is coming. One in which His will shall be ascendant.'

Willard raised his head. 'You may depend on our loyalty throughout whatever trials lie ahead.'

'Good. Then these, Colonel, are your orders.'

Willard, Vanderbilt reflected, lacked imagination, which was as much a blessing as a curse. He would carry out the orders given to him without thought or hesitation. As long as everything went according to plan, all would be well. His failing was his inability to extemporise in the face of the unexpected, resorting instead to brute force. While Vanderbilt intended for most of the Senate to dance at the end of a rope, it would not do for too many of them to die before he arranged a suitable show trial. The people must have their circuses.

Vanderbilt logged out of the workstation and stood. The chapter house was newly furnished as part of ongoing renovation works to the Richmond Temple. The state-of-the-art comms and cyber-security had persuaded him to leave the preferred workspace of his study. There were those, lacking the vision to see the necessity of his actions, who would view them as treasonous. Then it would be his own head in the hangman's noose.

Matters had ended badly in France for the historical predecessors of the order when King Philip IV had ordered the arrest of scores of Templars in Paris on the morning of October 13, 1307. Rumours had circulated for some time as to strange rituals being practiced by the Templars, and the king, who was heavily indebted to the order, had seized upon them for his own purpose. Pope Clement V, bowing to pressure from King Philip, had disbanded the order in 1312, and its last Grand Master, Jacques de Molay, was burned at the stake two years later. Vanderbilt did not intend for his Templars – and, more importantly, himself – to face the same fate. But the political parallels were undeniable.

A wood-panelled corridor led to the chapel, the walls of which were decorated with militaristic quotes from the Scriptures. His eyes alighted on a verse from the Book of Deuteronomy: *For the Lord your God is the one who goes with you to fight for you against your enemies to give you victory*. A sign of divine providence if ever there was one.

CHAPTER 23

Here, in the Syrian desert close the Iraqi border, there were few witnesses at the best of times. And at the height of the sandstorm, no one saw the white dome appear and disappear beneath the shifting dunes like the exposed bones of some long extinct mammal. Try as the probing tendrils of sand might, they could find no weakness in the hermetically sealed high-density polyethylene skin. Ismail had ordered the dome's erection at the first sign of the approaching storm, securing his mobile command centre from the hostile elements. If he heard the scouring winds, he gave no sign as he bent to study the satellite imagery. Lieutenant General Ahmad and Brigadier General Carim edged closer to observe the wide-scale evacuation of American troops from Syria and Jordan.

'If I did not see it with my own eyes, I would not believe it,' Carim said. 'Truly, Allah is great.'

Ahmad, though no less devout, was the shrewder of Ismail's commanders. 'How complete is the withdrawal?'

'Ninety per cent of troops, ninety-five per cent of materials. Those left behind are working with the underequipped forces of their appointed puppet administrations.' Ismail stabbed the projected map with his finger. 'With the Americans fighting one another on their home soil, Damascus is ripe for the taking. I will command a tank squadron and lead the assault on the capital myself.'

'Is that wise?' Ahmad asked.

'Perhaps not. But it is certainly proper. Our losses have been grievous of late, and we must set an example for the faithful.'

Ahmad bowed his head. 'As ever, you are correct.'

'Do not rebuke yourself too harshly, my friend. After our many tribulations, our time is surely coming. Soon we will drive the infidels from our lands.'

'And Israel?'

'Israel is a problem best left for another day. We must recapture and consolidate our heartlands before opening a fresh front.'

Privately, Ismail remained mindful of the Israelis' possession of a powerful nano-virus, a weapon they had demonstrated their willingness to use during the battle to capture Jerusalem. Israel was a dog best left to slumber. The occupied territory was not so great and the Palestinian people so reduced and scattered that resettlement might prove impossible. He took further comfort from the knowledge that Egypt and Saudi Arabia would not prove to be any more accommodating neighbours than they had in the past. Victory in Syria and Jordan would go a long way towards appeasing the people.

Unlike his predecessor, Abu Ahmad al-Nasr al-Qurayshi, the fifth and last caliph, Ismail neither believed nor relied on a divine right to rule. A good solider was forever assessing his opponent, amending and changing his tactics to suit. Strength alone was insufficient to hold onto power. He had to understand weakness too, both his own and the enemy's.

Ismail powered off the map. 'Come. It is time for *Asr*.'

Marshal Ismail swept the horizon from left to right with his binoculars, taking in the denuded skyline of his country's once prosperous capital. The City of Jasmine was fragrant no longer; the scars left by the American bombardment were all too visible. Much of what had been destroyed was irreplaceable, but they would rebuild regardless. First, they had to take it from the infidels and the treacherous dogs that supported them.

Sweeping down from the city, he examined the hastily assembled wall, formed of giant plascrete sections that had been craned into place on either side of the checkpoint on the International Road. Control of this road, which stretched all the way to Aleppo as it paralleled the western border, would be vital in the battle to recapture the conquered territories.

The red, white and black horizontal bars of the former Syrian Arab Republic flag flew above the wall, a symbol of the American's puppet democracy. Ismail increased the binoculars to maximum magnification and examined one of the soldiers guarding the manually operated booms that blocked access to the city. The angled helmet with the chin strap dangling free, the unbuttoned tunic, and the awkward manner in which he shouldered his rifle proved the adage that putting a man in uniform did not make him a soldier. He and his companions were here because they had no other place to be. Better to take the army's meagre pay and rations than subsist on parcels from the Red Crescent. Ismail saw little challenge in defeating such men, but one way or another, he would clear them from his path.

He lowered his binoculars and toggled on his microphone. 'All commanders, advance north, single file.'

The revving of the ancient Russian T14 Armata's double turbocharged engines filled the air, swiftly followed by the clanking of tracks as the tanks ground their way towards the checkpoint. Ismail remained visible, standing with the commander's hatch thrown back, effectively preventing the turret from traversing to the right. But if his assessment of the guards was correct, his authority would prove as effective as any shell.

The sound of the approaching armour column was unmistakeable, as were the black flags with the legend *ad-Dawlah al-Islāmiyah* in white calligraphy. Ismail watched the guards' hostility turn to uncertainty before finally transforming into fear. He waited until they were three metres from the barrier before ordering the driver to stop. The guard, his weapon forgotten, stared at Ismail.

'You know who I am?'

'Yes … sir!'

'Good.' Ismail grinned wolfishly. 'Then you will know that I am on a holy mission to clear the American infidels from our lands. If you are a true believer, you will not hinder my progress.'

The guard looked to his companion, who was manning the barrier across the middle lane for instruction. The grey in his beard and hair showed him to be a man of middle years. He appeared to ruminate for a few seconds and then shrugged.

'You may please yourself, Habib.' He pointed to the column of tanks. 'But I see no reason to die when we have not been paid in two months and the food is rotten.'

'Shouldn't we at least raise the alarm?'

'The Americans will know they are coming soon enough, I think.'

Habib looked at Ismail and then at his own poorly maintained rifle. Decision made, he stepped back to the boom and swung it into the air.

'Driver, forward,' Ismail commanded.

The T-14's engine roared and the tank ground forward. The remaining three tanks of Ismail's troop followed close behind, with the other two troops following at fifty-metre intervals. Ismail ducked into the tank and closed the hatch. He hoped the older man's pragmatism would rub off on Habib and the boy would see the wisdom of abandoning post and uniform. If not, he would be forced to hang him once the city was secure to make an example.

The streets were eerily quiet as they drove along the Amman and then the Ibn Al Abbas, striking north towards the People's Assembly of Syria. They turned northeast, passing Police Headquarters. Ismail checked the motion sensors. He felt discomfited by the lack of resistance and worried they were being lured into a trap. What few bodies there were remained indoors. His nerves tingled with the anticipation of action as they continued past the Khaled ibn al-Walid Mosque, with its twin minarets and distinctive silver domes. And still, no one tried to impede their progress. On they swept to Al Hijaz Square, Al Jalaa Park, all the way to Al Majlis El Nyaby, where the road was finally blocked by a barricade of plascrete-filled oil drums. Into the drums steel poles had been set, and between them hung coils of razor wire. Further razor wire, stretched between wooden crosses, blocked the access to the parliamentary buildings.

Ismail activated the tank's periscope and turned it in a slow arc as he examined the barricade's defenders. These men carried M8 carbines and wore the latest body armour and enhanced combat helmets. Their right shoulders were decorated with the Cross and Stars flag of the Religious States. But they fell into two distinct categories: grizzled middle-aged men and fresh-faced teenagers. Reservists. He watched them scurry for cover in response to the approaching tanks. The exception was a grim-faced sergeant, who stood his ground and raised an NLAW to his shoulder.

'Driver, reverse!'

Ismail knew the order was too late as he saw the flare of the missile's low-powered ignition systems, followed by the main rocket ignition. The missile deployed in an overfly top attack. A proximity fuse caused it to detonate above the tank, where the armour was weakest. In a conventional tank, the attack would have been devasting, but the Armat's turret was an unmanned automated weapons system. The three-man crew sat at the front of the hull in a special armoured capsule and were protected from the autoloader by a bulkhead.

The missile detonated before the APS could intercept it. The tank slewed to the side as the remote weapons station was ripped from the turret, together with the 12.7 mm Kord machine gun, its secondary armament. The aerials and APS went too, but the 44S-SV-SH steel and metal-ceramic plate armour held.

'Gunner, weapons status.'

Hamidi quickly scanned his console. 'Secondary weapons down but main armament still functional.'

The weapon the gunner referred to was a smoothbore 152 mm gun with an automatic loader containing thirty-two rounds.

'Select your targets and fire at will.'

The T-14 rocked back as the gun fired; the shell detonated with devastating force inside the barricaded area. The gun fired again and again as Hamidi sought out the sheltering defenders, throwing plascrete, steel and flesh into the air. Amidst the confusion, another missile struck the front of the tank but failed to penetrate the thick armour. A second tank slewed up to join the attack and directed a withering hail of machine gun fire into the crumbling barricade. Ricochets chipped the cream-coloured stone of the parliament's outer wall and rattled the metal railings.

Ismail caught a flash of white amidst the roiling smoke. It came again, together with a waving arm. It looked like the American reservists had already had enough of the unequal fight. Should he kill them? No. Their surrender and capitulation would be of greater value.

'All units, cease firing.'

The machine guns stopped their chatter and were replaced by the moans and screams of the wounded and dying. Ismail opened the hatch and clambered free of the tank. He unfastened the flap on his holster, although he did not think the Americans would resort to treachery. The last of the smoke cleared and the flag-carrying soldier stepped forward to stand at the shattered barricade. He was bareheaded, his skin almost as grey as his hair, with a stoop to his thin shoulders. Ismail noted the bars on his shoulders.

'You wish to surrender, Captain?'

'Captain Howerd, Eighty-first Readiness Division. Will you guarantee my men will be treated fairly as prisoners of war?'

'I will. But someone must take responsibility for the crimes the Religious States has committed against the Caliphate and pay the price. You, as the ranking officer, would appear to be the obvious choice.'

'What sort of price are we talking about?'

'The death penalty.'

'I see.' Howerd grimaced, but he knew his options were limited. 'And I have your word of honour that my men will be treated fairly?'

A soldier stepped into view behind the railings of the gates. 'Don't listen to him, Captain. You can't trust these Muslim bastards!'

'That's enough, Blackford,' Howerd warned the soldier. 'It would seem the fate of my men is in your hands, Marshal Ismail.'

Ismail kept his features impassive. It would appear that, despite his efforts, his face had become known to the American infidels. So be it. He spoke into his throat microphone and called in reinforcements to process the prisoners.

Including Captain Howerd, they took charge of fourteen prisoners. Two of them died from their wounds within an hour, while another was not expected to live to see the next day. As near as they could tell from the body parts, they recovered an additional seventeen dead. True to Ismail's word, the survivors had been given food and water and were now held in the cells of the nearby police headquarters. All except for their commanding officer.

Howerd knelt in front of the door of the parliamentary building, his face impassive as he looked down the flight of steps leading to the gates. The rubble and debris of the battle had been cleared from the front of the building for the camera's establishing shot. It rose upward, taking in the arch and the stone Hawk of Quraish, supporting a shield bearing the Syrian national flag, that crowned the building.

The camera dropped again to follow Ismail as he climbed the steps towards the kneeling man. His scabbarded scimitar slapped against his left thigh. Howerd remained silent as his executioner took up position on his left.

'Captain Howerd, you have been found guilty of participating in an illegal war against the Islamic Caliphate and all those who live under its protection. This war has resulted in the martyrdom of many thousands of its subjects and seen the unjust seizure of lands and properties from their rightful owners. It is the tribunal's verdict that you be sentenced to death by beheading. Do you have any final words before I carry out that sentence?'

'Just get on with this sham. My knees are starting to hurt.'

Ismail wasn't certain if the American was truly brave or simply seeking to mitigate his fear. Either way, the end result would be the same. The scimitar's blade reflected the midday sun as it was drawn. Ismail had sharpened the sword that morning. He took a step back, raised it above his head, and chopped down. Howerd's head sprang from his neck and bounced down the steps. A second later, his body slumped forward.

Ismail snapped his wrist, cracking the sword like a whip. Drops of blood spattered across the steps. One dead soldier would not turn the tide of the war, but symbols were important. He brandished the scimitar above his head and a cheer went up from the assembled crowd.

CHAPTER 24

Two pm on a Welfare Wednesday and Tipsy McStagger's was buzzing. The afternoon crowd was keen to get their drunk on as early as possible and so blot out another day with nothing to do. Jonesboro, like so many towns in the Religious States, had little to offer those who shunned military service, apart from grinding unemployment.

Donny Ackerman tilted back his glass and drained it. He burped as the glass banged down on the bar and turned to his companion. 'Your round, Mike.'

Mike Dunbar looked at his own half-full glass. It wasn't like him to lag behind, but he'd promised himself that he'd save enough of his welfare credit to buy his mom a birthday present. Maybe even take her out for breakfast at the diner. Was this the fifth or sixth round? He tried some quick mental arithmetic to reckon his tab, gave up, and held up two fingers instead. He would just have to borrow some money from his mom. She'd understand. Not like forty-three was a special birthday.

Joe, the barman, nodded his head and fished down a pair of glasses from the overhead rack. He angled the glass below the tap and pulled back the lever to dispense the beer.

A good two inches of foam formed on top, part of which oozed down the glass as he slid it towards Donny.

Mike finished his beer as Joe repeated the process, sliding his now empty glass across the bar as the fresh one arrived. He picked it up, saluted Donny, and drank down a good third. His forehead crinkled in response to the bitter note it left behind. He opened his mouth to say something and then snapped it shut. Wasn't like he was drinking the beer for the taste. If he were, there were more expensive brews on tap. But they all had the same effect if he drank enough.

'Holy shit! Joe! Turn up the sound, will ya?'

Mike looked up at the screen above the bar to see what had Donny so excited. He saw a talking head on a news bulletin, some middle-aged dude with a shaved head and HUD glasses, whose lips continued to move silently. Then the camera cut back to the person being interviewed and it was Mike's turn to swear as he recognised their childhood friend, Billy Ray Cooper.

'The sound, Joe!' Donny exclaimed.

Cooper's languid voice crackled from the speakers. 'When did I realise the war was wrong? What's that famous quote about how you go bankrupt? In two ways – first gradually, then suddenly.'

The camera stayed on Cooper as Lynch replied, 'I'm guessing the sudden part was the attack on the refugee column?'

Cooper's expression turned grim. 'I'm not trying to downplay my part. What Mac and I did was wrong. But it was a mistake, the result of heightened tension and stress. Tyler calling in the airstrike to wipe out the whole column was something else entirely. After Jerusalem was recaptured and Tyler committed suicide after you'd exposed him, I really thought I was getting out. But then President Hamilton was assassinated, and suddenly we were pressing into Syria in pursuit of the man behind it, El Zayyoud. We took him out, but that wasn't enough. On we went, ignoring the civilian casualties and misery, the child soldiers taught to hate us at their mother's breast.'

'Then you were captured by the de facto Caliphate leader, Marshal Ismail.'

'That's right. Me and Corporal Pete Goodman. We were rescued eventually, and I received a hero's welcome back home. But seeing the latest intake of Templars, one of them from my hometown, I just wondered where it would all end.'

'And that's what finally decided you?'

'I think so. Hell, I don't know. The only thing I'm certain of is that something has to change, for the sake of ourselves and future generations. We can't go on fighting this perpetual war in the Middle East, comparing our gods to see which has the biggest dick. Many will see it as betraying God and country, my joining with the Free America rebels. But it seems to me it's time for America to become whole again. To get back to the values that once made us the greatest nation on Earth.'

The video cut to the studio, where a male and female news anchor sat opposite one another. Their flawless skin and perfectly symmetrical features revealed them as sims.

'Well, John, that has to be the unkindest cut of all. One of our very own Templars defecting to the enemy.'

'It certainly is, Marlene. More pertinently, it makes President Gerrard's authority look shaky.'

An empty beer can sailed across the bar and crumpled against the wall. 'Turn that shit off, Joe. Don't want to hear any more about that stinking traitor.'

'You settle down, Davenport,' Joe warned. But he turned off the screen.

Denied a physical outlet, Davenport continued to vent. 'Can't believe I went to school with that dickwad. Fuck, I even shook his hand when he came home. If I'd known then…' Davenport's voice trailed off as he spotted Mike and Donny at the bar. 'Well if it ain't the traitor's buddies. Maybe we ought to take you down the sheriff's office in case you get any ideas about joining him. For all we know, you could both be fifth corners. Them folks are joining the rebels.'

Donny held up his hands. 'Stop right there, Mason. We had no idea Billy Ray was thinking of joining up with Free America. Only saw him the once while he was home, and up there on that screen was the first we'd heard of him since he went back to Fort Irwin.'

'Yeah, all right. Reckon his folks is more to blame.'

There was a rumble of agreement throughout the bar. Donny lifted his glass and drained it.

'Reckon it's time we left.'

Mike blinked. 'Is it?' He sighed as Donny flicked his eyes towards the door and finished his own beer.

Donny held the door for him and made sure it was shut before speaking. 'Those morons in there are a good temperature reading for the town. If they're starting to blame Billy Ray's family, others will be too. We should go and make sure they're okay.'

'I don't have money for a cab, and it'll take us forty minutes to walk.'

'Who said we were walking?'

Donny fished a fob from his pocket and pointed it across the road to where his truck was parked. The lights flashed on and off in response.

'You sure you're okay to drive?'

'Five and drive, man.'

Mike shrugged and followed him to the truck. If Donny wanted to risk a DUI rap, that was his affair. 'You could always use the auto-drive.'

'Don't trust those things. Besides, I know a couple of shortcuts.'

A horn sounded as Donny made to pull out. Mike caught a glimpse of the driver shaking her head as the car sped past. He checked his seatbelt twice as Donny finally pulled out. They ran a stoplight at the end of the road and turned right before veering left to disappear down a side street. By

Mike's estimate, the street cams must have picked up at least three traffic violations. He closed his eyes and waited for it to be over.

Mike saw the mob standing vigil outside the Cooper residence as the truck drew to a halt two doors down. Someone had painted "traitor" across the front door. He saw the living room curtains twitch as one of the Coopers peered outside. Donny opened the glovebox, removed a Glock 19, and ratcheted back the slide.

'Is that a good idea?' Mike asked.

Donny pointed to the mob, then opened the door and stepped from the truck. 'Better grab yourself the tyre iron.'

Mike swallowed nervously. Violence frightened him, but if it came to the crunch, he would rather dispense it than find himself on the receiving end. He turned in his seat and fished about the discarded fast-food wrappers that littered the rear footwell until his fingers closed around cold metal. Closing the door behind him, he followed Donny to where he now stood at the edge of the crowd.

The door swung open and Wayne Cooper stepped out onto the porch. His face darkened as he saw the faces of friends and neighbours stood outside his home in judgement. These were the same people he saw in the grocery store and at church. He made eye contact with several in quick succession until one of them finally looked away.

'That's right, Rufus Fortner, you bow your head there. How long have you and Zeke and Finch known me and my family? How long have our families lived together in Jonesboro?'

'A long time, Wayne. Not disputing that. But what your boy has done just ain't right. Surely you can see how it looks?'

'What I see is a passel of folks who ought to know better. Me and Patty are as shocked as y'all about Billy Ray. But as that boy is my blood, I'm sure he has his reasons.'

Fortner's reply was drowned out by the smashing of

glass as one of the youths threw a stone through the front window of the house. His shout of 'Traitor!' was picked up by the mob, who repeated the word until Donny pointed the Glock in the air and fired. Silence followed in the wake of the shot as the would-be rioters turned to face him. Donny kept the pistol in the air as he pointed with his free hand to the youth who had thrown the stone.

'You pick up another rock, Jeb Nash, and I will shoot you. Same goes for any of you as wants to cast the next stone. The right or wrong of what Billy Ray has done has nothing to do with any of his kin.'

'Says who?' Jeb demanded.

'Me and Mister Glock here. Now I suggest you all go about your business.'

Jeb looked set to argue, but Rufus Fortner shook his head. That mob started to disperse, drifting off in twos and threes with backward glances of varying hostility. Give them time and they would be back. Maybe not today. Maybe not tomorrow. But soon, and there would be no dissuading them.

Wayne Cooper looked midway between relief and embarrassment. 'Would you boys like to come in for a coffee, or maybe something stronger?'

'Coffee will be fine, Mister Cooper,' Mike cut in before Donny could reply.

Patty Cooper looked questioningly at her husband as he ushered Mike and Donny inside the kitchen.

'Don't worry. It's all under control now,' Wayne told her.

'Didn't sound under control to me. Sounded like a gunshot.'

Donny dipped his head sheepishly. 'Thought it might help some, Missus Cooper. Least they've left you in peace. For now.'

His words hung in the air for several seconds, then Patty Cooper went off to attend to the kettle, leaving Wayne to pick up a dustpan and collect the broken glass. Mike, spotting the fist-sized rock under the kitchen table, picked it up and deposited it in the pedal bin. Wayne, meantime, produced a roll of masking tape and a pair of scissors from a kitchen drawer.

'Should have some card in the recycling. That ought to keep the wind out until I can get a glazier.' Wayne shook his head. 'I've known Jeb Nash since he was knee-high to a grasshopper. What gets into people?'

Patty placed a tray bearing cups, sugar and milk on the table. She picked up the coffee pot and started to pour.

'Help yourself to milk and sugar. I have some cookies if you want one.'

'Please don't go to any trouble,' Donny said.

'It's no bother. Now, let me see.'

Donny turned as the door creaked open. A curtain of blonde hair appeared as Shania peaked round the door.

'Is it safe for the boys to come down now?'

Patty looked over to where Wayne was taping cardboard over the broken window. Her husband shrugged in response, as full an answer as she was going to get.

'I'll take that as a yes.' Shania caught sight of Donny and Mike. 'Hi, guys. I'll be right back.'

Shania's footsteps on the stairs were followed a few seconds later by the rumble of multiple feet returning. The door swung open again and a pair of brown-haired teenage boys appeared. Donny looked from one to the other but found their features impossible to tell apart. At least one was dressed in a green and black plaid shirt and the other a camouflage T-shirt, his hair noticeably shorter.

Shania pointed to the twin in the plaid shirt. 'Donny, Mike, you know Wade and,' she said, turning her head, 'Dale.'

'Grown a bit since we were last here,' Mike said.

'Boys will do that,' Shania replied with a wink.

Mike felt the blood rise to his cheeks. He hoped Shania didn't notice. She really was all grown up now. He watched her, trying not to stare as she poured the coffee. Judging by the sudden pressure of Donny's foot on top of his own, he was unsuccessful. His smile was brittle as he accepted the cup from Shania.

An uncomfortable silence followed as the Coopers and their guests concentrated on drinking their coffee and eating the Oreo cookies Patty had produced. The twins in particular appeared full of barely constrained energy.

Wade shuffled nervously, refusing to meet the eyes of any of the adults in the room. He eventually screwed up his courage to ask what was on his mind. 'Is Billy Ray a traitor?'

Dale curled his lip. 'Any dumbass can see that. He's shamed our family.'

'The only person in this family there's shame on is you, Dale Cooper!' Shania snapped, 'You've no idea of the hell Billy Ray has been through – and all for this family. The after-school classes you and your brother are getting are because of his service. Likewise, my job and the nano-therapy that treated Pa's arthritis. That's not counting the money he sends home. We've all got plenty to be grateful for. You can all ignore everything that's happening in this country if you want, but I'm glad he finally got out. I hope the rebels win! We need a change of government.'

Wayne stopped midway through tearing off a strip of tape, while Patty stood frozen with her cup half raised to her mouth. Wade stared at his feet, embarrassed at being the instigator of a family row, while Dale appeared to be in search of a suitable comeback.

Donny placed his cup on the table. 'You know what? I think I will have a cookie. Thank you.'

CHAPTER 25

L ynch, seeing his chance, tailgated the lab tech into the medical wing. It had been a hive of activity all morning; the buzz of excitement was visible among the white coated technicians as they went back and forth. But what had really spiked Lynch's curiosity was the delivery of a set of boxes stencilled with African Tech Corps logos. Was this the mysterious Project Phoenix?

The technician placed the box beside seven other identical ones on the stainless steel workbench. He nodded to Lynch as he left, presumably to fetch the next box. A tall, thin man, dressed in one of the ubiquitous lab coats, locked his workstation and crossed to the nearest box. Lynch recognised him as Doctor Bendix, Chief Medical Officer for Eagle's Nest. A frown creased his brow when he saw Lynch, but his attention was quickly drawn back to the box. He broke the seal carefully with a scalpel, then folded back the flaps to reveal a series of needle-gun phials packed inside injection moulded foam.

Bendix turned to the next box, and Lynch extracted one of the phials. It felt surprisingly heavy. The grey liquid inside had a metallic sheen to it. Some kind of nanotech? A prickling sensation on the back of his neck made him aware of the doctor's presence behind him.

'I don't think you're authorised to be here, Mr...'

'Lynch. Jefferson Lynch.' Bendix ignored Lynch's proffered hand. 'I work in Comms HQ. Ms Pulaski asked me to make a promo film.'

'I rather doubt that.' Bendix narrowed his eyes. 'I think it would be best if you left now, don't you?'

Lynch nodded, thrust his hands into his pockets and started to walk away.

Bendix held out his hand. 'The phial?'

'What?' Lynch pulled his hand from his pocket and stared at it. 'Gee, I clean forgot. Here you go, Doc.'

Lynch heard the maglocks engage as the door swished shut behind him, leaving him in a deserted corridor. His instinct hadn't failed him. Bendix – and by extension, Pulaski – definitely had something to hide. They would be watching him after this, so any more physical snooping was out for now. Time to dust off those old hacking skills. The African Tech Corps didn't do pro bono work, which meant a financial trail. First, however, he needed to use those skills to try and get a message to his daughter in Lexington, warning her and his ex-wife of the dangers they faced. As ever, it felt like too little too late. But the alternative meant entrusting Christine's fate to the emancipation of the Religious States.

Lynch's scheming was brought to a close by a message notification on his com-unit. His presence was required in Comms HQ. Had Bendix ratted him out that quickly? He hurried through the underground labyrinth of tunnels and arrived to discover Russell, Pulaski and Drummond watching a newscast on the holo-screen.

The newsreader's face was grim as he read from the teleprompter. 'Caliphate forces have today retaken Damascus, extending their control over the country. Several regions in Jordan have also fallen, with Amman now under siege.'

The bulletin cut to footage of a triumphant Marshal

Ismail stating the infidels will soon be scoured clean from Caliphate lands.

Pulaski smiled gleefully. 'See? It's progressing just as I predicted.'

Seeing Russell was keeping his own counsel, Lynch said what the ex-spook wouldn't. 'Can't you see that we're effectively turning the clock back here? And not for the better.'

Pulaski raised an eyebrow. 'I thought you were against American involvement in the Middle East?'

'I am. But abandoning the non-fundamentalists to their fate will have consequences in the mid- to long-term. A newly reunited America can do without them. Christ we've got almost a century's worth of examples from history to demonstrate what happens when we leave a vacuum. It's never good.'

'Only those who don't learn from history are doomed to repeat it,' Drummond said, 'Meantime, we need to focus on the troops being recalled from the Middle East. They'll be opposing us as soon as they're back on American soil. We need to step up the plan.'

'What plan?'

Drummond looked at Pulaski, who shook her head. 'Need to know only.'

'In case you've forgotten, you summoned me here '

'I'm forgetting nothing,' Pulaski said pointedly. 'We wanted you to see the news first-hand. Now get out there and write about it.'

Lynch knew better than to look to Drummond for support, but he was surprised and disappointed by the closed expression on Russell's face. Having saved his life seemed to count for very little now he was back in the bosom of Free America. But if his suspicions proved true, it would make what came next easier.

CHAPTER 26

Hopkins felt the Templar's eyes burn into her as she ascended the wide marble steps leading to the Congress Building – one for each of the original twenty-six states that had seceded from the US in 2049. The soldier was just the first in a series of obstructions she needed to navigate in order to gain access.

She forced a smile and tried to ignore the carbine slung across the Templar's chest. Armed soldiers in the heart of government appeared to go against everything democracy stood for. But Gerrard had insisted on their deployment – or, rather, Morrison had – which made her suspicious, given the Templars' fanatical devotion to their Grand Master. Thaddeus Vanderbilt, in her experience, was not a man for turning.

'ID, ma'am.'

Hopkins held out her pass for inspection. The soldier, whose name tape said Lomax, pulled the card towards himself, tightening the lanyard around her neck. Maybe he was longsighted, but most likely, he was just a macho dick. He dropped the card and it fell back against her chest.

'Right-hand door.'

Hopkins kept her ire in check as she walked by, heels

clicking on the flagstones. She moved diagonally, walking between two of the great Doric columns that held up the portico. Another pair of Templars stood on either side of the metal studded door. The cold indifference in their eyes reminded Hopkins of her former lover, the now deceased Colonel Tyler. She had gone to considerable effort in her attempt to deprogram his unthinking fanaticism. For a man sworn to celibacy, he had been only too keen to enjoy her body. But he was dead now, her effort wasted. Hannah was right; all she had left on the board to play were lesser pieces. If she did nothing else, she'd prove to the deputy director that he'd underestimated her.

The Templars checked her ID again and waved her through. A double staircase curved sinuously upwards at that the rear of the entrance hall, but first she had to undergo biometric verification and a body scan. Yet another Templar waved her forward and she presented her right eye and hand for scanning. The light turned green and the Templar stepped forward and held out a Faraday pouch. Hopkins placed her com-unit inside and signed for it with a thumb print.

'Any other electronic devices or sources of ignition?'

Hopkins shook her head and he ushered her into the body scanner. She felt faintly ridiculous as she stood with her legs apart and hands raised above her head while she waited for the inner cylinder to revolve back and forth.

'You're clear, Ms Hopkins.'

Hopkins managed to contort her mouth into another smile as she stepped towards the staircase. She followed the left-hand branch, climbing to the first floor, where the House of Representatives sat. But her business today concerned neither the House nor the Senate, and she took the elevator to the fourth floor, where the Majority Senators had their offices. In the wake of the Free America attacks, her own run on the Senate was faltering, and she needed to call in the few favours she had left.

The door of office 4-11 looked no different from its

neighbours. It was a slab of mahogany furnished with brass fittings. Hopkins ignored the red glow of the LCD panel's ENGAGED sign as she knocked and entered. She closed the door and made towards the leather chair in front of the occupant's desk.

Gerschwitz looked up from his workstation. 'Don't bother sitting.'

Hopkins rocked back on her heels, nonplussed. 'Guess you must have forgotten our arrangement?'

'Not at all. But they do say confession is good for the soul. I told Samantha all about my little dalliance with the intern. She's enough of a pragmatist to forgive me for the sake of the children. Particularly in the current climate.'

'Your wife might be okay with your infidelity, but the voters tend to be a lot less forgiving.'

Gerschwitz shook his head and laughed. 'You're deluded if you still think there's going to be a midterm. Believe me when I say the declaration of martial law is imminent. If you're even half as smart as you like to think, you'll get out now. Commercial flights are already grounded, but for those with contacts and money, there are still some private flights available. I'm getting out with my family while I can. You'd be wise to do the same. Even if we win the war, those associated with Gerrard's administration will have to carry the can. Not that I give a shit about what happens to you, Susanna.'

He shut down his terminal, picked up a case and brushed past Hopkins, who stared after him. It appeared Gerschwitz had more backbone that she had credited him with. Strike two. Was she losing her touch?

She dropped heavily into Gerschwitz's vacated chair and stared moodily into the distance. Her options were shrinking by the day. Hannah had made it abundantly clear that they were stuck with Gerrard for good or ill, and any lingering hope she had for a run at the Senate had just walked out of the door. But she would be damned before she went down with the ship. For all the predictable male posturing, the possibility of Free America winning the war was real. In such an event, she would need bargaining power.

Hopkins tapped the power button for Gerschwitz's terminal. Her eyes flitted over the desk as she slipped her hands beneath it in search of a concealed document holder. Nothing. She tapped her fingers on the desk next to the keyboard and then smiled to herself. Sure enough, his login credentials were taped to the underside of the keyboard. She typed them in, opened a second secure browser session, and navigated to the Senate Inquiries and Committees. After a pause, she downloaded them all. Better too much than too little. The policy section was next, particularly with regard to the prosecution of the war against the Caliphate, the deliberate targeting of civilian targets, and the use of "re-education" camps to further reduce the population.

She extracted the data-cube and slipped it inside her trouser suit pocket. If Free America prevailed, she had the evidence to send Gerrard and his staff to the execution chamber while saving her own neck. If, by some miracle, Gerrard won, the leak would be traced back to Gerschwitz, a man who had already fled or died in the attempt. The tricky part would be ensuring she survived either outcome.

CHAPTER 27

Cooper stared at his reflection as the makeup artist applied foundation to his face and touched up the shadows under his eyes. The door swung open to admit Jefferson Lynch. The journalist scanned the room, moving with that squirrely energy of his.

'You know, this wasn't quite what I had in mind when I defected to the Free America movement,' said Cooper, smiling to take the sting out of his words.

Lynch ignored the no smoking sign and the tutting of the makeup artist as he took out a cigarette. He switched on the extractor fan above the mirror and lit up, exhaling the smoke upwards.

'Reckon we've both been sold a pup.' He shrugged. 'Here's the thing. You can shoot a gun, stab a man, even beat him to death a whole lot better than the average Joe. But they got so goddamn many willing to fight that your contribution is hardly worth it. But as a symbol, as propaganda, with your Templar background, well that's pure gold. Pulaski is going to milk that for as long as she can. Then, depending on how the war is going, she might let you take up arms and actually fight for something you believe in. Personally, I wouldn't hold my breath.'

Cooper waved the girl away and pulled the protective cover from his shoulders. She gathered up her brushes, powders and creams, pausing only to give Lynch a dirty look before sweeping from the room. He made sure the door was closed before turning back to Cooper.

Cooper hopped nervously from foot to foot, his fists clenching and unclenching. 'Why can't I catch a single fucking break? God only knows what they're doing to my family back home, and all I'm doing is making shitty videos. If you've got any juice with Pulaski or Russell, persuade them I need to get back in the fight.'

'Trouble is, they're fanatics of a sort you and I know only too well. Turns out there ain't much by the way of good guys in this here fight. Reckon I've outstayed my welcome, as will you. There's something big in the offing. They won't say what, but I don't think it's anything good. I've got its scent, but so far, I've not been able to run it to ground. I asked you to come with me in Jerusalem, but you turned me down. I get the feeling you're ready for a partnership now. Am I right?'

'I ...' Cooper fell silent. He wanted to join Lynch but didn't want to become a liability. Something was wrong with him, and he couldn't ignore it any longer. He took a deep breath and let go.

'I've been having these ... episodes since I got back from Syria. Blackouts, lost time, a sense of being outside myself, of not being in control. They sent me to see a shrink. He said I had PTSD, but I think it's something more than that. You heard about Goodman, right? How he went crazy and attacked the men who rescued us from Marshal Ismail. I think Ismail might have done something to me too. Or maybe Steiner's also been fucking with me. This is going to sound crazy, but I think I might have tried to kill Vanderbilt. Stupid, huh?'

'This war's made us all crazy. Some more than others. Maybe you should get a second opinion?'

'What?' Cooper felt a sudden surge of panic. 'These Free

America guys don't trust me as it is. Reckon Jones and Drummond would like nothing better than to lock me in a cell and throw away the key.'

'Look, I'm no psychologist, but it sounded like you were reaching out for help there. Why speak up in the first place, if that isn't so?'

'I just felt I owed it to you to be honest. You said it yourself – something's been different about me. Thought you had a right to know what you're letting yourself in for.' Seeing the concern in Lynch's eyes, Cooper tried to de-escalate the situation. 'Shit, I'm probably overreacting. I mean I've hardly noticed it all since I've been here – one or two minor incidents at most. Probably environmental, right? Now that I'm out of the Templars and away from Fort Irwin, it'll probably sort itself out.'

Lynch lit a fresh cigarette from the butt of the first one. He exhaled the smoke from his nostrils and smiled. 'Reckon so. But you have any more *incidents*, you can tell me. Okay?'

Cooper nodded.

'They say people don't believe in America no more. Well, you and me, we're gonna give them back the dream. We're going to march into Richmond and pull the whole rotten establishment down, including Gerrard and his cronies. The people deserve better, and that's what we're going to give them. Meantime, we keep our heads down and sniff around. If Pulaski has something to hide, we're going to find it.'

Cooper forced a smile. He agreed with Lynch, but he couldn't quite shake his doubts. Still, he couldn't deny the relief he felt in finally coming clean about it. Seems there was truth in the old adage that admitting he had a problem was the first step to recovery.

CHAPTER 28

Albright parked the car in the pool of shadow between two of the streetlights that lined the drive to Vanderbilt's house. Unlike Bishop Gibson, a kidnapping was out of the question, so it had to look like an accidental death. His SOC coveralls rustled as he unzipped the seatbelt and reached out to open the glove compartment. He retrieved a fresh pair of nitrile gloves, snapped them over his hands, then removed the needle-gun. He had two ampoules. The first contained succinylcholine, intended to paralyse Vanderbilt. The second was filled with a fatal nanotech that would cause a haemorrhagic stroke by rupturing a blood vessel in his brain. How convincing a stroke would be in a man as fit and healthy as the Grand Master remained to be seen. But rumour would only strengthen their hand. If a man as powerful as Vanderbilt could be assassinated, no one was safe.

Albright slipped the needle-gun into his pocket and exited the car. Hannah had supplied him with the codes for Vanderbilt's security system, and it had been simple to disable the alarms and loop the cams.

A tall laurel hedge surrounded the perimeter of the grounds, disguising the plascrete wall behind it. Access was via reinforced steel gates, which closed at an angle to form a prow-like point to deter ramming. Albright pointed his com-unit at the sensor pad and the gates swung silently open. He entered and moved to the right, using the shadows to conceal himself from anyone looking out from the house. A light shone in the glass panel above the front door. The only other light showed around the drawn blind of a window to the right of the door, which the floor plans identified as a lounge. Heat and motion detectors, however, showed no evidence of habitation.

Albright stepped back closer to the hedge and started to work his way counterclockwise. The kitchen and library were similarly devoid of life, but as he rounded the gable, he saw a pool of light cast across the flagstones from the study. Infrared showed a single occupant kneeling in the centre of the room. Albright edged forward until he could look through the patio doors.

Grand Master Thaddeus Vanderbilt, bare-chested, knelt on the boards of the study floor. The geometric pattern of a rolled-up rug was visible to his left. His back was a crisscross of fresh welts and old scars, which he added to with each stroke of the leather scourge he held in his right hand. His blood mixed with his sweat to form pink rivulets. His right shoulder carried the puckered scar of an old bullet wound, a souvenir of the Fall of Jerusalem. At fifty-six, his body showed none of the softening one might expect. Albright was reminded that the Templars used nanotech to augment their bodies. Age, in this case, did not mean weakness. It meant cunning.

Albright overrode the door locks and slipped carefully inside. The rhythm of Vanderbilt's strokes increased as he worked himself into a frenzy, spattering the boards with blood. Albright took the needle-gun from his pocket and primed it. He crept forward, spreading his weight carefully, conscious of the bare boards. One step. Two steps. Three.

A shrill chirping sounded as the floorboard shifted beneath his heel. Albright instinctively glanced down. By the time he looked up again, Vanderbilt was on his feet, facing him. The Grand Master's arm chopped down, driving the edge of his hand into Albright's wrist. The needle-gun slipped from nerveless fingers.

'It's called a nightingale floor. Simple mechanics. Unhackable.'

Albright nodded, acknowledging his mistake as he rubbed life back into his right hand. He was four inches taller than Vanderbilt and a quarter of a century younger. Vanderbilt, in acknowledgment of this, stepped back into a defensive pose. The two men circled one another, neither willing to make the first move, until Albright lashed out with a straight arm jab. Vanderbilt blocked the punch with his forearm and stepped back, opening the space again. Albright pivoted on his left heel, swinging his right leg in what should have been a devastating roundhouse kick, only for it to be blocked once more by the corded muscle of the Grand Master's forearm. The kick left him off-balance, and Vanderbilt capitalised on it by landing a knuckle strike below his right deltoid. Albright's guard dropped in response to the pain and Vanderbilt caught him on the chin with a right cross, snapping his head back.

Albright spat out a mouthful of blood. Bastard was playing with him. Time to up the ante. He feinted left, kicked right, and heard the crack of his foot against Vanderbilt's knee. A hiss of pain informed him that the blow had landed true, and Albright risked stepping in close. He brought his knee up sharply, smashing it into Vanderbilt's groin, but instead of soft flesh, he hit some kind of re-enforced jockstrap.

The split-second pause was all the opening Vanderbilt needed. He locked his arms around Albright and started to squeeze. Albright tried to jab him in the kidney with his fist but lacked the leverage. He pulled his head back instead and smashed his forehead into Vanderbilt's nose, which broke with a satisfying crack. Albright pressed his momentary advantage, using his greater height and weight to force

Vanderbilt to the floor, rolling him as he went and establishing a headlock. He locked his fingers tight behind Vanderbilt's neck and pushed forward. The corded muscle of his neck and shoulders resisted every millimetre, but Albright kept the pressure on. The Grand Master's feet and hands beat a desperate tattoo on the floor as the pressure increased. He had him. Just another few seconds. Hannah would not be pleased, but in time, he would see the advantage of being able to blame Free America rebels for the assassination. A scenario that was likely to hold more credence than a stroke.

Albright caught the flash of movement out of the corner of his eye, but by then, it was too late. He heard the hiss of the needle-gun as Vanderbilt pressed it against his thigh and fired. Too late, he realised the panicked slapping of Vanderbilt's limbs had been a cover while searching for the fallen weapon. His hands slipped from Vanderbilt's neck as his own limbs became impossibly heavy, and he relaxed into the floor.

Vanderbilt pushed himself to his knees and sat back on his heels. He rubbed the back of his neck and spat out a mouthful of blood. Then he began a search of Albright's pockets. He discovered the ampoule and held it up to the light. Albright watched helplessly as he ejected the spent ampoule and loaded the deadly nanotech.

'You don't strike me as the sort of man who would talk, so let's see what you had in store for me, shall we?'

Albright tried to shout out as Vanderbilt pressed the needle-gun to this thigh, but no words came. The sibilant whisper of the needle-gun now heralded his own death. He closed his eyes as the pain exploded in his head.

Vanderbilt placed the needle-gun on his desk and hit the intercom to summon Lachlan. He returned to his would-be assassin and examined the body. The clothing, as he had suspected, was generic, with all tags and labels removed. He peeled back the gloves and saw his attacker's fingerprints had also been removed. A check of his teeth showed them to be suspiciously healthy, most likely stem cell replacements.

He looked up in response to Lachlan entering the room. If his adjutant was surprised to discover his master stripped to the waist and bending over the corpse of an unknown man, he gave no outward sign as he stood awaiting instruction.

'Ah, Lachlan, see if you can get an ID on this fellow.'

Most likely a fool's errand, as his would-be assassin would almost certainly prove to be a ghost. Full body X-rays might help, but odds were that nanotech had been used to strengthen and regenerate the bones, removing evidence of any previous fractures. Not that he was in any doubt as to who had sent the man. But this time, Deputy Director Hannah had overstepped his bounds.

CHAPTER 29

Comms HQ was a hive of activity. Lynch did his best to remain unobtrusive as he hunched over his workstation, filtering multiple newscasts through his earpiece. Air superiority, facilitated by a seemingly endless supply of drones, was allowing the RSA to make tough retaliatory strikes against the civilian population. Morale had plummeted accordingly. Despite an increase in donations of lethal aid, the possibility of Free America losing the war now seemed very real.

If Bendix's experimental nanotech was truly capable of turning the tide of the war, now would be a good time to reveal it. But they were keeping it under wraps, and Lynch's own efforts had yet to determine its scope and nature. Worse still, base comms was locked down so tight, it had proved impossible to get a message to his daughter. His efforts in other directions had proved more fruitful. He had identified direct financial contributions to Free America from Europa City's Tessler Corporation and North Africa's Bamako Tech Corp; the former acquiring controlling interests in Pfizer Inc and Gilead Sciences Inc, and the latter six million acres of land in New York state. Not so much Free America as Sold America.

Russell entered the room and made a beeline for one of the data analysts. His face clouded as he spotted Lynch lurking in the corner.

'Shouldn't you be preparing the latest press releases?'

'You mean the latest propaganda claiming we're winning the war?'

'Jerusalem should have taught you that the first casualty of war is truth.'

'Then what's the point of re-uniting America if we're no different to the zealots across the border?'

'It's the end, Lynch, not the means. I thought you were more of a pragmatist. Hope that Templar headcase isn't infecting you with his idealism.'

'Perish the thought,' Lynch muttered under his breath.

The door banged open, and Lynch spotted the white, peaked cap of a military police officer. Lynch rose as the MP strode towards him. Had his cyber infiltration attempts been detected? The officer's fingers wrapped around his bicep. Lynch tried to shake them free, but the grip was like iron and he had no choice except to conform as he was steered towards the door.

'Hey, I can walk unassisted.'

'Can you? Because Brigadier General Drummond requested your presence fifteen minutes ago.'

Lynch felt the tension flow out of him. He recovered quickly. 'Guess I got distracted. But I'm a hundred per cent focused now.'

'It's all right, Tucker. I'll take it from here.' Tucker turned at the sound of Russell's voice. When he looked hesitant, Russell added, 'Return to your post.'

Tucker glowered at Lynch, then turned on his heel and marched back the way he had come.

'You're welcome, Lynch.'

'I'm welcome? Remind me who recruited who here?'

'I don't see how that puts me in your debt. Or maybe you're fixing to remind me again how you saved my life?'

'Shit.' Lynch ran his palm across his scalp. 'Look, this

isn't just about me. You know the situation with my daughter. Can't you at least get word to her? Let her know what's coming. Surely, that's not too much to ask?'

'All my operatives are engaged in depleting the enemy. I'm sorry, but your daughter will have to take her chances for now.'

'Thanks for nothing.'

Lynch pulled ahead, leaving Russell staring after him. He let the briefing room door swing shut behind him, even though Russell was only a few paces behind. A small and petty victory. It did nothing to help his daughter. He turned and pulled the door open to admit Russell.

The staff officers snapped to attention as Pulaski entered the room. 'Sitrep.'

Drummond cleared his throat, buying himself a moment to phrase the bad news more positively. 'We've been unable to capitalise on our initial gains, primarily due to RSA air superiority. I've utilised all available kill-sats, but it's impossible to stop every drone. Thirty to forty per cent are getting through, targeting our infrastructure.'

'Then we need to retaliate in kind,' Pulaski said.

'What happened to winning hearts and minds?' Lynch demanded.

'You of all people should know our attempts so far have been less than a glowing success.'

'You're going with that? Seriously?'

'What's that supposed to mean?' Pulaski retorted.

'It means once a hawk, always a hawk. You never wanted a peaceful solution. You might be selling the idea of a reunited America, but it's just the means to an end. And that end is Gina Pulaski on top, no matter how many corpses you have to crawl over in the process. You and Gerrard are just two sides of the same coin. I was a fool to think any different.'

'Much as it might shock you, I didn't call this briefing just so you could assassinate my character. So, perhaps we can continue?' She took Lynch's shrug as acceptance and continued. 'Our fortunes are about to change. We've received additional donations of fast attack craft and increased kill-sat coverage, which should address some of your concerns, Brigadier General. But now is not the time for defence.' She shot a look at Lynch. 'We need to go on the offensive – strike fast and hard at the heart of our enemies.'

Lynch straightened in his chair. Pulaski's plan was bold, dangerous, and more than a little crazy. And yet, if he were part of it, he could be back in the RSA and closer to his daughter. And there was only one ally in the whole of Eagle's Nest he trusted to accompany him.

Lynch found Cooper in the rec room, watching Al Jazeera's coverage of the war. The sense that America was getting its just desserts was palpable as the news anchor listed heavy civilian casualties and infrastructure damage on both sides against a backdrop of bombed power stations, refineries and hospitals. America was tearing itself apart, much, Lynch imagined, to the delight of the Caliphate.

'You wanna turn that shit off?'

Cooper raised the remote and the holo-screen fizzed out. 'Shouldn't you be creating something to counter that?'

'Counter the truth? I don't think so. Besides, even Pulaski sees where this is going. We need to end the war quickly, while there's still something left of America to be free.'

'You'll get no argument about that from me. Question is, does she have a strategy for victory?'

'Much as I hate to admit it, she does. They're putting together a fast strike team. Gonna punch straight through to the Capitol and arrest Gerrard. This is the chance we've both been waiting for.'

Cooper was suddenly interested. 'Go on.'

'Stealth technology with air support. An additional three wings of suborbital attack crafts have been delivered, plus control of a dozen kill-sats turned over from Bamako. It's a now or never moment. You in?'

'Is this you or Pulaski asking?'

'You know how this works, kid. Of course, she's signing off on it, and yes, it's all about the optics. No point acting coy about it. That's how it is. Our ride is in the motor pool if you want to check it out.'

'You're definitely going, then?'

'From where I'm standing, there isn't any other option. Not if I want to get to the heart of this war and discover the truth. I wouldn't be Jefferson fucking Lynch if I did anything else.'

CHAPTER 30

Cooper ran his hand along the side of the JLTV, feeling the tiles of its Adaptiv armour. Although it looked unappealing, the advantage afforded by the thermal camouflage made it forgivable. The Tessler X10 was a full generation above the latest model supplied to the Religious States, an indicator that corporate opinion in Europa City was beginning to turn. Or perhaps it was nothing more than pragmatism. There was profit to be made from supplying both sides while prolonging the conflict.

He opened the rear door, climbed inside, and commenced an inventory, starting with ordnance: two UCIWs, two M4 carbines, one M42 IAR assault rifle, four Glock 19 pistols, fifteen 30-round STANAG magazines, eight 18-round polymer magazines, six fragmentation grenades and four Marine Recon FS knives. Seen side by side, Cooper realised the Ultra Compact was essentially a chopped-down version of the M4 he had trained with. He took one from the locker and hefted it experimentally. Overall, the feel was very similar. He flipped up the front and rear backup iron sights and squinted through them, taking spot aim around the cabin. Weight and balance were good, and the length of twenty-two inches made it ideal for operating in confined environments. Fit a decent set of optics and it would be a fine weapon. He made a note to see the quartermaster.

A pair of battlefield med-kits were stowed beneath the rear seats, together with a fire extinguisher and blanket. He lifted the floor panel and confirmed the water tanks were full and the purity monitor showed clear. Lastly, he popped the overhead bins and sifted through the ration packs, a two-week supply for a four-man crew. The obvious readiness and preparation took a little of the edge off his worries. Free America was at least a properly funded and equipped concern.

Cooper closed the bins and jumped from the JLTV to discover Lynch waiting outside.

'How's it looking, kid?'

'Weapons' locker is full and there's a stash of MREs.'

'I'd say I'd missed eating those fuckers, but I'd be lying. You sure you still want to fight against your former comrades?'

'No.' Cooper paused. 'But it offers me the best chance of helping my family. They'll never be safe while the RSA stands. Everything I've done, good and bad, has been for them. Don't know about you, but I've not seen anything here that convinces me life under Pulaski will be any better than it is under Gerrard.'

'Yeah. Been getting that vibe for a while now.'

'Which makes me wonder what we're doing here.'

'Playing the hand that we've been dealt. Neither of us can overthrow Gerrard on our own, so we're stuck with Free America for now. But the intel I'm gathering will help ensure the right people get put in charge of the peace. Reckon that's a victory worth fighting for. So, are you in?'

Cooper nodded. He wasn't sure if Lynch was crazy, and if he was, what that said about himself. But the Templars had taught him the value of keeping busy to avoid dwelling on his thoughts.

He waved Lynch away and climbed into the driver's seat. The instrumentation was almost identical to those of the units he had driven in Israel and Syria, although he had been informed that the auto-drive would handle all duties except combat. He cycled through the menus, familiarising himself with how to deploy the thermal camouflage and countermeasures, as well as programming the navigation. The specs listed the 475kW engine as producing 633 horsepower and 840 Nm of torque. Bastard was going to shift. Just as well, considering the drone saturation.

He thought about Evelyn Rivera: tall, blonde, blue-eyed, remotely piloting the Religious States' various engines of destruction. She did her job without ever concerning herself with the consequences. It felt like a million years ago since he had lost his virginity to her in the front passenger seat of her car. Another victory for the adrenaline junkie; corrupting the Templar novitiate prior to his vow of celibacy. The seven-year age gap between them equated then to a lifetime. And yet, in Jerusalem, it had seemed he might become more to her than just another notch on her bedpost. But he had pulled back, already too embittered by war to risk becoming her plaything. Although, he reckoned the hurt that she showed could have easily been injured pride, rather than wounded feelings. Either way, he doubted she would lose much sleep were she later to discover one of her missiles had put an end to him.

The convoy travelled by night without lights, using GPS navigation software. Cooper refused to relinquish the driver's seat. He peered into the Stygian dark, as though the road might somehow be persuaded to give up its secrets. Behind him, Lynch sat with his finger pressed to his earpiece, sifting the coms in an attempt to determine the true course of the war. Tom Keogh, possessed of the red hair and green eyes of his Irish ancestors, compulsively stripped and reassembled his M42 IAR by touch alone. Terri

Jablonski sat with her arms folded in the passenger seat. The muscular staff sergeant appeared to view her assignment to the JLTV with Cooper and Lynch as a personal affront. Cooper's attempts at conversation were met with one-word answers and grunts. He couldn't decide if this was better or worse than the icy silence she meted out to Lynch. Theirs had already been dubbed the "oddball wagon".

Cooper shrugged it off and called up the navigation map. So far, the convoy's course had cut almost directly west through Jersey, for the intention was to enter the RSA via Delaware. Then would come the perilous journey through Maryland to Virginia, with the Capitol as their ultimate goal. It seemed madness to go overland, but with RSA kill-sats and drones dominating the airspace, a suborbital attack was currently out of the question. An amphibious assault would be launched on Sandbridge Beach as a feint. Would it be enough? Probably not. But he had spent the last two years dodging death, so what was one more roll of the dice?

'Got movement to the northwest,' Jablonski stated. 'Two … three … no, five contacts. Travelling in convoy.'

Cooper scanned the console, looking for an available satellite. He found one and synched its imagery to the display. It lit up with the eerie green of night-vision. He zoomed in and spotted the lead PLS heavy tactical truck; its demountable cargo bed was laden with a surface-to-air battery. The following four trucks were similarly loaded, doubtless on their way to engage with Free America's dwindling supply of drones.

Cooper toggled the comms. 'Are you seeing this, Captain Jones? Do we engage?'

'Do not engage. Repeat, do not engage. Sending alternative route to navi-comp.'

'But they'll …'

'But nothing. The mission comes first.'

Jones killed the connection before Cooper could reply. That he had made the right call didn't make it sit any better with Cooper. He'd been trained to take out all available targets and deny assets to the enemy. He stared moodily through the windscreen into the dark.

'No glory for you here, Templar boy,' Jablonski sneered. 'Lay off him.'

'Word from the peanut gallery.' Jablonski looked Lynch up and down. 'Still don't know what you're doing here. Unless we need to bore the enemy to death.'

'You see, that is the problem with you grunts, Lynch said 'We ain't fighting the enemy. We're fighting fellow Americans. Ones we hope to reunite with once Gerrard is done.'

'Now I know you aren't a military man, but let me fill you in on the basics. Anyone pointing a weapon at me is the enemy, and you better believe I'm going to take that fucker out.'

'That's because you're a real first-class human being, Jablonski.'

Lynch ignored the proffered middle finger. Truth be told, he didn't think Jablonski was particularly stupid or cruel. Her attitude was no different from most of the Free America rebels. More's the pity.

CHAPTER 31

Wayne Cooper's jaw jutted forward as he crossed his arms in front of his chest. Donny knew that look of pride as the old man tried to reconcile the need to protect his family against the shame of abandoning his home. He kept his eyes deliberately downcast to avoid his wife's look of mute appeal. Behind him, Shania sat at the kitchen table with the twins, trying to keep them occupied while the grown-ups decided their fate. Dale's expression remained truculent.

'I'm sorry, Mister Cooper. I really am. But it ain't safe to stay here no more. This war is splitting families, making neighbours into enemies.' His eyes flicked over to the twins. 'And turning brother against brother. That mob out on your lawn earlier tonight hasn't forgotten about you. Sooner or later, they're gonna screw up their courage and come back, and when they do, they'll be out for blood.'

'Sounds an awful lot to me like you're saying we should run and hide. But hide where? And do we keep on running? That don't strike me as doing right by my kin. No. This here is my home. I'll be damned if I let my friends and neighbours run me off of it.'

Donny chewed his lip. Wayne Cooper had given little

indication as to how he felt about the Free America movement and his son's defection. But he could see he needed to offer something concrete to persuade him to uproot his family.

'There's a place we can go – a safe house operated by a pro-Free America militia.' He saw Wayne open his mouth to protest and cut him off. 'Just hear me out. Whatever you think of the right or wrong of their cause, these are good people. They'll see to it that your family is kept safe. I sort of know their leader. When she hears about the bind you're in, I'm sure she'll want to help. It's a couple of miles out of town, on the old back road.'

'You mean Bill Driscoll's old place? Didn't the daughter inherit?'

'That's right. Lena.'

'She cooking meth out there like her daddy?'

'Wayne Cooper!' Patty's voice was disapproving. 'That is ancient history. You don't have to dig too far back into either of our families to find worse.'

'That might be so, but the Driscolls have always been no better than they should be. From what I hear, the apple hasn't fallen far from the tree. Didn't the sheriff lock her up for breaking George Scanlon's jaw?'

'I believe that was after she told him to take his hand off her … well, away from somewhere it had no business being without her permission.'

'So, you're happy for our kids to be under her roof with the rest of those lunatics she calls kin?'

It was Shania who replied. 'I recall you and Ma teaching me right and wrong, and that ain't something I'm going to forget just because I'm in a stranger's home. Seems to me you ought to have a bit more faith in how you raised us. There's no denying we're in a bad situation, but life ain't always fair. Sometimes you just got to face up to it and make do.'

Wayne Cooper looked from his daughter to his wife and saw the resolution on their faces. Beside him, Donny breathed a sigh of relief. Although, he suspected this was only the start of his problems.

Donny told them to pack quickly and bring a change of clothes and toiletries, the bare essentials. His gut told him the mob would be back sooner, rather than later, and he didn't want to contemplate what would happen then. Shooting the sky was a whole lot different from shooting a person, particularly when that person was someone you lived next-door to or had gone to school with. The minutes seemed to stretch to hours as he waited, but then the Coopers finally assembled in the kitchen. He looked at their various rucksacks and packs, wondered if he should search them, then abandoned the idea.

Donny stepped outside and swore. Denied their initial target, the mob had taken out its anger on his truck, slashing the tyres and smashing the windows. He had previously questioned the wisdom of putting Shania, the twins and Mike in the bed while Mr and Mrs Cooper rode in front with him, but now the decision was made. It was a little over three miles to the Driscoll property. He could do it in less than an hour but reckoned he should allow a third again for Wayne and Patty. He had to roll with what he got.

He motioned for Mike to take the lead as they set off at a brisk walk. Shania and the twins fell in behind Mike, while he brought up the rear with Wayne and Patty. The pistol was a malignant lump pressing against the small of his back, but he could not abandon it. The houses thinned as they passed through the suburbs and turned off the main road. Outside the municipal boundaries, the road became dusty and cracked, leading through waste ground and scrub before rising up a thickly wooded slope. Donny felt the incline in his legs and looked over at Wayne. The old man's face was flushed, his brow beaded with sweat, but he strode doggedly on with Patty at his side. Mike, a good thirty years his junior, looked little better. Donny scanned the path. There was a natural plateau about ninety metres into the assent. He would call a rest there.

It took a full ten minutes to reach the plateau, with Patty moving slower and slower in order to spare her husband's pride. Donny made a show of beathing heavily and threw himself on the bed of old pine needles that covered the ground. He watched the others drop down in relief, except for Mike, who stood doubled over with his hands on his thighs, panting heavily. Shania moved over to her father, but he waved her away with an impatient gesture.

'Ten minutes,' Donny informed them. 'Then we move out.'

He took up position on the edge of the plateau, where he could look down. The road stretched through the trees, winding back towards town. He looked for telltale clouds of dust or other signs of pursuit and found none.

Dale stood up. 'I'm just going to … you know.'

Donny watched him disappear into the trees and then lay back and closed his eyes. He could feel the sun on his face and shadows flickered on his eyelids. Suddenly, he was very tired, and the ground below him was soft and comforting.

'Dale!'

The cry was loud, tinged with concern. Donny sat upright. How long had he been asleep? Surely, only a matter of minutes. He climbed to his feet and saw Patty and Shania in the fringes of the wood. Both women were shouting now, and Donny felt a sudden sense of dread. He moved over to the wood and peered through the trees, but the truth of what had happened was already clear to him.

'Do you think he's wandered off and gotten lost?' Patty asked.

A long pause followed before Wayne voiced what Donny feared. 'He's made his choice. We should get moving.'

'What?' Patty's voice was strident, tinged with hysteria. 'We can't just leave him. He could be hurt or …'

Wayne lumbered forward and took Patty's hands in his own. He bowed his head until their foreheads touched.

'You teach 'em right and wrong and hope they make good decisions. Who's to say he isn't right, and Billy Ray is wrong? Like him or not, Charles Gerrard is still our legally elected president. Even if we find Dale, we can't keep him with us against his will.'

'But Pa!' Shania protested.

'But nothing. I've a duty to keep what's left of this family together.' Wayne waved a hand in Donny's direction. 'Lead on, son.'

Before Donny could react, Shania ran past him and disappeared into the woods. He looked helplessly at Wayne and Patty, then started after their daughter, calling out to Mike to stay with the remaining Coopers. Branches whipped his face, adding to his anger as he chased after Shania, following glimpses of her red jacket. He cursed as her shouts echoed through the trees, identifying their position to any pursuers. But had their situation been reversed, he knew he wouldn't have abandoned his kin either. He swore as he tripped over a root and took a headlong tumble, his fingers digging into the mulch of the forest floor. Staggering to his feet, he brushed the pine needles from his clothes and breathed a sigh of relief as he saw Shana standing a few meters to his left in front of a fallen tree. She turned as he moved forward, revealing Dale perched on the trunk.

Donny approached slowly to avoid frightening the boy. 'Hey, we were worried about you. Ain't that right, Shania?'

'I ain't going back!' Dale said, his bottom lip jutting out petulantly.

'Then where are you going to go?' Shania asked. She continued, doing her best to sound reasonable. 'There's only a few days' food in the house, and that mob could be back at any time.'

'It's not fair! We shouldn't have to run away because of Billy Ray. He's the criminal, not us.'

'Now don't you go blaming your brother for this.'

'You're right, it's not fair,' Donny interrupted. 'But if you want to be the bigger man, you have to do what is right.' He held up a finger to silence Shania's protest. 'The right thing is to stick by your family. Your ma and pa have enough worries without you adding to them. They need your support, as do Wade and Shania.' Seeing him start to waver, he added, 'It might all blow over once people have a few days to cool off. We could be home again by the end of the week.'

Dale slipped off the tree trunk and thrust his hands into his pockets. He kept his head down as he threaded his way between the trees. Shania mouthed her thanks and followed him. Donny wasn't convinced he had won the argument, but he hoped the boy would settle once the reality of their situation sank in.

Patty rushed forward as they exited the wood and caught Dale in an embrace. He tried to twist out of it before submitting. Wayne glowered but held his anger in check. He avoided meeting Donny's eyes, embarrassed that he hadn't gone after his son himself. Donny diplomatically held his peace.

They set off again, picking up pace as they began the descent. The mood grew increasingly sour as they pressed on; fear for the future pressed down on them all. Donny turned the day over and over in his head, searching for alternate choices that didn't involve them hiking towards Lena Driscoll's. And yet, wasn't this what he had wanted all along? To take a stand against the corrupt state that had been gaslighting the nation for generations about the threat posed by the Caliphate? He should be triumphant. Why, then, did he feel so scared? Had he expected everyone to unite once the truth was known? A tsunami of public indignation that would sweep the old order away? But all he saw was division, anger, and an unwillingness to accept the truth. The old certainties were gone, replaced by fear and confusion.

The first sentries were posted a hundred metres from the house, a pair of wiry men in their late twenties dressed in army fatigues and carrying assault rifles. Donny thought he recognised one of them as Lena's cousin, Ty Wade. He nodded a greeting and received a steely-eyed stare in return.

'This here is private property. You wanna hike, go back to the woods.'

'We're here to see, Lena. We want to join the militia.'

The other sentry laughed, but Ty waved him to silence. 'Is that so? Thing is, Ms Driscoll recruits soldiers. I see two.' He flicked a glance at Shania. 'Possibly three. And a lot of dead weight. She ain't running no care home.'

Donny felt Wayne Cooper bristle behind him and hurriedly spoke up. 'Maybe not, but this here is Billy Ray Cooper's kin and it ain't safe for them in town. They need protection. In return, Mike and I will fight for you.'

Ty appeared to consider this for a moment, then flipped down the mic from his headset. He spoke quickly and the reply was equally rapid. 'Connor, you're to take these good folks up to the house.'

'Seriously?'

'That's an order.'

Connor muttered something under his breath, but he shouldered his rifle and peeled off to the side to allow them to pass. He fell in behind them, forcing a quick pace. The house turned out to be a two-storey wooden shack with a shingle roof, the front of which was lined with a raised wooden porch. A ragged Stars and Stripes flew defiantly from a flagpole fixed at an angle to the railing. As they drew closer, Donny spotted Lena sitting out on the porch, flanked on either side by another pair of armed men.

Lena stood up as they drew to a halt at the foot of the steps leading up to the porch. She was a tall woman and wore her blonde hair shaved close to the scalp. The sleeves of her army shirt had been hacked off at the shoulders to reveal full arm tattoos. She rested her hands on the butt of a pistol and the hilt of a wicked-looking Bowie knife; her pose managed to look both studied and casual.

'You, I know,' she said, looking at Donny. 'Who's your friend?'

'Mike Dunbar.'

'Haven't seen him on any of the forums or at the meets. You vouch for him?'

'He's good people.'

'Uh-huh.'

The utterance was non-committal. Donny realised he had effectively put Mike, and therefore himself, on trial. Best press on.

'This here is…'

'I know who Wayne Cooper is. You and my Daddy never did see eye to eye. Reckon you thought you were better than him, even though neither of you had a pot to piss in.'

'He was a criminal.'

'Daddy preferred the term "outlaw". Point is, he did what he had to for his family. Seems that's something you can relate to. If not then, certainly now, as you stand here looking for my protection.'

Wayne turned to Donny. 'Told you this would be a waste of time.'

'Point is,' Lena said, cutting him off, 'I'm not my Daddy. Lotta water under the bridge since then. If we're gonna build a new America, we need to put old enmities aside and work together. That said, nobody gets a free ride. There's cooking, cleaning and maintaining the weapons and vehicles to be done. Help with this, Wayne Cooper, and you and your kin are welcome under my roof.' She waited for Wayne to nod his assent, then turned to Connor. 'Take these two boys to be kitted out – uniform, knife, pistol, rifle and ammunition.'

Donny produced the Glock from his waistband. 'I'm all right for a pistol.'

The colour drained from Lena's face as she turned on Connor. 'I'm guessing neither of you pair of dickwads thought to search our *guests* here?'

'You said to bring them up to the house.'

'And if I told you to take a leak, would you need me to tell you to take out your pecker and hold it, or would you just piss in your pants?'

'Sorry, Ms Driscoll.'

'That don't cut it. You and Ty are on sentry duty tonight as punishment.' She looked meaningfully in Donny's direction. 'I sure hope you boys shape up better.'

CHAPTER 32

They pulled the truck off the road half a klick from the checkpoint. Reconnaissance showed two soldiers on guard at the barrier, with another one in the cabin. Best estimate for the depot itself was another half a dozen. All of them were Middle East vets, recalled from the front to tackle the crisis back home, which made Donny nervous. Dealing with the National Guard or state troopers was one thing, but these men were professional soldiers, hardened in battle. Lena might talk a good fight, but she and her men remained amateurs, and he and Mike more so.

He checked his M42 was set to fire three-round bursts and attached the SureFire SOCOM556-MG2 suppressor. Opposite him, Mike continued to stare at his com-unit, examining the depot floor plans. They needed fuel and ammunition, and the depot was stocked with both. Ty's suggestion that the sheriff's office was an easier target had been shut down. Lena wanted a statement; hitting the depot fulfilled that role, while also denying vital material to government forces.

Connor was at the wheel. Beneath the patchy beard, Donny had revised his age down to match his own. He spoke loudly and brashly to cover his nerves, but his handling of the truck was faultless. Escaping with it fully loaded would be a different matter. He'd settle for himself, Mike, Ty and Connor escaping with their lives.

Donny checked the time on his com-unit and lowered his night-vision goggles. He squinted through the Aimpoint Pro scope. The sentries manning the barrier looked bored. It was a little after two am, with their relief not due until six. Clear skies during the day had led to a significant drop in temperature, and both men wore their jackets fastened to the neck, with the collar turned up. He looked to Ty, who nodded. They exited the truck, with Mike following.

The light was on in the cabin, showing the soldier sitting with his back to the door. Ty signalled for Mike to enter, then waved Donny on. They circled round through the woods, arrived at the opposite side of the checkpoint, and selected their target.

Ty stepped out, with Donny following. The red dot of his sight was steady on his target's chest, while Donny's jumped around. Lena had stressed lethal force was to be a last resort; they might be the enemy, but they were still Americans.

'Easy, boys,' Ty warned. 'Lose the rifles and the sidearms, then let's have your hands where we can see 'em.'

A heartbeat passed while Donny prayed neither man got the urge to be a hero. The sentries looked at one another and then laid down their weapons.

'Good. Now hands on heads and turn around – slowly.'

Donny shouldered his own rifle and stepped up to the first sentry. He produced a pair of flex cuffs and fastened the man's hands behind his back. He repeated the procedure for the other sentry and then stepped clear.

'Are you going to kill us?' the nearest captive asked.

'Could have done that already if we'd been so minded,' Donny replied.

'Don't engage,' Tyler warned. He addressed the prisoners. 'Move when told. Speak when spoken to. Stick with that and we're all good.'

They herded the prisoners into the cabin and sat them down on the floor next to where Mike had already placed their comrade. Donny bound their ankles with more flex cuffs and then roped the men back-to-back and gagged them. It wouldn't hold against a determined effort to escape, but all they needed was twenty minutes in the depot

He radioed Connor, who drove the truck past the barrier. They followed it into the depot at a walking pace, skirting the admin block, mess hall and barracks to arrive at the main storage facility. The metal-skinned building covered two hundred square metres. The relief guard would be sleeping, which left the duty officer, comms officer and possibly a mechanic to account for. Heat and motion detectors showed no life inside the shed. Ty motioned for Connor to reverse up to one of the loading bays.

The bay was accessed by an old-fashioned roller-door. Donny pulled nervously on the chain as the slats rattled and clanked upwards. He stopped at the three-quarter point, leaving sufficient clearance for the truck. Ty waved him inside and they sprinted across the loading bay. POL supplies were at the rear of the bay. Ty climbed aboard a forklift and manoeuvred into position to insert the tines into the top-tier pallet, which was loaded with 55-gallon drums. He paused the operation and shouted over at Donny and Mike.

'Munitions are stored on the right. Should be some heavy cal in addition to the rifle ammo. Get some nine mil as well.'

Donny crossed over to the crates and read the stencils on the side. He picked up a case of 5.56 x 45 mm ammunition and heaved it back to the truck. Mike followed with a crate of 9 mm.

Donny was sweating by the time they returned. 'This is stupid. Let's sort out what we need.'

He lifted down another crate of 5.56 ammo, used by both their carbines and assault rifles, and set it down. A quick search turned up another crate of 30-round STANAG magazines, but he'd yet to see any calibre larger than 9 mm.

Mike let out a whistle and slid a smaller crate across the floor. 'Frag grenades. We take 'em?'

'What do you think?'

Donny stacked a final crate of rifle ammunition and looked round. Keen to impress Lena, he headed deeper into the shed, skirting a portacabin as he went in search of .50 calibre rounds. A major supply depot like this had to have some. He spotted some racking ahead stacked with metal ammunition cases and hurried over. A yellow stencil on the olive paintwork identified it as .50 cal with M9 links – food for the M60 Lena was so proud of. He lost his grip as he lifted it off the shelf, and it landed with a clatter. Seconds later, a light appeared in the portacabin, and the door swung open to reveal a figure silhouetted in the light. Donny raised his gun, but his finger refused to pull the trigger.

'Drop your weapon. I won't warn you again.'

Time slowed as he watched the guard raise his rifle to his shoulder, ready to fire. His own weapon was similarly poised. All he had to do was squeeze the trigger. But he didn't want to kill this young man who looked no different from himself.

A muffled shot sounded, and the young man spun back into the room behind him. Fingers dug into his shoulder and spun him about.

'Leave the box. We need to go!'

Donny followed Mike blindly, sprinting for the truck as he tried to process what had just happened. Another couple of seconds and it would have been his blood pooling on the concrete floor.

Ty reached out from the rear of the truck and hauled him inside as Mike opened the passenger door. The wheels were already turning as Conner put it in drive. Ty slammed his hand on the side of the truck, and it suddenly shot forward. More lights had appeared in the admin building, and the first shout of alarm sounded as they exited the loading bay. Conner floored it and the truck accelerated, leaving confusion in its wake. He spun the wheel and the truck veered hard right, taking a forestry path.

In the back of the truck, Ty completed a quick inventory of the stolen materials. He grinned as he spotted the grenades.

'M67s. You shouldn't have.'

'Do you think that kid had a family?' Donny asked.

Ty shrugged. 'Most people do. He was unlucky. Don't beat yourself up over it. Collateral is unavoidable.'

'Wasn't me that pulled the trigger.'

'Don't beat yourself up over that either.'

When they arrived back at the Driscoll homestead, Connor drove past the house and parked up next to a dilapidated-looking barn. But the outer shell was just a façade for a secondary building of polymer and steel erected inside, providing a climatically controlled environment for storing ordnance.

Lena stepped out of the shadows, flanked by her ever-present guards; their names, Donny had learned, were Duke and Errol. She nodded to each of them, then stepped up to the truck, shining a flashlight inside. She allowed the beam to play over the fuel drums and ammunition crates. Her expression gave no indication as to whether the haul matched her expectations.

'Any trouble?'

'Got disturbed by one of the support crew,' Ty said. 'Mike had to put him down.'

'Unfortunate. Could lead to some civilian reprisals. They'll definitely step up patrols. You'd best get this gear stowed and the truck under cover. Once you're done, come up to the house for some chow.'

'You heard her, boys. Quicker we load in, the quicker we get fed.'

They worked quickly, the fear of spy-sats a greater motivation than food, and soon had the fuel and munitions safely stored. When Connor went to park the truck, Ty tossed Donny the keys to lock up. It was the first time he and Mike had been alone together since the shooting.

'I guess I ought to thank you.'

Donny held out his hand, but Mike swatted it away. He clenched his fists. For a second, Donny thought he was about to swing at him, but the moment passed. He stepped back anyway, confused by his friend's anger.

'Are you happy now, Donny?'

'Happy with what?'

'Happy that you've made a killer out of me.'

Mike pushed past him, not waiting for a reply. Donny stared helplessly after him. It wasn't supposed to be like this. The guilt, the fear, the doubting. He wondered if this is what it was like for Cooper at the front: split-second reactions during the adrenaline rush, followed by endless self-questioning. He would do better next time. He had to. Lena would accept no less.

CHAPTER 33

War had not made the Panopticon's Outer-Circle any more welcoming. Its granite walls reflected the dull grey of the clouds on a windswept afternoon. Hopkins shivered as she looked up at the alabaster finger of the Watchtower. She told herself it was a reaction to the cold and nothing to do with the pair of Templars guarding the entrance. They were young men, hard and lean, with eyes and faces devoid of emotion, just like their comrades at the Capitol Building.

The soldier on her left, whose name tape identified him as Adler, held out his hand and barked, 'ID.'

Hopkins produced her ID card in response to the order and handed it to Adler, who held it out in line with her face. He studied it for so long that she was about to ask if there was a problem when he suddenly returned it. However, as she made to step forward, he held up his hand.

'I need to see inside your bag, ma'am.'

'You've never needed to before.'

'New protocol. You can hand over your bag to Templar-Private Sanderson, or you can turn around and go back the way you came.'

Adler's expression made it clear he didn't care which

choice she made so long as she made it quick. Hopkins, reckoning her meeting with the president would be fraught enough without antagonising him by being late, handed over her clutch bag. Sanderson snapped it open and proceeded to empty it by handing her back the contents one by one. Hopkins accepted her com-unit, a small compact, lip gloss and a pair of tampons. She waited while Sanderson checked the lining for secret compartments. Satisfied it contained nothing untoward, he returned the bag and indicated that Hopkins was now at liberty to approach the biometric scanner.

Hopkins hurriedly repacked her bag before presenting herself for verification. The hairs on the back of her neck rose as she felt the Templars' eyes bore into her back. They seemed unusually keyed up, and she wondered if they had been made aware of some threat or imminent danger. Surely, they were safe here, hundreds of miles from the front line. The sight of their reflections in the polished steel door stalled her enquiry on her lips.

The door slid open and she stepped into the curving corridor, turning to the right. Additional Templars had been posted inside, with pairs guarding the doors to the Cabinet and Situation rooms. They were dressed for front line combat in full body armour and armed with rifles and sidearms. Hard eyes studied her, assessing her capabilities and threat level. They were meant to be on the same side, so why did she feel like the enemy? Employing zealots to fight for the country was all well and good, as long as they did the fighting in a foreign land.

Her perambulation brought her to the door of the Lyndhurst Room, where her ID was checked again by another set of guards as a prerequisite for accessing a second biometric scanner. She breathed a sigh of relief as the door slid shut behind her and took a moment to centre herself. Woody Lyndhurst, first president of the Religious States, seemed to smile mockingly at her from his portrait on the far wall.

Ignoring Lyndhurst's apparent scorn, Hopkins used her pass to summon the elevator and pressed the button for the sixth floor. The tension left her as the door pinged open to reveal the empty reception area outside the Central Office. She took a moment to smooth down the front of her suit, then knocked smartly on the door and entered.

The blast shutters were closed, shutting out the view of the Panopticon's Outer-Circle. Gerrard sat with his elbows on the desk, fingers tightly interlinked, his features underlit by the glow of the holo-screen. Behind him, a pair of Cross and Stars flags mirrored the steepling of his arms. The information on the screen scrolled in response to his eye movement as he continued to read. Hopkins cleared her throat, and he waved her to the one remaining vacant chair.

Hopkins swivelled her chair slightly to the left and then back again, repeating the arc every few seconds as she waited for Gerrard to finish reading the report. Kordowski's lugubrious features stared impassively at the presidental seal between the flags. Given the civil war, should the vice president be in the same building, let alone the same room as the president? Not that any of these men would listen to her.

Morrison, by contrast, was full of nervous energy, not dissimilar to the Templar guards. She tried to catch his attention, but he refused to make eye contact. The staff doctor had probably shot him full of uppers. She shook her head, sending a ripple through her long auburn hair. One minute, they were surging towards victory in the Middle East with the Caliphate in full retreat, and the next, they were conceding their newly won territories as troops were recalled to fight a brutal civil war. What-ifs were dangerous, but she couldn't help wondering if they would be in this mess if they had left Hamilton in place as president. She certainly wouldn't be in this room, but that was by-the-by. And yet, it was obvious that Pulaski and Free America had been preparing for war for a long time.

Deputy Director Hannah interrupted, joining the

meeting by video link. 'After an admittedly rocky beginning, we're making progress against the rebels. But vital infrastructure has been destroyed, resulting in an exodus of refugees across our borders, to Canada in the north and to Mexico in the south, sparking a growing humanitarian crisis. It threatens both us and Free America.'

'Frankly,' Gerard snarled, 'I don't care, so long as our enemy's pain is greater than our own. If I haven't made myself clear, I want the Free America states bombed back to the Stone Age, then levelled to the point they won't ever be able to rise again.'

'With all due respect, that's precisely the sort of optics that are harming us,' Hannah critiqued. 'The harder we retaliate, particularly with regard to civilian casualties, the more lethal aid pours in from Europa City, Canada and North Africa. Our forensic accountants haven't managed to trace all the money, but it's clear the rebellion has been funded for some time by outside forces, including the Caliphate. International Brigades are forming as volunteers arrive to fight for a re-unified America. We're going to need all the allies we can foster if we're to prevail.'

Gerrard looked at Kordowski and Morrison. 'Perhaps it's time to remind the world that we are still a nuclear power. I want our nuclear units placed on active standby.'

'Christ almighty,' Hannah blasphemed. 'Don't you think that's a step too far?'

'I don't hear anyone offering me any alternatives.'

Hopkins cleared her throat. 'Might I suggest we concentrate on defence? With the troops returned from the Middle East, we should have sufficient numbers to defeat the FA military. It'll be difficult, but it should halt some of the sympathy towards the rebels. Voters love a victory.'

Hannah turned away from the camera as an armed Templar burst into this office. The video link went dead. Gerrard swiped the holo-screen, and the casualty lists were replaced by the securi-cam feeds. The screen filled with the image of Templars attacking the Secret Service agents assigned to his protection. Grand Master Vanderbilt had finally launched his long-suspected coup.

Gerrard pushed back his chair and stood. As he started towards the elevator, intending to take refuge in the briefing room bunker, Morrison pulled out a ceramic pistol and levelled it at him.

'You're going nowhere, Charles.'

'Have you lost your freaking mind? What's gotten into you?'

'You really have to ask? Hannah became Deputy Director of the Agency. Kordowski got to be Veep. Even Hopkins is getting a run at the Senate. All I got was a pat on the head. Even a dog would have been given a biscuit to go along with that.'

'That's what this is about? You feel passed over? Why didn't you come to me, Lee? I would have sorted something out.'

Morrison sneered. Kordowski, seeing him distracted, made his move. The pistol fired once as he sprang forward. The vice president looked in disbelief at the spreading patch of crimson in the centre of his shirt, then collapsed to the floor.

Hopkins, whose fingers had been edging along the desk towards a heavy glass paperweight, froze.

CHAPTER 34

The door of the Central Office swung open to reveal the imposing figure of Grand Master Vanderbilt. He was dressed for war in full body armour, with a carbine slung across his chest. A heartbeat passed as he regarded his enemies. Then he entered the room, flanked by Colonel Willard and Sergeant Jackson. Morrison, seeing his captives covered by the Templars, lowered his pistol and moved towards Vanderbilt.

'Signed, sealed and delivered as promised.'

'Indeed.'

Vanderbilt smiled, opened his arms, and stepped forward. Morrison returned the smile as he accepted the embrace. He heard a click, and his eyes widened as pain tore through his gut. Looking down, he saw the hilt of the gravity knife embedded in his stomach. Vanderbilt ripped the blade upwards and out, disembowelling Morrison. Hopkins screamed as Morrison folded to the ground, his intestines spilling through his fingers.

'We had a deal ...'

'We did. But a man who would betray one master would just as easily betray a second if he thought the circumstances warranted it. I'm afraid you'll have to settle for getting your reward in Heaven.'

Vanderbilt cleaned the blade on Morrison's shirt, then retracted it. He looked over at the deceased Kordowski before turning his attention to the president.

'He was the lucky one, Charles. You, Hannah and Hopkins will wish you got off so lightly before your trial is over.'

'Trial?' Gerrard's voice was full of indignation.

'For the murder of your predecessor. Don't try to deny it. I have my sources. And I have no doubt that Hannah will, in the fullness of time, provide a full confession. After all, he's familiar with all the techniques that will shortly be applied to him.'

'And then what?'

'Then the people of these great Religious States of ours will see how they have been lied to and misled by those they elected to serve them. Then the Templar order will unite Church and State and rule in its stead.'

'With you as its head?'

'Naturally.'

'Careful, that sounds like vanity.'

'Perhaps. But it was your pride that led you here. You thought you could kill with impunity and humiliate me in public with no consequences. Unfortunately for you, Deputy Director Hannah's choice of assassin was found wanting. But I am a just man. You'll be tried for your treachery in public and given the opportunity to defend the indefensible. After that, you can expect an equally public execution.'

'You could be right,' Gerrard conceded. 'Guess it rather depends on whether you can defeat Free America. Otherwise, you might find yourself joining us.'

'I'm certain God will oversee the victory of the righteous. Colonel Willard, Sergeant Jackson, take them away. I trust I need not stress that no harm is to come to them.'

210

CHAPTER 35

The JLTVs were parked off-road in a copse of trees, shrouded in camouflage netting to shield them from satellite surveillance during the day when the Adaptiv plates were of limited use. The majority of the Free America troops were using the break to get some sleep, but Lynch was too keyed-up for that. He looked enviously at Cooper, who slept with the practised ease of the professional soldier, snatching rest whenever he could. He returned to scanning the news feeds on his com-unit, monitoring the progress of the war.

Luck had been with them so far, and they'd reached Maryland without incident. Government forces and rebels were mainly clustered around Richmond, Virginia as Drummond sought to create a noose around the city. Most states had been subject to so-called terrorist attacks, carried out by fifth columnists seeking to undermine the government. But scan as he might, he could find nothing relating to Lexington. He hoped that meant his daughter was safe.

A notification pinged up on the screen and suddenly all he feeds were being dominated by the same story.

Lynch shook Cooper awake. 'You're going to want to

see this.'

Grand Master Vanderbilt stepped up to the podium and began his address. 'Earlier today, a handpicked squad of Templars arrested President Gerrard and a number of co-conspirators for the assassination of his predecessor, President Hamilton. In accordance with due process, they will stand trial for treason and, if found guilty, be sentenced to death, as the hideousness of such crimes justly merits. I have taken the difficult decision to suspend Congress and, in conjunction with the Church, have taken charge of the country and the fight against the rebels. A state of martial law now exists. For your own safety, you are urged to remain indoors unless employed in an essential role. Stay tuned to the Emergency Broadcast System for updates.'

The colour drained from Cooper's face and his focus appeared to shift to some faraway point. He spoke in an eerie monotone. 'Vanderbilt has to die.'

'Steady on there, kid. Let's not get ahead of ourselves.'

Cooper's knuckles whitened as he clenched his fists. 'He has to die.'

'Okay...'

Lynch, disturbed by the sudden change in Cooper, backed away. He hoped whatever it was would pass quickly. In the meantime, he needed to speak to Drummond. He stepped around the slumbering Jablonski and set about opening a secure comms channel to the brigadier general.

'What the hell are you doing on a secure line, Lynch?'

'You've seen the news?'

'If you're referring to Vanderbilt's little coup, then yes. What of it?'

'What of it?' Lynch hopped from foot to foot. 'Don't you see? This is a game changer. The more they tighten their grip, the faster people will slip from their control. We'll finally get our popular uprising.'

'Or maybe they'll just knuckle under like before. Did you consider that?' Drummond continued without waiting for a reply. 'No. If anything, this only makes our mission more critical. Vanderbilt's zealotry is a danger to us all. You're to press on for Richmond. We have additional kill-sats online to secure a no-fly corridor all the way to the Capitol. I'm transmitting coordinates for a rendezvous with a special convoy. Their cargo is to be protected at all costs. Drummond out.'

Lynch stared at the dead connection. He should have known Drummond was too intent on having his war to backdown. He would just have to hope his faith in the spirit of the American people was justified.

They cut across country, travelling at maximum speed, often exceeding driving conditions for the road, relying on the split-second reflexes of the navi-comp. Whatever they were rendezvousing with, Drummond clearly thought it worth risking their necks. Jablonski met Lynch's questions with a series of dismissive grunts, and Keogh simply shrugged in answer. With Jones unlikely to be any more forthcoming, he settled for staring moodily at the passing landscape. His one hoped-for ally proved no more communicative as Cooper obsessively unloaded and reloaded the bullets from his various magazines.

Lynch took out his hip flask and shook it; it was half-full. He unscrewed the cap and took a drink, looked around the interior of the JLTV, and took another. For all his other flaws and addictions, he had never been much of a gambler. Yet here he was, betting his life on black at the roulette wheel of fate. What was it the Cheshire Cat had said to Alice when she asked how he knew she was mad? "You must be. Or you wouldn't have come here." He laughed mirthlessly as he screwed the cap back on the flask.

An hour later, Jablonski snatched up the headset in response to a coded squawk on the comms. She listened intently for a few seconds before toggling off the channel. The JLTV slowed in response and a few seconds later Lynch felt a steady vibration through its wheels; something large and heavy was on the road ahead. He craned his neck to see out the window as they drew alongside a HEMTT military transporter. Its cargo was shielded inside a container, and the cab was armoured with a GPK machine gun mount. The gunner waved to them as they sped past. Lynch counted twenty vehicles in the convoy before they pulled in front.

'You gonna spill, Jablonski? I'm guessing it's not tractor parts in there.'

'You might be closer than you think,' Jablonski replied with a laugh. 'Don't worry. It'll become clear soon enough. Meantime, sit your ass back down and enjoy the ride. Richmond, here we come.'

Cooper paused midway through reloading a magazine. 'It's siege equipment.'

'How the fuck…'

'Educated guess,' Cooper cut Jablonski off. 'We all saw the footage of the barricades being airlifted into place around the Panopticon. Only a fool would try and assault it directly, so it stands to reason this high-value convoy of ours contains some sort of equaliser. Plasma breachers or industrial lasers.'

'Not even warm, Templar boy.'

Cooper shrugged and resumed reloading the magazine. Lynch waited for him to finish, then reached out and grabbed the magazine as Cooper made to eject the first round again.

'Think you've checked that enough.'

For a moment, he thought Cooper was going to argue, but then he tucked the magazine into a pouch on his vest.

'Everything okay?'

'Just dandy,' Cooper replied.

Before Lynch could continue, he produced a whetstone, unsheathed his knife, and started to sharpen it. Lynch took the hint, dropped his HUD in place, and polarised it as dark as it would go. Situation normal, all fucked up.

CHAPTER 36

Hannah screwed his eyes shut against the sudden glare as the hood was pulled from his head. He inventoried his surroundings. A windowless room tiled in white, and a single chair bolted to the floor, to which his ankles and wrists were secured to with cable-ties. A trolley with a car battery, leads, crocodile clips, and heavy rubber gauntlets. Two buckets of water. A table and a towel. Torture – or as the Agency preferred to call it, Enhanced Interrogation Techniques 101. Let the prisoner see the implements and method, then allow his anxiety and fear to build as he anticipates the pain to come. In time, the imagined pain would be worse than the actual pain. Hannah nodded his approval.

The snatch squad that had abducted him from his office had been quick and efficient, bundling him into a waiting vehicle. A series of interminable turns suggested a circuitous route intended to disorientate and confuse. For all he knew, he might now be less than a klick from his original location. No one spoke as he was led from the vehicle and into a building, where the same process was repeated up and down stairs and along corridors until he reached his present location. He took some comfort in the fact he hadn't been put onboard a plane and flown out of the country, but that could change soon enough.

His interrogator stepped forward, revealing himself as a tall, muscular man dressed in military fatigues, the epaulettes of which bore a major's golden oak leaves. In common with many Templar veterans, he favoured a crew cut and a full beard, cut square at the bottom where it rested on his chest. He halted a couple of paces in front of Hannah, forcing him to tilt his head back in order to meet his gaze.

'How the mighty have fallen. One day you're a deputy director of the CIA, the next … But then the Good Book warns us of the dangers of pride, and you, Matthew, have been so very sinful.'

'Is that a fact, Major…'

'Lomax. Kyle Lomax. Five hundred and first Templar Military Intelligence.'

'Isn't that an oxymoron?'

'It's good that you have a sense of humour, Matthew. Because you're going to need it before the day is through. But I forget, I'm talking to a man well acquainted with the process of interrogation.'

'Yeah, have to say, I like the setting. What are you running? Tessler VR sim Z5 series? Or is this something newer?'

The corners of Lomax's mouth drooped in an exaggerated fashion. 'I'm afraid this is quite real. Some of my younger colleagues favour virtual methods, but I've always preferred the hands-on approach when it comes to extracting information. When you look into the subject's eyes, see the rapid pulse in their neck, hear the stentorian rasp of their agony, you know how much more it will take to break or kill them. It's an art form that cannot be replicated by pressing a button.'

'Why do I get the feeling you're hard right now?'

'Ah.' Lomax wagged his finger. 'That humour of yours. But as one professional to another, I will extend the courtesy of offering you a chance to confess.'

'Confess to what, exactly?'

'Your part in the conspiracy to assassinate President Hamilton. A false flag operation blamed on Omar El Zayyoud and used to justify military action in Syria. Confess your guilt, name your co-conspirators, and I promise you a mercifully swift execution.'

'You had me right up until the execution part.'

'Regrettably, that part is non-negotiable. Your final destination was set from the moment of your arrest. You will not leave this room without confessing your guilt. You can do so swiftly or with encouragement. I can assure you that you will not enjoy the latter.'

'Perhaps not. But I've been trained to resist such techniques.'

'Indeed. And now it's time to put that training to the test. I do hope you don't disappoint me.'

Lomax pulled a knife from the sheath on his hip and proceeded to cut the shirt from Hannah's body. He cast the shredded fabric aside, picked up one of the buckets and poured water over his captive's head. Hannah tried to shake it off, but the water was already running down his back and chest, soaking into the waistband of his trousers. Lomax crossed to the trolley, pulled on the heavy rubber gauntlets, and attached the leads to the battery. A spark flashed as he touched the crocodile clips together.

'Are you sitting comfortably? Then I'll begin.'

CHAPTER 37

L ena held up her clenched fist and the squad crouched in the undergrowth. Donny craned his neck, trying to see what had caught her attention. Movement drew his eyes, and he spotted a government patrol point-man cutting across the path ahead. He then counted a further four, all of which were wearing full body armour.

Since the declaration of martial law, government forces had been cracking down on the rebels and those suspected of aiding them. Donny, Mike and Ty had been out on patrol for three hours, gauging the strength of the enemy in the hope of formulating a counterattack. Truth was they were outnumbered, outgunned and outclassed. Hit and fade was the only tactic left to them, and even that was becoming less effective. They were fleas irritating a hound.

Donny looked askance as Lena. She shook her head and held position for a further five minutes. Then, having convinced herself there were no additional patrols or rearguard, she finally moved out.

Donny fell in behind as Lena took the lead. Ty brought up the rear, looking nervously from side to side. It took them an hour to return to the house, circling the long way through the woods to remain under cover. As they drew close to the house Lena seemed to sense something was wrong and again called a halt.

Donny took out his field glasses and scanned the porch. At first it looked empty, but then he spotted the crumpled forms of Errol and Jake. The dark pools beneath them could only be blood. He felt the familiar knot of fear form in his gut. Panning round, he spotted the APC parked at the edge of the road. The side door was open, and he could see a shorter figure dressed in civilian clothes sitting between two soldiers. Donny zoomed in and swore as he recognised Dale. He must have been picked up in the woods and given up the location of the house.

Lena hissed and he offered her the glasses. She shook her head and pointed at the front door, which had opened to reveal Wayne Cooper standing with his hands on his head. Patty, Shania and Wade followed him outside. They spread out in a line in front of the house before being herded to the side by a trio of armed soldiers.

Another pair of soldiers appeared, dragging Connor between them. His right thigh was soaked with blood, and he groaned in pain as they lowered him onto the steps. One of his captors took out a med kit and applied coagulant to the wound, which looked like a through-and-through. He wrapped it in a dressing and then stabbed Conner in the other thigh with an injector pen. Some kind of painkiller, judging from the relief on Conner's face. He helped Connor to his feet and got him aboard the APC.

The APC shook as it started up. The troops began walking the Coopers towards it. Wayne stopped and clutched at his chest. Patty screamed as he sank to his knees. She turned and attempted to go to his aid but was held back by one of the soldiers. Shania's attempts met similar resistance. One of the soldiers dropped down and, after checking Wayne's airways and breathing, commenced CPR. Another ran towards the APC, while the others kept the Coopers back from the patient. The second soldier returned quickly, carrying a defib. He tore open Wayne's shirt, then used his knife to cut open his vest, while the first stopped chest compressions. Then he opened the defib, took out a razor and shaved an area on Wayne's chest. He attached the shock pads while his buddy continued to deliver rescue breaths.

An electronic voice crackled through the air. 'Analysing. Move clear of the patient. Shock being delivered.'

The first soldier lifted his hands off Wayne's chest and watched his patient's back arch in response to the shock. He checked for signs of breathing and then swapped places with his partner, who resumed CPR. They went through another three shock cycles before powering down the defib.

Patty pushed forward as they started to peel off the shock pads. 'Please, you can't stop. I need you to keep going.'

The soldier who had first examined Wayne stood up and walked over to Patty. 'I'm sorry, but he's gone. We did everything we could for him in the field, but it wasn't enough.'

He caught Patty's elbow and held her as her knees buckled. Wade started to cry, and Shania pulled him to her. Donny cuffed a treacherous tear away and raised the glasses again.

The second soldier had finished packing up the defib. He toggled on his radio. 'Sarge, Rodriguez. Casualty is Tango Uniform. Orders?'

'Leave in situ. Clean-up squad will collect the body along with the other casualties. Return to base.'

'Understood.'

Shania screamed and refused to move as the soldiers tried to direct her towards the APC. Patty took her hands and wiped the tears from her face.

'Now, girl, I need you to be strong. Carrying on like this isn't gonna help no one. I need you to look after your brothers. Can you do that for me?'

'Yes, Ma.'

Patty took the lead and walked calmly towards the APC; Shania and Wade followed. She refused the offer of assistance and climbed aboard the APC. Wade was the last to be loaded. He kept turning to look at his father, perhaps expecting a miracle. His was the last face Donny saw as the soldiers closed and locked the side door. A Jeep appeared and the remaining troops climbed aboard. It kicked up dust as it pulled away in the wake of the APC.

Lena tapped Donny's arm. 'Go check on Errol and Jake. We'll follow the APC into town. See what we can do.'

Donny stumbled forward. The air felt thick around him, and he had to force himself through it. Mike shouted something, but his voice sounded slow and distorted. His world shrank to the figure lying on its back, which had come to symbolise all his mistakes. Time continued to stretch as he closed the distance step by step. Despite all he had seen and heard, he knew he wouldn't accept Wayne's death until he checked for himself.

Donny hunkered down beside Wayne. The old man was ghostly pale. A sheen of sweat covered his skin, while his eyes stared sightlessly at the heavens. He closed Wayne's eyes and said a silent prayer. Dying like this seemed stupid, cruel and arbitrary. Maybe he'd always had a weak heart, and this was on the cards. But he couldn't help thinking the shame of Billy Ray's defection and the stress of being on the run had played their part.

'Hands where I can see them. Now!'

Donny cursed. He should have known they wouldn't have left the house unguarded. Not when they knew members of the militia were unaccounted for. He felt a flash of rage, for his own stupidity and at the seemingly callous manner in which Wayne Cooper's body had been left to lie in the dirt. Time for a dirty trick of his own.

'Please, man. He's still got a pulse. I can save him.'

It was a fleeting moment of conscience, but Donny seized it. As the soldier's rifle dipped, he pulled the pistol from the front of his waistband and spun around. The rifle stuttered an instant before he fired, kicking up dirt to his right. Something stung his temple, but by then he had already squeezed the trigger twice. Double tap, centre mass, just as Lena had taught him.

The soldier threw his arms up in the air and fell backwards. Donny was already on his feet. He kept his pistol sighted on the fallen soldier as he kicked away the rifle. His shots had gone high, one hitting the right shoulder and the other just grazing it. Donny looked into the soldier's eyes and saw acceptance rather than fear. His finger tightened on the trigger. This was one of the men who had killed Errol and Jake, and he had him at his mercy. All he had to do was squeeze the trigger. But what would that make him?

Donny holstered the Glock and then searched the soldier, removing his pistol and knife. He opened the man's med kit and applied coagulant, just as he had seen them do to Connor's wound. It bubbled and hissed as it formed a crust. Next, he applied a dressing and administered pain relief, then assisted him to the steps of the house.

'Name's Simpson, Eighty-second Airborne,' the soldier introduced himself. 'Guess you need to decide what you're going to do with me. Might have been simpler just to put a bullet in me when you first thought about it. Don't get me wrong. I'm glad you didn't.'

Donny hesitated, but there seemed no harm in talking. 'Donny Ackerman. Jonesboro Militia, fighting for a free America.'

'Doesn't that come free with a box of Cheerios?'

'Is this a joke to you?' Donny pointed at Errol and Jake's bodies. 'Did you kill my friends and laugh about it?'

'War's no joke, which is why you should be certain what you're actually fighting for. Take a look around. You see all that spent brass around your buddies? We gave them the chance to surrender. They didn't take it. That's how it goes in war.'

Donny fell silent. He removed the radio from Simpson's

lapel and ground it underfoot, then took the flex cuffs from his belt and secured the paratrooper's wrists and ankles. After another moment's hesitation, he removed his canteen and set it beside Simpson.

'Your sergeant called in a clean-up crew. Sit tight and you'll be okay.'

'Fair enough. I'm going to give you some advice, which I'm sure you won't like and even more sure you won't take. Quit playing soldier before you get yourself killed. You got lucky earlier, but if I'd had backup, you'd be dead. You didn't think to secure the house before treating me. There are only two kinds of soldiers in war: professionals and the dead. I see you again, I'll kill you.'

'I'll take that as fair warning.'

Donny initiated his GPS tracker and set off in pursuit of Lena and the others.

CHAPTER 38

The sky lit up with tracer rounds as the JLTV and HEMTT gunners poured a steady stream of fire into the government lines. The hastily dug trenches offered little protection from the heavy calibre rounds. They had entered the city from the north, travelling along Interstate 95. They encountered only light resistance until Bryan Park, where a detachment of state troopers had chosen to make their stand. The troopers were poorly disciplined and equipped, making for easy targets. If they weren't shooting fish in a barrel, it wasn't far from it.

Cooper picked up a fleeing trooper on motion sensors and sent a burst after him. He watched the man spin around before collapsing onto his back. Their progress seemed too fast, too easy, and he wondered if they were being led into a trap. But the mission parameter remained unequivocal: capture the Capitol.

The last ragged line of defence broke. Cooper, sickened by the butchery, let the survivors run. He caught hold of a grab handle as the JLTV lurched back into motion. The white ziggurat of the Capitol was dead ahead. Above, the heavens blazed with fire as opposing kill-sats fought for supremacy, for whoever controlled the skies would command the land below. He heard the buzz of a drone overhead but had no means of telling if it were friend or foe.

The JLTV gathered pace as it homed in on the Capitol. Two more vehicles followed in its wake, trailed by the snaking convoy of HEMTTs. Small arms fire rattled off the JLTV's armour as they encountered pockets of resistance, but the column had developed an unstoppable inertia. One foolhardy soul tried to attach a magnetic mine and disappeared under the wheels. Cooper felt the JLTV bounce twice as the front and rear axles ground the body into the road.

The JLTV braked sharply as the white stone of the Capitol filled the windscreen. With the exception of the external lighting, the building remained in darkness. The politicians and support staff had already fled or been evacuated. The ornate wooden doors at the top of the steps stood open, inviting the unwary inside.

'Is it just me, or does that look like a trap?' Cooper asked.

Jablonski nodded. 'Anything from booby traps to an assault force waiting to attack the rear. Take your pick.'

'So what's the plan?' Lynch asked.

'For you and the Jesus' sunbeam here to keep your asses in this vehicle, while Keogh and I neutralise any threat.'

Cooper clenched his teeth. 'Still don't trust me?'

'Not overly. But if we smoke anyone out, I want someone who knows what they're doing manning the M60.'

The debate apparently over, Jablonski grabbed a bandolier of CS grenades and popped the door. Keogh grabbed a second set and followed the sergeant. Lynch raised a questioning eyebrow and Cooper shrugged in response. He climbed up into the turret and checked the M60 was locked and loaded. He swung the gun on its mount to cover Jablonski as she pumped the grenade launcher mounted below her carbine. The first shot went through the open doors, the second a first-floor window. Keogh joined in until they had covered the building floor to ceiling. As the sound of the final shot reverberated away, plumes of gas drifted from the shattered windows; the sodium lights transformed it into an orange-yellow haze.

Jablonski radioed in and Cooper felt the thrum of the engine starting up again as she and Keogh made their way back to the JLTV. He stayed in the turret as they rode away, covering the first of the HEMTTs to take up position behind them. Here, the road was wide enough for a second JTLV to ride parallel to the transporter. Cooper recognised it as belonging to Jones. It kept station until the barricade around the Panopticon came into view, then peeled off as the transporter convoy parked parallel to the fortification.

A mobile command carrier drew up alongside Jones' JTLV and the comms crackled to life. 'Eagle Leader to all Eagles, assemble for briefing.'

Lynch patted Cooper on the back as he descended from the turret. 'Looks like we're about to discover what's inside those transporters. Which is good, 'cause that wall locks like a tough nut to crack.'

Cooper checked his rifle for the fifth time as a distraction from his thoughts. He had seen too much combat to be frightened, but he felt uneasy at the prospect of fighting against his former colleagues. Up close, the prefab barricade looked even more daunting. The huge plascrete blocks, with cast-in fire steps and loopholes, formed an impenetrable wall around the Panopticon, reinforced at regular intervals by anti-aircraft batteries. As he looked at that three-metre-high off-white wall, he imagined Jackson and Adler patrolling behind it, possibly accompanied by some of the latest intake, pressed into service at this hour of need. Men – boys, he corrected himself – such as Porter, Dwight and Hollister. For what felt like the millionth time, he found himself asking where the cycle of violence would end. Certainly not with Pulaski, if Lynch were to be believed.

Cooper turned his head to the command carrier, where Lynch had been installed to broadcast the assault on the

Panopticon. His mood had been dark since the news of Vanderbilt's coup had broken; his views were increasingly at odds with the Free America leadership. Cooper knew him well enough to suspect some craziness was brewing. He hoped it wasn't the kind that would see him locked up, or worse.

A gull-wing door opened in the side of the carrier and Jones stepped down. Following a field promotion, he had swapped his captain's bars for a major's oak leaves. Cooper was troubled that such a relatively low-ranking officer was in charge of the assault, but knowing he was here on sufferance kept his peace. Brigadier General Drummond, a man who clearly preferred to lead from the rear, had remained at Eagle's Nest and would be relaying his orders via satellite. *Disapprove all you want*, he told himself, *but you volunteered for this.*

Habit kicked in as Jones approached and Cooper snapped to attention. Jones returned his salute with a lazy wave of his arm.

'Hand me your rifle.'

Cooper handed over the M8. Jones took out a triangular bandage from his med kit and fastened it to the rifle. He stepped out into the open ground between the command carrier and the barricade, then waited for a few seconds to ensure his flag of truce had been acknowledged before approaching the Templar defences.

'I am Major Jones of the Free America Second Battalion. I wish to speak with the commanding officer.'

Cooper recognised Willard as he appeared on top of the barricade. A shiver ran down his spine as he recalled the siege of Jerusalem. Only this time, he and his former comrades were on opposite sides of the barricades.

'Colonel Willard, First Templar Division's Combat Aviation Brigade. Say whatever you have to say and be done with it.'

'Your men are outnumbered, Colonel. And while your defences are formidable, you have limited access to food and water, precluding a lengthy siege.'

'If this is the point where you ask me to surrender,' Willard interrupted, 'I'll save you wasting your breath.'

'If you don't value your own life, at least think of the lives of your men. Brigadier General Drummond guarantees they will be treated fairly and honourably as prisoners of war.'

'Since you speak of honour, let me remind you that those men, like myself, are Templars. We took a sacred oath to defend the faith. There will be no surrender. Look to your own men, Major, for you'll lose many if you insist on attacking. We fight to the last man and the last bullet.'

'You'll find my men are equally willing to die for their beliefs.'

'Then may God have mercy on the fallen.'

Jones stalked back to the command carrier and thrust the rifle into Cooper's hands. He took out his radio and initiated an uplink. 'Eagle's Nest, this is Eagle Leader. You are clear to commence bombardment. Repeat, you are clear to commence bombardment.' He clicked the radio off, glanced at the sky, then addressed Cooper. 'To your station, soldier.'

Cooper acknowledged the order, pulled the bandage from his rifle, and slung it over his shoulder. The roar of the suborbital attack crafts filled the air as they dropped through the atmosphere. The Templar anti-aircraft batteries moved in response, rocket tails criss-crossing the sky as they laid down their wall of defensive fire. Cooper saw the first fireball blossom high above as one of the suborbitals exploded. Men had died. More were about to die. And all for what he knew to be a diversion.

Beyond the command carriers, the convoy trucks had been circled like an old-fashioned wagon train, with stealth awnings drawn out to form a second outer circle. It was beneath this infrared and radar shielding that Free America's great equaliser waited: the mole-miners. Cooper approached the first of the cylindrical yellow and black checked tubes.

A metre and a half in diameter and four metres long, they carried a crew of three and had been designed for exploration and rescue work. The drill bit's triple tungsten carbide cones would make easy work of tunnelling below the barricade.

Jablonski was standing with one foot on the bottom rung of the mole-miner's launcher, a cigarette dangling lazily between her lips. She took a final draw, dropped it to the ground, and twisted the butt beneath her heel.

'Time to see whose side you're really on.'

'Don't worry, I'll do my bit. You do yours.'

Cooper pushed her away from the ladder and climbed into the mole-miner. Keogh was already seated in front, monitoring the status board. The drill would be run from the command carrier. All twenty units would be synched together to breech the surface simultaneously, and the vibration and noise would be covered by the aerial bombardment. At least, that was the hope, for there would be several seconds of vulnerability when they exited the mole-miner.

Jablonski climbed in behind Cooper and closed the hatch. A two-minute countdown appeared on the status board. Cooper fitted his earpieces, which would double as comms and hearing protection. He strapped himself into the four-point harness as the launch module's hydraulics elevated the mole-miner to sixty degrees. Vibrations rattled through the outer hull as the drill bit spun up to speed. Drill time was estimated at just under two hours to cover the twenty-six-meter distance. Cooper closed his eyes as the countdown hit zero and the vibration increased.

Cooper watched the mole-miner inch towards its target. Due to the short distance, they had almost immediately started to climb again on reaching their target depth. The breech point was the lawn surrounding the Panopticon's outer ring, an area identified by satellite imagery as being clear of defences. However, the imagery was now forty-eight hours out of date, as a brutal war of attrition in the heavens had rendered both sides effectively blind. Willard, in Cooper's experience, was an unimaginative soldier. As such, he would not waste resources guarding what he believed to be an impenetrable rear. Not unless someone overruled him.

Cooper turned his attention to the battle aboveground. The first two attack waves had taken heavy casualties, but with the anti-aircraft batteries running low on rockets, they were now starting to once again exert air superiority. A flight of RSA drones had been launched and beaten back, but not before one of the transporter trucks was taken out. Cooper thought of Evelyn Rivera, ensconced safely in an UAS pod, as she mechanically went about her duty. He doubted she would be troubled by whose flag she flew under. Like so many before her, she would doubtless claim she was only obeying orders. But if she represented the banality of evil, men such as Gerrard and Vanderbilt were its true architects. Was Gerrard even still alive? Lynch had thought it likely when they'd spoken; Vanderbilt needed a big show trial to endorse his authority. As ever, it was all about the optics of the politics.

'Three minutes to breech!' Keogh warned.

The vibration decreased as the mole-miner moved from bedrock to substratum. Cooper locked and loaded his M8, then lowered his goggles into place. The men above weren't brothers or comrades; they were Tangos. Nullify them. Move on. Complete the mission objective. In the white-hot heat of action, there was no time for thought. Hesitation meant death.

'Breech!'

The mole-miner appeared to hover for a moment before crashing back to the level. Jablonski threw open the hatch and fired a wild burst as she jumped free. Cooper heard similar shots as the Free America troops sprung their trap. They were amateurs wasting ammunition. The Templars would make every round count.

He paused in the hatch. The Templars were already

turning to face the new threat, jumping down from the fire step and sheltering behind supply crates. Cooper sighted on one and dropped him before moving clear of the mole-miner. This was the weak part of the plan, for the Templars still had vestiges of cover, while the FA troops were brutally exposed. He dropped to one knee and targeted the troops still manning the barricade, shooting them in the back. He took out three before they accepted the untenability of their situation and abandoned their posts.

The return fire increased as the Templars smoothly picked off their targets. He heard Keogh scream but had no time to check if he was wounded or dead. The slower FA troops had been killed as they left the mole-miners; others had been shot while trying to close with the Templars. Cooper reckoned fifty percent of their force was down, compared with maybe a quarter of the Templars. They were now outnumbered by almost eight to one.

A bullet grazed his shoulder. He spun and directed fire at a pair of Templars, forcing them to take cover. He changed magazines and rolled over to where Keogh had fallen, using his body for cover. Five meters to his left, Jablonski was attempting to crawl forward. Machine gun fire ripped up the turf in front of her and she pressed herself into the ground. On his right, Jones had piled two of the dead into a makeshift barrier, occasionally popping above it to fire off a shot. It was a stalemate that showed no immediate sign of being broken. Where were the troops Drummond had promised would scale the barricade while it was undefended, trapping the Templars between two forces? Doubtless history would record it as too little too late. Not that Cooper would read it; he, along with the rest of the assault force, would be long dead.

Others had already reached that conclusion. Cooper heard a scream of rage as Mendonza jumped to his feet and rushed the Templar line, ripping the pin from a grenade. He staggered back once, twice, three times, as bullets tore into him, but rage and momentum kept him moving long enough to throw the grenade. It rolled to a halt in front of the Templars' makeshift barrier. Cooper turned his head away as it exploded in a shower of deadly shrapnel.

The gap was there, small and temporary, and Jablonski made to seize on it. Cooper came back to one knee to provide cover fire; the muzzle flashes to his right indicated Jones was doing the same. But the Templars were quick to recover from their disarray and blood and brains exploded from the back of Jablonski's head. The half dozen troops following in her wake were similarly cut down as the Templar line closed again.

Silence fell as wreaths of smoke drifted across the battlefield. Cooper looked to Jones, but the major had no strategy. They had been relying on surprise to roll up the Templar defences. Everything had hinged on taking control of the barricade. All the Templars needed do was wait. The Free America forces had no cover and no means of retreat.

Cooper toggled on his throat mic. 'Eagle's Nest, this is Eagle Nine. We need aircover. We need it now!'

'Negative at this time, Eagle Nine. Hold. Repeat, hold.'

The line stuttered and crackled as they closed Cooper's com channel. Hold for what? He gripped his rifle tight, fighting back his frustration. *Slow is smooth, smooth is fast. Regroup and assess the situation.* He signalled to Jones to withdraw, but the major instead directed Cooper to look left.

Jablonski's body had started to twitch and writhe. The Templars pulled back to the barricade, fearing a bomb. Cooper started to back away as well.

'What the fuck…'

Jablonski's corpse stood up.

CHAPTER 39

Jablonski's eyes stared sightlessly ahead. The back quarter of her skull was missing where the bullet had exited, and her shoulder was covered in blood and brain matter. Next to Cooper, Keogh's corpse began to twitch, and he saw two more Free America casualties rise from the dead. Jablonski jerked as a three-round burst hit her in the chest, exiting her back in a bloody spray. She raised her own rifle and returned fire, making the Templars scramble for cover.

'Fuckers are using Lazarus tech!'

Keogh was on his feet, as were Pemberton and Wilson, whose corpses were also animated by the outlawed nanotech. They would burn hot and fast, fading in a matter of minutes, but during that time the AI controlling their hardwired nervous system would drive them to inflict as much damage on the enemy as possible. No wonder Pulaski was so secretive about what her troops were being injected with. They were breaking every convention and accord.

Cooper flattened himself against the ground as the firefight intensified. In the face of an enemy that refused to die, Templar discipline started to break down. Knowing there was a rational explanation was one thing, but fear of fighting the dead was quite another. Jablonski and

Pemberton broke the Templar line and started rolling it up, like an ancient trench. As the dead continued to pour into the gap, they turned left or right, driving the Templars clockwise or anticlockwise around the perimeter. Jablonski eventually collapsed, as did Wilson, but there were others to take their place. As their ammunition ran out, the Templars fought on with rifle butts and knives. Their numbers dwindled until they formed a small defensive circle. But the Lazarus drones were fading too, dropping one by one. Keogh was the last of them to fall, but the damage was done. Only three Templars remained standing, surrounded by the bodies of their comrades. Jackson, his helmet lost and his face bloody from a scalp wound, pulled the trigger of his pistol reflexively as it clicked empty.

Cooper staggered to his feet, shocked by the destruction of his former comrades. Had he really expected anything different when he had volunteered to be part of the attack? And yet, maybe some last shred could be salvaged.

'It's over, Sarge,' Cooper called out. 'You fought well, but you're beat. Surrender and let us treat the casualties.'

'You know I can't do that. You might have forsaken your vows, but with God as my witness, I'll hold to mine. We fight to the last man and the last bullet. Just like Commander Maxwell at the Fall of Jerusalem.'

'I'm begging you, if there was ever any friendship between us, don't do this. There's been too much blood spilled already. Don't add to it needlessly. Don't die for nothing.'

'One man's nothing is another's everything. But if you understood that, you wouldn't be standing opposite me.'

Jones pushed Cooper aside. 'That's enough jawing. Time to finish this.'

Jackson uttered a grunt as the major raised his sidearm. His eyes widened in surprise as blood frothed between his lips. Then he pitched forward, revealing the knife in his back. Cooper recognised Porter as he raised his hands in surrender. As he had suspected, the young novitiates he'd been training at Fort Irwin had been pressed into service.

Cooper caught the tensing of the other Templar's muscles and stepped in as he leapt at Porter, catching him across the throat with the edge of his hand. Jones stepped forward, but Cooper waved him away.

'It's okay, Major. I don't think Novitiate Hicks will be causing us anymore trouble.'

Hicks turned his head and, between gasping breaths, coughed a glob of phlegm onto Cooper's boot. 'Traitor.'

Lawerance, at Jones' signal, came forward to secure the prisoner, leaving Cooper to face Porter.

'I had to do it. You understand, right? He would have gotten us all killed. It's over. We lost. End of.'

Cooper nodded, suddenly too tired for words. Jackson would never have surrendered, but that didn't make it any less painful. He owed the sergeant his life, as the sergeant had owed him his, so perhaps in the end they were quits. And yet, Jackson had been a good man, a decorated career soldier who had served his country proudly and never once shirked his duty.

Cooper became aware of other troops around him as the reserve force belatedly scaled the barricade and fanned out to secure the area. Porter was cuffed and led away. He looked impossibly young, little more than a child. Would he stand trial for murder or become a hero of the reunited republic? Whatever served the narrative best. Cooper shook his head. He had clearly been spending too much time in Lynch's company.

He began his own search, checking each of the Templar casualties for familiar faces, hoping he might find some other survivors.

There were none.

Cooper took a roll of the dead as he went: Dwight, Fielding, Diego. Thompson really had been lucky that day, when he fell from the aerial assault course and shattered his leg. Was he watching this on the vid, full of regret or relief? The one that got away.

Only there was another notable absence: Colonel Willard. He looked to the tall alabaster finger of the Watchtower in the centre of the Panopticon. Somewhere inside, the colonel was waiting for him, as was the Grand Master. Cooper gripped his head as a wave of unthinking rage tore through him. He pushed it down, confused again as to why Vanderbilt had become the sudden focus of his anger. Steiner could deny it all he wanted, but Cooper couldn't shake the conviction that Marshal Ismail had programmed him during his time in captivity, just as he had done to Goodman. Perhaps that, more than anything else, had driven him to defect. Ismail be damned, he wouldn't give in. Not when he was this close to being free of the war and returning to his family.

But first there was one last member of the dead to honour.

Cooper knelt beside Adler's body. His eyes stared accusingly at his former brother. He had taken two rounds in the chest and drowned in his own blood. Cooper closed his eyes as an image flashed in his head: Adler, the first of his intake to cross the chapel floor to the altar and receive the coveted red cross pattée from Colonel Tyler. They were all dead now, with the exception of himself and Goodman, who remained locked in the secure ward of the military psychiatric hospital in Barstow. What a waste of hopes, dreams and ambitions. Then again, wasn't that the story throughout the ages of young men who had gone to war?

Jones laid a hand on Cooper's shoulder. 'Having second thoughts?'

'If they didn't die here, they'd probably have died in the Middle East. We need to end this war.'

'Then we should press on to the Panopticon. Vanderbilt is holed up there. Once he's gone, the rest of his people will follow.'

Cooper picked up his rifle. 'Vanderbilt!'

CHAPTER 40

Donny caught up with Lena, Mike and Ty in the diner opposite the local sheriff's office, where the Coopers and Connor had been imprisoned with other rebel sympathisers. He accepted the field glasses from Ty and scanned the building. A cordon of sandbags had been erected in front of the office, protecting two soldiers manning a heavy machine gun. At least three more were visible through the office windows, with a pair of snipers positioned on the roof. There was no sign of the sheriff or his deputies; the office had been completely given over to the military. It would be a tough nut to crack, since a frontal assault was nothing short of suicide.

Lena shook her head and ordered them to fall back to the mall. The automatic door swished open and Donny felt the instant relief of the air-con. An empty mall was a curious thing, with the store lights dim, the escalators at a standstill, and the absence of the white noise hubbub of families. They fanned out as they moved further inside, away from the exposure of the doors.

She tried to hide it, but Donny could see that Lena was rattled. She had lost Errol and Jake, Connor was wounded and captured, and the men they were facing were well-armed and well-trained. The smart move would be to fall back, stay operational, but despite her initial reluctance, it was obvious she now felt a duty of care for the Coopers. All Donny felt was guilt. It played with him as they took up position behind the coffee kiosk. The echo of their footfalls faded away as silence fell once more.

In the hush, the opening of the security office door and the footsteps that followed were loud. Donny's rifle was at his shoulder before Lena finished shouting the order. The four of them found themselves facing off against the sheriff and two of his deputies. Sheriff Foster's pistol was pointed directly at Lena, while his deputies covered the group with combat shotguns. A zero-sum game.

'Now don't you stand there acting the fool, Lena Driscoll,' Foster said. 'I've known you and your family since you was a little girl. I might have put your daddy in jail a few times, but I never did shoot him or any of your kin, and I ain't about to start now. So why don't we all just take a breath and lower our weapons?'

The standoff continued for several seconds before Lena reluctantly holstered her pistol. Donny exhaled slowly as rifles and shotguns were pointed towards the floor. Foster holstered his own pistol. The skin around his eyes crinkled as he smiled.

Lena placed her hands on her hips and tilted her head defiantly, trying to hold onto the illusion of being in charge. 'This is all well and good, Sheriff. But what are you aiming to do about the Coopers and other political prisoners?'

'Going to reason with them, is what I'm going to do. These are regular army folks, not the hardcore fanatics that have seized control. Anyone with a lick of sense can tell the smart thing to do is stand down and let what's happening in the Capitol play out. In case you haven't heard, the rebels have taken control of Congress and are closing on the Panopticon. Vanderbilt's coup might prove to be short-lived.'

'That's as may be,' Lena replied. 'But they've killed ours

and we've killed theirs. They just gonna forget about that?'

'I don't know. But people kill one another in war, and that don't stop peace from breaking out. And peace always begins with people talking. So I'm going to walk out here with Deputy Amos and Deputy Reed and see if I can't do some negotiating. You can stay here, or you can come with.'

Foster, good to his word, set off, with Amos and Reed at his back. They were halfway to the entrance when Lena shook her head. 'Damn it. Let's go.'

The heat was oppressive. At least that's what Donny told himself was making him sweat. Foster walked slowly, almost as if he were doing a foot patrol, making sure the soldiers saw him and his deputies approaching. It was less than four hundred metres between the mall and the sheriff's office, but, as if responding to an unseen message, people began to emerge from their homes. They came in one and twos and threes, forming up around the sheriff until a sizeable crowd had gathered. If Foster could not name every single one of them, after twenty years of service he was familiar with most. Donny recognised some of them from the mob that driven the Coopers from their home. Now, faced with a common enemy, they were all on the same side.

The snipers trained their weapon on Foster as he stepped to the front of the crowd. He positioned himself in front of the machine gun post, arms neutral at his sides.

'My name is Bill Foster. And as you can see from this here badge on my chest, I am the sheriff of Craighead County. I'd like to speak with your commanding officer. If that's okay with you boys?'

One of the soldiers spoke into the radio on his lapel. A short while later a tall, lean man in his early thirties emerged from the office. He folded his arms, revealing the paratrooper wings on his sleeves, and fixed Foster with a stare.

'Major Robert Stanley, Eighty-second Airborne Division. Sheriff, you know by what power I'm authorised to act during this period of martial law. You also know this crowd constitutes an illegal gathering, which I'm required to disperse – by force, if necessary.'

Foster nodded. 'That's all true, Major Stanley. But I know you don't have enough cells to arrest the whole town. More to the point, are you willing to start killing civilians who are merely exercising their right to peaceful protest? If you'll pardon me for saying so, that don't seem like the act of no soldier to me.'

'I take it you're proposing something to the contrary?'

Foster looked up at the big holo-projector in the town square. 'Why don't we put on the vidcast, settle back and wait and see who should be surrendering to who?'

Stanley looked from the tired faces of his men to the hopeful faces of the crowd that far outnumbered them. He didn't doubt he could take them, being for the main part unarmed and comprising largely of women, children and the elderly. But the sheriff was right. It would be a cowardly and despicable act.

'Sergeant Chisolm, see if you can patch comms through to the screen.'

CHAPTER 41

Hopkins tried the door again, as if she might magically find it unlocked. Despite the blast shutters being in place she could hear and feel nearby explosions as battle raged outside. Without visuals she had no way of knowing who was winning and what that meant for her future. She grabbed the edge of one of the shutters and pulled. It remained obstinately in place, so she started a fresh circuit.

'Will you stop pacing?' Gerrard complained. 'You're driving me crazy.'

'We need to come up with an escape plan!'

'If that's rebels outside, we might be safer staying put.'

'You do that, Charles. I'll take my chances with the rebels. Yes, they might kill us, but Vanderbilt definitely will!'

As if summoned by his name, the door opened to reveal Vanderbilt and Colonel Willard. Vanderbilt's blank expression gave nothing away as he ordered the colonel to take charge of the prisoners.

Willard marched them to the elevator at gunpoint and kept them covered while Vanderbilt called the carriage. It would be cramped with four of them, limiting Willard's ability to use his pistol. Vanderbilt, seemingly sensing

Hopkins' intention, smiled and drew his sidearm.

'Like the animals into the ark, we shall go two by two. After you.'

Vanderbilt selected the button for the briefing room, taking them below ground. Hopkins kept her face impassive as the beginning of a plan formed. The Grand Master's arrogance would be his undoing.

The conference table was lit up with holo-displays showing the progress of the war. The blocks of blue and red painted a picture of disaster for the Religious States.

'The Capitol,' Vanderbilt needlessly explained, 'is already in rebel hands. The regular army has stood down, and only the last of my Templars stand between them and the Panopticon.'

Gerrard laughed. 'Guess your coup is going to be short-lived, Grand Master.' His pronunciation of Vanderbilt's rank was mocking.

'Perhaps. Then again, perhaps not. I'm willing to offer you and your staff amnesty. All you have to do is address the armed forces and get them back on our side.'

'And if I don't?'

'If you don't, the RSA will fall into the hands of apostate scum like Gina Pulaski. Is that really the legacy you want to leave behind you? The man who lost the Religious States to heathen scum?'

Gerrard straightened himself and looked Vanderbilt in the eye. 'Frankly, if it's a choice between giving America to religious zealots such as yourself or to Pulaski, that dried-up husk of a Democrat gets my vote.'

Vanderbilt nodded his acceptance and started to turn away. Then he stopped and spun around, delivering a powerful backhand blow to Gerrard's face. Caught off-guard, Gerrard dropped to one knee. He wiped the blood from his face from where a heavy ring had burst open his cheek.

'Thought you had a bit more class than to bitch slap a man when he isn't looking, Thad.'

'That was always your mistake, Charles – thinking we're equals. Let's be clear on one thing. I will not lose this war and concede our country to atheists and heathens. If you won't address the army, you'll give me the nuclear codes, and I'll put an end to the United States once and for all.'

'Are you crazy? The fallout will poison Canada, Mexico and much of our own lands. You'll govern over a wasteland.'

'God will protect the righteous.'

'Go to hell.'

'I see you're not going to be civilised about this. Willard, start with his left pinkie.'

Gerrard made to run, but Willard was too fast for him. He caught the president in a headlock and dragged him over to the conference table. Steel flashed as he pulled a dagger from its sheath. He splayed Gerrard's hand out on the table.

'Struggling will only make it more painful.'

The blade chopped down and blood sprayed through the projection of the Panopticon. Vanderbilt smiled coldly in response to Gerrard's scream. In the distraction, Hopkins seized her chance and dived towards the door. Her hand slapped the panic button as she rolled through, causing a secondary blast door to slam down and seal the room.

Hopkins' heart hammered in her chest as she staggered to her feet. Apart from herself, now that Morrison and Kordowski were dead, only Gerrard had the codes to reset the system. Of course, it was only a matter of time before he gave them up.

She skirted past the elevator, knowing it would be out of service, and made for the end of the corridor. The outline of the panel was faint; her nails scraped across the surface as she tried to prise it open. She swore, paused, then tried again. The panel clicked free, exposing a sensor pad. Hopkins pressed her right palm against it and a hatch slid open in response to the biometric scan. Lights fluoresced to life as she climbed through, illuminating the steep slope of the tunnel that would take her to freedom. She closed the hatch behind her and started to climb.

CHAPTER 42

L ynch swapped between feeds from his camera drones, choosing the best angle to broadcast. The assault on the Panopticon had reached its final stages, with FA forces having gained air superiority. The blackened ruins of offices and rooms in the outer circle were like missing teeth, with the smoke-wreathed Watchtower the final point of defiance. Lynch spiralled the camera around its soot-blackened stone, taking in the heavy steel blast shutters that covered the windows. He pulled back sharply to show the circle of men and steel that surrounded the Watchtower before focusing on the assembly of a railgun. A countdown appeared on his HUD and he toggled on his mic.

'Jefferson Lynch, broadcasting for Free America. You join me at eleven-fifty-two on the twenty-third of July, a day that will surely mark the end of the Religious States of America and the birth of a reunited republic. The last vestiges of government forces, under the command of Grand Master Thaddeus Vanderbilt, are trapped inside the Panopticon. The fate of President Charles Gerrard and his staff remains unknown. The final assault can only be an hour or two away, perhaps as little as minutes. Stay tuned for real-time coverage of events as they unfold.'

The door of the command carrier banged open and Jones climbed aboard. 'Rousing stuff, Lynch. Only Pulaski thinks it will play better if we give them the chance to surrender.'

'I take it you're otherwise minded?'

'Vanderbilt doesn't strike me as the type to meekly give up. But you'd probably know better than I.'

'Never met him.'

'Then it's your lucky day. Pulaski wants you to cover the negotiation.'

Lynch keyed up a "Broadcast On Hold" image. He pulled on his vest with its PRESS markings and strapped on a helmet. Nominally, they would be under a flag of truce, but times were desperate, and he hadn't come this far only to catch a bullet at the end.

Cooper was waiting for them outside. Something in his expression told Lynch it wasn't his idea. Doubtless Pulaski was looking to parade her Templar defector. Good optics. Poor negotiating. Typical careerist politician.

Lynch walked across the scorched lawn with Cooper and Jones, doing his best to ignore the serried ranks of body bags. This was not the sort of reunification he had been hoping for. Cooper's jaw tightened. Fighting the rank-and-file troops was one thing, but facing off against men he had trained and fought with was another. Lynch had been sorry to hear about Jackson. Knifed in the back by a frightened kid who wasn't willing to unquestioningly lay down his life for his country. It wasn't enough to win the war. They had to win the peace.

They stopped five metres from the Watchtower in an area that had been cleared of the detritus of battle. Lynch launched the drones and waited. The blast shutter rolled back on a first storey window to reveal a standing figure. The silhouette was wrong, but Lynch zoomed in to confirm his suspicion. This man was shorter and heavier built than Vanderbilt; his head and face were clean shaven. If Lynch was at all uncertain as to his identity, the clerical collar put it beyond doubt. It was Chaplain-Commander Du Pont.

Du Pont stepped forward as the window slid open. 'Ah, the hack and our wayward heretic. I suppose I shouldn't be surprised to see you here, Cooper. A dog always returns to its own vomit. But you, Major, are not known to me.'

'You have me at a similar disadvantage, sir,' Jones said. 'I was expecting to negotiate the surrender with Grand Master Vanderbilt.'

'You can expect all you want. But the Grand Master doesn't wish to speak with you. His instruction, however, is clear. There will be no surrender. Not to a rabble of heretics who have attacked a legitimate democracy. The world is watching, Major Jones. As is God. He will not allow this outrage to stand.'

Du Pont turned away as the window closed and the blast shutter rolled back into place, sealing off the room. Lynch recalled the drones to the docking station on his belt.

'That went well.'

'Laugh it up all you want, Lynch. But the appearance of our clerical friend suggests Vanderbilt is either incapacitated or dead.'

'Maybe. But it doesn't put us any closer to ending this war.'

'Says you. I've got four railguns in position,' Jones said. 'All I need is the word and that tower is toast. If these guys are so keen on God, I'm happy to send them to meet His ass in person.'

'Just as well you're not running the show.'

'Sometimes I wonder whose side you're on.'

'Same side I've always been – that of the ordinary American. The kind of people who are going to have to pick up the pieces once you and Drummond are through with playing soldiers.'

Jones' retort was blotted out as a hopper passed low overhead, setting down on the lawn in front of them. The nose was decorated with the Stars and Stripes and the fuselage with the old presidential seal of the original republic. Looked like Pulaski was ready to declare herself president elect.

The tail ramp descended, allowing Pulaski to step down, followed by Russell and Drummond. Two security officers brought up the rear. Jones snapped to attention and Cooper reluctantly followed suite. Lynch took out his hipflask, raised it in an ironic salute and took a swig. He fumbled for his cigarettes as Pulaski told them to stand at ease.

'The clock is ticking, gentlemen, and the Watchtower remains in enemy hands.'

'Permission to speak freely, Ma'am?'

Pulaski nodded at Jones.

'We gave them a chance to surrender, and they turned it down. Let's level the Panopticon and turn it into Vanderbilt's mausoleum.'

'Unacceptable, Major. At the very least, Gerrard must stand trial if we're to have any semblance of legitimacy in the eyes of the world.'

Pulaski's voice trailed off. Lynch followed her gaze over to the Panopticon's outer wall, where one of the pickets stood with his rifle trained on a tall woman with auburn hair. The interloper raised her hands.

'Hold your fire! I surrender.'

The security officers tried to block Pulaski's way as she made to step forward, but she waved them away. Her eyes narrowed as she squinted. 'Is that Susanna Hopkins? How the devil did she get here?'

She set off towards the newly captured prisoner, forcing her security detail to fall in behind. Lynch, sensing a story, paused long enough to launch his camera drones. He circled them round, getting a close look at Gerrard's spin doctor. Her normally smart appearance was somewhat undermined by an untucked blouse and missing shoes. Dirt smudged her trouser suit and sweat streaked her makeup, but she held herself up straight.

'Susanna Hopkins.'

'I know who you are,' Pulaski said. 'What I don't understand is what you're doing here. Can't imagine Vanderbilt released you to negotiate.'

'No, I escaped.'

'That much would appear obvious.'

'I initiated the lockdown protocol and shut Vanderbilt, Willard and Gerrard in the briefing room.' She pointed at the opening behind her. 'Used the escape tunnel. Only Gerrard's authorisation codes can release them. It's a question of how long it takes Vanderbilt to torture those and ... the nuclear codes out of him.'

That final statement hung between them.

Finally, Pulaski continued, 'You were in the room with him. What's Vanderbilt's state of mind? Is he really willing to use them?'

'He's a fanatic, and few things are more dangerous than a cornered fanatic. The prospect of losing the war has driven him over the edge. You won't reason with him; I can tell you that much.'

'Damn it.' Pulaski pinched the bridge of her nose between forefinger and thumb. 'There must be some alternative to just bombing the bastard.'

'There is.' Hopkins' smile failed to hide the calculation in her eyes. 'But before I give you anything, I want your guarantee of immunity from prosecution.'

Pulaski shook her head. 'In case you haven't noticed, we're a little short of notaries or attorneys. Nothing I offer you will be legally binding.'

'Oh, but we have something so much better.' She pointed to the hovering camera drones. 'I'm sure Truth and Justice there will hold you to account. So, do we have a deal?'

Pulaski's stare was baleful, but it was equally apparent that she had little alternative. 'Okay, but any deal is dependent on your information securing the Panopticon.'

'I can work with that.' Hopkins pointed to the dark maw of the escape tunnel. 'Insert a strike team and use my override codes to enter the briefing room. Worst case scenario, Gerrard is already dead, and you have to kill Vanderbilt, but at least you stop Armageddon.'

'I don't like it,' said Russell. 'How can we be sure it's not a trap? Her escape could have been orchestrated precisely for that reason.'

Doubt clouded Hopkins features as she sought to resolve some inner conflict. She uttered a sigh. 'If one of you gentlemen would like to reach into the right inside pocket of my suit jacket and take out my com-unit.'

Pulaski nodded and one of her security guards retrieved the com-unit. The other levelled his pistol at Hopkins' head.

'Hold the screen in front of my face to unlock it. Good. Now open the authenticator app and the shortcut to tesslerlocker.com. Username is Hopkins. Password Black Diamond. Got that? The pin number for the authenticator is one, three, one, zero, one, nine, three, zero. Type in the code it generates. Okay, now it also needs my thumbprint.'

Hopkins pressed her thumb against the screen.

'Reckon Russell is the best person for this if you pass him the com-unit. What you'll see there are a series of policy reports and Senate meetings relating to the prosecution of the war against the Caliphate. Highlights include the deliberate targeting of the civilian population and the use of "re-education" camps to achieve further depopulation. There's enough there to hang Gerrard a dozen times over, assuming Vanderbilt hasn't already tortured him to death. The longer we stand here debating, the more likely that becomes. And the more likely we'll see a mushroom cloud on the horizon.'

Pulaski turned to Russell. 'Is the information legit?'

'Reckon so.'

'Can't say I like it, but we don't have a choice.' Pulaski looked at Hopkins. 'But if this is some kind of a trap, I'll personally put the rope around that lovely neck of yours.'

If Hopkins had a reply to that it was cut off by Cooper snapping back to attention. 'Permission to volunteer,

Ma'am.'

Pulaski considered it for a moment and then nodded. 'Major Jones, go with him. You have ten minutes to secure the target before I send in a strike team to clear the building. Hopkins, time to give up those override codes.'

Lynch, unable to shake the bad feeling from earlier, caught Cooper by the arm as he made to ready himself. 'You know it's a suicide mission, kid? Going in blind, the place crawling with God knows what.'

'Maybe. But it's the only way I can stop carrying the weight of the war. You get that? I have to face Vanderbilt and Willard. I'll never be free otherwise.'

Lynch nodded. 'Good luck.'

'Any chance I can bum a cigarette off you?' Hopkins asked.

Lynch almost refused but then relented. No point being petty. He extracted his pack from his vest pocket and shook one free. As Hopkins bent to receive a light, he smelled sweat mixed with whatever floral scent she was wearing. Her hand barely shook at all.

Hopkins took a long draw, exhaled through her nose, and smiled bitterly. 'I underestimated you. If I'd known then what I know now, I'd have let Tyler execute you. He'd still be alive, and who knows how this war would have turned out?'

'That's where you and I differ. I always knew you were a viper.'

'No. I'm a survivor. Just you wait and see.'

CHAPTER 43

Cooper pulled ahead of Jones as they descended. The nagging pain was back behind his ear. He tapped the spot a couple of times. The major's presence was a complication, but he knew Jones wouldn't stop him from doing what needed to be done when the time came. He slowed down, allowing Jones to catch up. Best not to raise any suspicion beforehand.

Slow is smooth. Smooth is fast.

The angle of the tunnel levelled out and Cooper signalled Jones to stop. Cocking his head, he heard a whining noise. He opened the hatch a crack and looked out into the corridor. Two Templars were operating a tripod-mounted industrial drill, the bit of which was skipping and jumping against the seemingly impervious blast door. The whine rose to a screech as the operator put his full weight behind the drill. The drill bit bent, then a sharp ping sounded as it snapped, sending the tip spinning across the corridor.

The two Templars looked at the faint scratches on the door and then at one another. The drill operator shook his head and powered it down.

'Fuck it. Let's go and get some nano-corrosives.'

'Are you sure that's a good idea?'

'Reckon it's preferable to facing Du Pont and the lash, don't you?'

The two men moved back to the elevator, the door of which had been forced open. A pair of ropes dangled inside the empty shaft. The first man clipped on his ascender and activated it, and his body quickly disappeared upwards. His companion gave him a twenty-second head start before following. The coast was clear.

Cooper opened the hatch and crossed the corridor. Jones covered him as he opened the keypad beside the door and typed in the code Hopkins had given them. The blast door shot back into its housing and the main door swung inwards. Cooper dived through, rolling to the left and coming up into a crouch. Jones angled to the right, his rifle trained on Vanderbilt, who stood impassive as he watched Willard cut off Gerrard's right thumb. A collection of severed fingers and an ear lay in a bloody pile on the conference table.

Cooper sighted on Willard. 'Step aside, Colonel. This will be your only warning.'

Willard raised the bloody knife and Cooper shot him in the head. Gerrard, his eyes glazed with shock, started to crawl towards his liberators, the stumps of his fingers leaving bloody trails across the floor. He saw Jones step forward to secure Vanderbilt and shook his head frantically. The warning came too late, as the Grand Master triggered the gravity knife and stabbed Jones through the heart. Jones' mouth formed a perfect "O" of surprise as Vanderbilt pushed his body aside.

Cooper felt a stabbing pain behind his ear as he sighted his rifle for the kill shot. He put the weapon aside and drew his fighting knife. After what felt like months of torment, he now had clarity. Complete the mission. Kill Vanderbilt.

Vanderbilt bowed his head in prayer. 'Hear me, Heavenly Father, and strengthen my hand against the apostate!'

'I don't think He's listening. Ask me, He hasn't been

listening for a long time.'

They sparred back and forth, neither man able to penetrate the other's defences. Cooper fought defensively, inviting Vanderbilt to attack in the hope of wearing the older man down, but the Grand Master's righteous anger powered him on. His strategy failing, Cooper darted forward, and the point of his knife scored a shallow wound in Vanderbilt's cheek. The move left him overextended and he felt a white-hot pain as Vanderbilt slashed his bicep, forcing him to transfer his blade to his left hand. He parried a second thrust and caught Vanderbilt across the forearm with a riposte. A second stroke cut across the Grand Master's thigh, but neither was the disabling wound Cooper needed.

His breath felt ragged as they circled one another again. Neither man spoke; the time for words had long since passed. He watched Vanderbilt's eyes, waiting for his move. A feint to the right fooled him, and the backstroke sliced across his chest. He fell back, opening up a gap, buying time to assess the wound. Painful but not life-threatening. They continued to circle round, taking them back to where the president lay huddled on the floor.

Gerrard, seeing Cooper losing and fearing for his own life, stuck out a foot. He failed to trip the Grand Master, but the resulting stumble was the opening Cooper had been waiting for. He sprang on top of him, twisted back his arm and pressed until he heard it snap, sending the gravity knife flying. Forcing him to the ground, he locked his fingers around his throat. Vanderbilt tensed the muscles in his neck, fighting against Cooper's grip, but the younger man's fingers tightened relentlessly, choking the life from him.

He was close to being free. Just a few more seconds of pressure and Vanderbilt would be dead, consigned to the trash can of history. As Vanderbilt's face turned blue it shimmered and transformed; the skin became darker, younger and beardless. The world slowed, distorting and extending sound, until the gunfire became a long, drawn-out moan. Glass shattered in a time lapse of spidering cracks as the hot sun shone mercilessly upon the bus. Cooper watched himself in his own private horror movie as he and Mackinlay emptied their magazines into the refugee bus. It ended as it always ended, with a single perfect bead of blood falling from a child's outstretched hand.

The present snapped into place, like a stretched elastic band returning to its point of origin. Cooper stared at Vanderbilt's swollen face. The Grand Master deserved to die; of that he had no doubt. But he had shed enough blood fighting a war he had never believed in. Today, as of this moment, he was done with killing.

Cooper released his grip and Vanderbilt sucked in a wracking breath. The room was suddenly crowded, with Lynch standing over him and a pair of medics attending to Gerrard. He felt Lynch's hands on his arms and let the journalist help him to his feet.

'Decided to let the old bastard hang for his crimes? Good for you, kid.'

One of the medics peeled away from Gerrard and approached Cooper. 'Do you need any help?'

'I'm fine.' Cooper jerked a thumb over his shoulder. 'Guess you better check him out.'

Vanderbilt managed to lever himself onto his knees. His right arm hung uselessly at his side. The medic squatted next to him and jabbed a fentanyl pen into his thigh.

Cooper heard muffled gunfire and explosions from the tower's upper storeys and looked at Lynch. 'Guess my ten minutes must be up.'

Vanderbilt raised his head and winced in pain as he tried to square his shoulders. 'That's the sound of patriots dying for their country. Men like you wouldn't understand.'

Lynch shook his head in disgust. 'Just what the world needs. More bloody martyrs.' He looked at Cooper. 'C'mon, kid. It's time to get out of here.'

CHAPTER 44

Du Pont grunted as he pushed at the desk, bracing his feet against the floor. It inched stubbornly forward with a screech. He paused to wipe the sweat from his brow with the back of his hand before turning round.

'I could use a little help here.'

Lomax paused in the middle of thumbing a bullet into his pistol magazine. 'Get the big fellow to help. For all the good it'll do.'

'That's defeatist talk. You'll face the lash for that!'

'I doubt it.' Lomax waved his hand, indicating the confines of the Central Office. 'We're trapped. Surrounded by enemies. Barricading the door is going to make little difference. We'll be dead before dawn. The only question is whether we die with honour, like true warriors of the faith.'

The conversation might have soured further if Bitoni hadn't limped forward and braced his hands against the presidential desk. Sinews stood out in his neck and forearms as the Templar sword bearer applied his considerable strength. Du Pont also bent himself to the task. Together, they forced the desk across the room, where they turned it on its side and placed it in front of the door.

Bitoni grimaced as he staggered back. Fresh blood leaked through the bandage on his right thigh. He searched his vest for a field dressing, patting the same pouches repeatedly. Du Pont opened his own med-kit and handed over a sachet of blood coagulant.

'Thank you, sir.'

Du Pont waved away Bitoni's thanks as he turned his attention back to the Central Office. Beside the desk, there were three chairs and the pair of flags fixed to the wall on either side of the presidential seal. Not exactly the world's most effective barricade, but he didn't see the Good Lord providing anything else. The sardonic quirk of Lomax's lips as he wheeled over two of the chairs suggested he had reached the same conclusion.

Du Pont, recognising the grimness of their situation, offered an olive branch to the intelligence officer. 'I'm open to suggestions, Major.'

'Like I said, we fight and die now, or we surrender and die later. Either way, I'd suggest it's time for the Rites of Absolution.'

Du Pont nodded, doing his best to hide his disappointment. Only a few months ago victory in the Middle East had seemed all but assured, and with it, the future of the Templar order. Now those lands were lost, the Caliphate resurgent, and the Templar order reduced to a handful of troops surrounded by enemies. Had they really displeased the Lord that much? If He had a plan, it remained opaque to the chaplain-commander.

Lomax, once again displaying an apparent ability to read Du Pont's thoughts, said, 'Dwelling on "might have beens" is the road to madness.'

Du Pont motioned for Lomax and Bitoni to come forward and kneel. The sword bearer winced as he bent his wounded leg but obeyed the instruction. Du Pont, ignoring the muffled cries from the other side of the door, clasped his hands together in prayer. In the circumstances he was sure the Lord would excuse brevity.

'Forgive us, Heavenly Father, for our failure to defend the faith from the heathens and apostates who defile your holy laws. We are but frail creatures of flesh and blood and prone to weakness. Forgive us also our failures this day, and remember the good works we have done in thy holy name, so that when we are summoned from this sublunary abode, we may ascend to the Heavens above and hear the words, well done, good and faithful servant. Amen.'

The upended desk shivered and shook under a sustained barrage of blows against the door. At most, they had a few seconds before their enemies forced their way inside the Central Office. Du Pont's pistol was empty, Bitoni had half a clip left in his carbine, and Lomax had half a dozen rounds in his pistol. Surrender was unthinkable, death was inevitable, and the trick was dying as well as possible.

Du Pont placed two fragmentation grenades on the floor in front of him. He looked at Bitoni and Lomax and received nods of acceptance. Bitoni produced a grenade of his own and Lomax picked one up from floor, leaving Du Point to retrieve the other. They pulled the pins together and waited. The desk fell with a crash and the door inched open.

'For God! For faith! For glory!'

Du Pont felt the bullets tear into his flesh, but in that moment all he saw was the retribution of the Lord nestled in his hand. And then the light of Heaven was all around him, bearing him upwards.

CHAPTER 45

*I*nterview *Transcript #1: Jefferson Lynch in conversation with former US Senator Gina Pulaski, Panopticon Watchtower Central Office.*

Jefferson Lynch: Hello and welcome to the inaugural broadcast of my Truth & Justice cast. I'm joined by Gina Pulaski, leader of the Free America movement, on the eve of their historic victory over the Religious States. For forty-one years America has been a nation divided, but no more. With me tonight, the woman whose vision made it happen.

Gina Pulaski: That's quite the introduction, Jefferson. I hope I can live up to it. But first, let me reassure your followers that reunification will not be arbitrarily imposed. Consultation and due process will be followed to ensure the democratic will of the people takes precedence.

JL: And yet, you've just used military force to overthrow a democratic government. Many of the citizens of the Religious States are, perhaps rightfully, apprehensive about what that portends for their future freedoms.

GP: First, let me say, I hear their concerns and I understand them. But it must be remembered that the Religious States were founded through conflict, creating an ideological schism in this once great nation of ours. Those of the Free America movement who took up arms did so in the spirit of the Second Amendment to the Constitution of the United States. These men and women, these patriots, recognised the need to defend the security of their country so that it could once more be a free state. They did so without prejudice. And I would urge those listening to remember we are all Americans. Together, we have a bright future.

JL: Again, some would wonder about that future. Cyber-attacks, aerial bombardment and sabotage have destroyed critical national infrastructure on both sides of the conflict. An estimated three million people remain off supply. Hospitals and A&Es are at breaking point. Crops have been destroyed or left to rot, unharvested. Death and War have already ridden across our lands. Many fear that Famine and Pestilence won't be far behind. Ours may be a nation reunited, but it's currently on its knees.

GP: While it's true we have some challenges ahead of us, I fear you're overstating the issues. Given this is a new launch, we can forgive you a touch of sensationalism. America doesn't stand alone. Our allies in Canada, Europa City and the North African Free States, who supported us in the War of Reunification, are willing to supply financial aid, equipment and skilled personnel. In what will be the greatest air mobilisation since the Berlin airlift in 1948, supplies averaging sixty tons a day are scheduled to land at the points of greatest need. America does not stand alone. This I promise.

JL: Apparently not. Although, with those same allies having already supplied billions of dollars of lethal aid, it's not unreasonable to wonder what will be demanded in return for this latest generosity. Who will ultimately own this new America?

GP: I'm not certain I follow your line of reasoning here.

JL: No? Then, if you look to the screen, I'll provide some examples. Document One, dated October nineteenth, 2091, details ongoing negotiations between yourself and representatives of the Canadian government over the ownership of Alaska.

SH: How the hell... [pause] No such discussions, to my knowledge, has taken place. I suggest you check the source of your information, as it's clearly fake. That said, as one of our largest neighbours, fostering good relations with the Canadians is essential to our future. To this end, we are currently discussing a number of trade agreements. Perhaps there's been some confusion?

JL: I rather doubt that. Let's move on to Document Two, dated November third, 2091, which details the sale of controlling interests in Pfizer Inc and Gilead Sciences Inc to Europa City's Tessier Corporation. Or we can look at Document Three, dated November seventeenth, 2091, which grants a twenty-five-year lease of six million acres of arable land in New York state to the Bamako Tech Corp for GM crop development. I can continue, if you wish?

GP: That won't be necessary. Again, you're looking for a conspiracy where none exists. Deals such as the ones you've highlighted are essential if we are to rebuild and grow our economy. Like any country, we have our preferred trading partners.

JL: But we're not any country. We're a country without any functioning federal or state governments, and which is effectively still under military control. I'm sure I won't be alone in asking who decides how to distribute the pieces of the pie.

GP: I don't think I care for that insinuation.

JL: That's your prerogative. But we're beyond insinuation and into the realm of fact. Document Four is a forensic audit trail. I've got to hand it to you – that's an impressive nest of shell companies and dummy corporations, but it wasn't quite slick enough. The offshore account listed can be traced back to a trust fund set up by your maternal grandfather. The current balance is just north of two hundred million dollars. That's quite a war chest. Perhaps you can enlighten me and *my followers as to how it was assembled? Investments? Political donations? Facilitation fees for the deals I've previously mentioned?*

GP: No comment.

JL: No? Well, I guess the source of the money isn't strictly as important as its purpose. We all know presidential campaigns are very expensive to run. Sorry. I forgot. You've not publicly confirmed if you intend to run.

GP: That's right. But if I do, Jefferson, you'll be one of the first to know.

JL: Okay, then let's move on. I see we're almost out of time, but before I go, the elephant, or perhaps that should be minaret, in the room is the Middle East. President Gerrard withdrew the majority of troops from Syria and Jordan to assist with the war against Free America. The skeleton force left behind proved inadequate to combat a resurgent Islamic Caliphate, led by its de facto ruler Marshal Ismail. With almost all occupied territory in Syria ceded to the Caliphate, is there a withdrawal strategy? If so, what sort of time scale are we looking at?

GP: Firstly, I'd like to state categorically that the endpoint is the withdrawal of all American forces from the Middle East theatre. We are, however, looking at a quarter of a century of intermittent conflict, and our withdrawal must take into account the safe transfer of power, thus protecting the civilian population while not disadvantaging our strategic allies in the area. At this stage of planning nothing can be presented as absolute.

JL: Guess we're dealing with the unknown unknowns here. Thank you for your time, Ms Pulaski. I'm sure my subscribers have found it enlightening.

GP: You're welcome ... [mumbled] sonofabitch.

Transcript Ends.

CHAPTER 46

Patrick Donaghy parked a hundred metres from the substation gate and turned off the truck's engine. This was a close as vehicles were allowed to park. The fear of further attacks was still very real, only this time it would be Religious States sympathisers.

He scrubbed at his face with his hands, but it did nothing to dispel the bone-deep weariness he felt. Like the other members of the ERCOT field team, he had been working twelve-hour shifts with a single day off every fortnight. But the truth was, with thousands still off supply, they were barely scratching the surface. They were repairing what they could, but the electricity network was a mess and would remain so for the foreseeable future.

He collected his datapad and toolkit from the back of the truck and set off towards the substation. Two members of the National Guard were stationed at the gate. One of them trained his rifle on Donaghy, and the other prepped a scanner. He and his possessions would be scanned for explosives while his identity was verified with ERCOT. Then, and only then, would he be granted entry to begin his shift.

'You're clear to proceed, Mr Donaghy.'

Donaghy picked up his toolkit and stepped through the gate. The metal-clad side of the GIS Hall loomed up ahead. The gable end was a "mushroom farm" of GPS antennas. They had re-gassed the Main Bus Section last night and were due to conduct breaker timing tests this morning. All being well, they would move onto the feeder circuits next. It would be a long day, with the promise of more of the same to come.

The ninety-minute commute each way didn't help either. He could do it faster, but after Dan Walters ran his truck off the road, Stephanie had made him promise to drive carefully. Keeping to that promise felt like the least he could do, given she kept everything running without a word of complaint. She put his dinner on the table when he arrived home, filled his lunch box in the morning, and looked after their son Chad. At times, the extra money he was earning seemed poor compensation for the time he was losing, but he reminded himself he was helping put the country back together. It didn't help that they were chronically shorthanded.

Donaghy badged his way into the GIS Hall. He spotted Hal Lawson, waved to him, and received a nod in reply. He was a competent engineer, if a little standoffish. Donaghy had worked on and off with him for seven or eight years. It occurred to him that he knew little about Lawson beyond that he was married with a couple of kids. Donaghy hadn't given it much thought before, but his experience with Andrew Fleming had changed that. Maybe he ought to get to know his colleagues better.

But to what end? The SCADA engineer had held him hostage for three days before finally surrendering. This was a man he had worked with for years. A man he thought he knew. Someone he considered a friend. During those three days he'd had a lot of time to reflect on what he knew about him, to search for signs that he had missed as to Fleming's double life. But Fleming had always come across as a good family man and a conscientious employee. No indication that he harboured extreme political ideals. No spouting of manifestoes as he held a gun to him. Fleming conducted hostage taking with the same quiet professionalism he brought to the day job. In many ways the encounter had been all the more disturbing for that. As had its end, when Fleming simply handed over his pistol and informed Donaghy that he could open the gates and admit the police. He did so and then called his wife to let her know he was okay. She had been understandably unhappy about his return to work, but what else was he going to do? The system wasn't going to fix itself.

Fleming was arrested, but his case never went to trial. He, along with other sleeper agents who had not used violence, were pardoned by the emergency government. ERCOT had dismissed him, along with eight other employees who had taken part in sabotage. Donaghy assumed they would find employment in one of the former US states, where they would no doubt receive a hero's welcome.

Donaghy swiped open his datapad. 'Okay, Hal. If we're set, let's start with a trip.'

Laura Byers checked the monitor, noting pulse, heart rate and oxygen saturation level. The readings were all within acceptable limits, which was something of a miracle, but then that was how Byers thought of Pamela Downey – the miracle woman who had survived forty per cent full-thickness burns. Her insurance didn't cover nano-therapy, so they had treated her with skin grafts. They kept her shrouded in a sterile tent, the sterility of which had been threatened after they lost power following an attack on the hospital backup generator. And yet here she was, pulling through on the long road to recovery.

Laura felt a catch in her throat and cuffed her eyes angrily with the back of her hand. Not all of the patients in Mercy Heights General ICU had been so fortunate. Those reliant on ventilators had died within minutes, and with no means of maintaining oxygen to the blood, their organs were lost to the transplant list as well. As an ICU nurse, she got used to losing patients. Sometimes their injuries were too severe or their illness too advanced to save them. But for them to die as the result of a deliberate and callous attack was reprehensible. One thing was for sure: she would be damned before she voted for Gina Pulaski in the upcoming election. The woman was a terrorist, pure and simple. For all the talk of reparations and justice, to her knowledge not a single Free America soldier had been charged.

Laura took a deep breath. There she was, getting all worked up again. She breathed out, took a last look at Pamela Downey's vitals, and moved on to the next patient. Brian Teirnan, age fifty-three. Blunt-force trauma to the back of the head after falling in the bathroom. He currently scored a seven on the GCS, and they did not expect him to regain consciousness. A reminder that everyday life contained danger enough without war and insurrection. She checked his chart and nodded.

Adjusting his pillows, she kept her voice bright and airy. 'Hello, Brian, how are you tonight?'

Ford Sutherland had been staring at the screen of his com-unit for the best part of the last half-hour. It was a simple enough question, requiring a yes or no answer, but he had yet to figure out what a win for either side would look like and how it might change his life, if at all. The single line of text continued to blink at him: Should the United States and the Religious States be reunified as a single nation?

He had studied the campaign literature from both sides and found only claim and counterclaim. Was one side lying? Were both sides lying? If the truth was out there, it eluded him. The separatists claimed reunification would triple the national debt, while the unionists pointed out that the country would be able to reduce its reliance on imported food by sixty per cent in three short years. The Caliphate was a clear and present danger. Peace was possible with the Caliphate. The currency would be devalued, leading to hyperinflation. The military would be defunded. Members of the Armed Forces would be retrained to rebuild the emergency services.

The ifs and buts went round and round in his head, but here in Louisburg some facts remained inescapable. The city was subject to rolling blackouts, with power outages between ten am and three pm daily. The shelves of the grocery stores were bare, and even if they had been stocked, he had not received a welfare payment in over three months. Every Tuesday the inhabitants gathered at City Hall, where food and medicines from Canada, Africa and Europa City were dispensed to the needy, which was everyone.

Normality looked a long way off to Sutherland. He had to wonder if merging with the rebel states would only add to the pain. But what choice did they really have? They were a conquered nation. President Gerrard was in prison, scheduled to stand trial for treason and genocide. His fate was almost certainly sealed. Realistically, how much worse could things get?

And there he had his answer. He checked the "Yes" box and clicked submit. For good or ill, it was time to embrace a new future.

Porter looked around the cell, staring at the bare plascrete walls and floor, the bunk bed with its neatly folded sheets, the stainless steel toilet and washbasin. Anything to avoid returning to the holo-screen in the corner, where the Chief Justice of the Supreme Court was hammering the final nail into the coffin of his hopes and ambitions.

His own trial, conviction, and sentencing for killing Sergeant Jackson had been swift: twenty years for voluntary manslaughter, to be served in Arkansas' Maximum-Security Unit, near Tucker. It was a little over a three-hundred-mile round trip from Jonesboro to the prison, and so far, his parents had visited just once. It had been an awkward meeting for all concerned. His mother and father were confused as to how their son had gone from Templar selection to convicted felon in a matter of weeks. Porter wasn't sure himself. All he knew was that with the Free America troops surrounding them, continued resistance would have been nothing short of suicide. Had he intended to kill Jackson from the outset? He didn't think so and had pled as such at his trial, but that didn't stop him from waking screaming in the middle of the night.

Realising he could avoid it no longer, Porter pointed the remote at the holo-screen and resumed the playback. Lionel Becker, a veritable Methuselah who had held the position of Chief Justice for over thirty years, turned his washed-out blue eyes on the prisoner. Grand Master Vanderbilt squared his shoulders and raised his chin defiantly. Medals glinted on the breast of his dress uniform, a reminder of the service he had given his country.

'Thaddeus Hiram Vanderbilt, it is my duty to inform you that this court rejects your appeal and upholds the following charges against you. Treason; that on August third, 2091, you and members of the Templar order entered the Panopticon and used force to remove the legally elected president of the Religious States from office. Murder in the first-degree; that on the same day, you did wound Lee Patrick Morrison with a knife, causing his death. False Imprisonment: that on the same day, you did unlawfully imprison Charles Stuart Gerrard and Susanna Hopkins. Torture: that on August fifth of the same year, you did torture Charles Stuart Gerrard in an attempt to gain access codes he was in possession of as the lawfully elected president of the Religious States. The sentence for these crimes, as passed by the Eastern District Court of Viginia and upheld by the Court of Appeals Fourth Circuit, is death. Accordingly, at a date to be set, you will be hanged by the neck until dead. Does the prisoner wish to address the court?'

'Only to reiterate that I do not recognise its authority, or that of the so-called emergency government. I am a soldier, sworn to defend the faith. The acts you call treason and murder were legitimate acts of war taken in defence of the country and its citizens.'

'Are you merely going to repeat the contents of your appeal, or do you have anything new to add? To talk in terms you might understand, you have been judged and found wanting.'

'Judged, you say? The Lord alone will judge me, and He shall not find His good and faithful servant wanting.'

'Well, it looks as though you're certain to meet God before I do. Moving on, I have reviewed the findings of the Senate inquiry into the Templar order, and I accept all recommendations. Namely, that the order be disbanded and declared a proscribed society, with all ranks and privileges suspended immediately. It will be an offence for former members to associate, and a felony to display any of its insignia in public. Bailiff.'

The court bailiff in charge of Vanderbilt stepped forward and tore the red cross pattée from his chest. The colour drained from the former Grand Master's face, but pride prevented him from making any further public display.

Becker motioned to the bailiff. 'Take him away.'

Porter pointed the remote at the holo-screen and it fizzed out of existence. The emergency government needed a scapegoat and the Templars fit the bill. Porter was not surprised by Vanderbilt losing his appeal, nor by the Senate committee's recommendations as to the fate of the order. He had already reconciled himself to his own fate. In truth, prison was not so bad. They fed and clothed him, and they told him when to eat, sleep and exercise. In many ways it was not so different from the army. As a holder of so-called extremist views, he had been given a cell of his own, and this, too, suited him. With time off for good behaviour, he could be out in a little under seventeen years. Assuming the Religious States didn't rise again before then.

Porter dropped to the floor and started his daily routine of push-ups, crunches and thrusts. It was important to stay physically and mentally active for the day when he would be called upon to serve his country once more.

CHAPTER 47

*D*ebrief Transcript #1: Jefferson Lynch and Susanna Hopkins, Panopticon Outer-Circle, Lyndhurst Room.

Jefferson Lynch: Ms Hopkins, for the record, you're seeking immunity from prosecution for your part in the conspiracy to assassinate President Michael Hamilton in return for your testimony against your fellow conspirators?

Susanna Hopkins: I know I relied on your footage outside the Panopticon, but shouldn't this interview be taking place at a police station or some other government office? No offence, but you don't have the authority to offer me shit.

JL: None taken. You're right. I'm not here to offer you a deal. This is what you might call a preliminary hearing to … establish the facts.

SH: In other words, Pulaski wants to extract every last nugget of intel from me before she makes it official. Probably run it by some focus group, see how well my walking away plays with the voters. Guess I should have seen that one coming.

JL: I'm sure you can see her problem. Lee Morrison and Gene

Kordowski are dead. Deputy Director Hannah is locked up in a secure ward, flinging his own shit at the nurses. Seems those enhanced interrogation techniques of Lomax's took a toll. That just leaves you and Gerrard available to stand trial – unless you can give me anyone else. How about we start with who actually fired the shot?

SH: [bitter laughter] Not going to help much. It was a ghost, an off-book Agency assassin by the name of Jon Albright. He was also responsible for Bishop Gibson being found dead after apparently strangling a sex worker. Took care of Hannah's pet shrink, Steiner, too. Made it look like a heart attack.

JL: Getting a lot of past tense here.

SH: Finally met his match when Hannah lost patience and sent him after Vanderbilt. So Pulaski won't be parading him through the courts either. Sorry.

JL: It's a good story, but can anyone corroborate it?

SH: [lengthy pause] Hannah mentioned an agent by the name of Paxton who did some work with Albright. Think his first name is Sam. Probably rounded up along with Hannah, so don't ask me if he's alive, dead, or in possession of all his appendages. Still, I hear they managed to reattach Charles' fingers.

JL: Uh-huh. I'll ask them to look for Paxton. But right now, it's beginning to look a lot like he said, she said. What's to stop him saying it was all your idea?

SH: The thing you have to understand about Charles is his vanity. There's no way he'll accept being portrayed as a clueless rube who had no idea what was going on. Not even to prevent a noose around his neck. He'll cop to it as a noble act for the greater good of the American people. Play the martyr.

JL: You better hope so, or else Pulaski will make good her threat to stretch your neck.

SH: And how does that make you feel? Jefferson Lynch, the great liberal arbitrator of right and wrong.

JL: Makes me feel like we're done here.

Transcript Ends.

CHAPTER 48

Cooper held out his arms. His mother took his left hand, his sister his right, and the circle continued, passing through his twin brothers, then Donny and Mike, leaving a noticeable gap at the head of the table. Apart from that empty chair and the scarred surface of the kitchen table, the room looked much the same as it had almost three years ago, when he had come home on furlough prior to taking his vows. The youth who had sat here while his father said grace was not the same person who now thanked the Lord in his stead. The young, innocent and naive Billy Ray Cooper had been lost forever in the deserts of Israel and Syria.

During that first tour he had heard it said that a veteran never truly went home. He'd angrily dismissed it at the time because the belief that he would one day go home was all that he had to cling to. It had sustained him throughout the horror and violence he had participated in, during his captivity at the hands of Marshal Ismail, and later, when he had broken his vows and chosen to fight for Free America.

But now that he was finally home, sitting with family and friends, he knew it was true. Part of him would always be a stranger, an outsider, separated by experiences he could never share. It went beyond the confirmed diagnosis of PTSD, and it went beyond the neuro-link they had found and removed from his brain, the source of his murderous rage towards Vanderbilt. Only those who had trained and fought with him could understand, and they were either dead, in prison, or insane. Lynch had a glimmering, but he was a man with his own demons, ones that continued to put him at odds with the new regime. Cooper was certain he hadn't heard the last of the crazy bastard.

'Something funny?' Shania asked. 'Only you're smiling.'

'Just remembering something. Anyway, food's getting cold.'

Cooper carved the turkey and dished out the meat as the potatoes, gravy, biscuits and vegetables went round the table. He had paid for the day's largesse out of his savings from accumulated backpay, but the money wouldn't last for long. He glanced at his mother, then went back to eating.

With the main dishes cleared, Shania brought out a freshly baked pumpkin pie. Patty Cooper poured coffee while the pie was dished up. Cooper felt a lump form in his throat as his mother lingered by the head of the table. Everything came at a price.

An alert pinged on Cooper's com-unit. He glanced at the screen and then waved on the holo with an apology. The news sim smiled a perfect smile and commenced with her bulletin.

'Following the signing of an historic agreement with Marshal Ismail of the Islamic Caliphate, all remaining troops will be withdrawn from Syria, Jordan and Lebanon prior to midnight on the thirtieth of November. Peace keeping troops will remain stationed in Israel and Saudi Arabia, subject to future negotiations.'

The feed cut to footage of Gina Pulaski standing in front of a lectern. The discoloured and cracked dome of the original Capitol Building in Washington was visible behind her, shrouded in scaffolding as restoration work continued. She tapped the mic to confirm it was on.

'Today, my fellow Americans, it is my humble privilege to announce the first US elections since reunification. As you know, the American Reunification Referendum was held on the fourth of July, with sixty-three per cent of voters endorsing a reunified United States of America. Following this historic decision and the formal dissolution of the Senate in Richmond, I and other members of the emergency government have worked tirelessly to enact the will of the people, for which many of our citizens made the ultimate sacrifice during the War of Reunification. It is therefore, with all due reverence and humility, that I announce my intention to stand for the presidency of the United States of America on behalf of the Democratic party.'

'Traitor,' Dale spat. He looked pointedly at Cooper and muttered, 'Just like you.'

'Dale Elliot Cooper, you will apologise to your brother!'

Dale looked at his mother, bit back whatever retort was on his lips, and scraped back his chair. When Shania stood to go after him, her mother waved her back to her chair.

'The boy's best left alone. He's angry. No doubt blames himself for what happened to his father. We all need to work through that.'

Shania, hoping to change the subject, turned to Cooper. 'You know Ms Pulaski. What's she like?'

Cooper thought it over for a moment. 'She's a politician.'

Donny snorted. 'Ain't that the truth!'

Cooper fixed his friend with a stare. 'Let's not spoil the meal talking politics. There'll be plenty of time for that later.'

Cooper stared at his father's empty chair again and then at Dale's. Wade, his food barely touched, put his fork down and plucked up the courage to speak.

'What are you going to do? I mean, now that you're no longer a Templar.'

It was a good question. He knew he couldn't avoid answering it any longer. 'There are a lot of jobs going in construction as part of the regeneration of the old US states. It would mean travel and time away from home, but it would be good to build something after all I've helped to destroy.' He looked at Mike and Donny. 'We could apply together, if you've got a hankering. Pays top dollar.'

Mike looked set to decline, but Donny cut across him. 'Sounds like a fine idea.'

'Surely you don't have to go right away?' Patty asked. 'You've barely been home two months. I mean, with your father gone, we need a man around the house.'

'I'm sorry, Ma, but those jobs will go fast. I can't risk losing out. I promise I'll call and write you. And there will be long weekends for travelling home. It won't be so bad. You'll see.'

'I guess you got to do what you got to do.' Patty's voice faltered as she continued. 'No, I can't be holding you back.'

'It won't be forever. A year or two at most. Meantime, as you said, there's a few things need doing round the house. I'll get started on them tomorrow. I'm sure Wade would like to help ... maybe Dale too.'

Another pause followed, then his mother said, 'You know your father was proud of you. Not for joining up, but for realising the war was wrong and doing what you believed in. He'd have told you that if he was here. Some folks might be minded to see it different, but don't you pay them no head, you hear?'

Cooper nodded. Much as he hated to admit it, that was another reason for going away. The Templar Order had been dissolved, its insignia and symbols proscribed, but there would be those on either side who would view him as a hero or villain accordingly. Best to keep his family out of it while the dust settled. Seemed a small enough penance for his sins.

CHAPTER 49

The supervisor closed the door behind Lynch and took up position beside it. His presence made it feel more like visiting time at the penitentiary than a custody visit. Lynch forced it from his mind, determined not to ruin what he had fought so hard for: the chance to see his daughter for the first time in over four years. He strode purposely to the cheap table and pulled out the chair opposite his daughter. Christine sat with her fingers interlaced and her legs crossed at the ankles. Her shoulder-length brown hair was held out of her eyes by an Alice band. Lynch noticed the tilt of her head and spotted an earbud.

'What you listening to?'

Christine tapped the bud, pausing the music. 'Brandi Devine.'

Lynch nodded as though the name meant something and made a note to check on it later. Doubtless it would prove to be whatever sim was flavour of the month right now. Namedropping her next week would probably earn him an eyeroll. He cleared his throat, buying time as he tried to think of a suitable conversation opener.

'You look so grown-up.'

Christine stiffened. 'There's a big difference between

nine and thirteen. Perhaps they didn't do biology when you were at school? Or maybe you cut class, preferring to smoke weed behind the bleachers?'

'Is that what your mother told you?'

'Hate to burst your bubble, but she barely mentioned you after the divorce. While you might be a long way from the A-list, you're still a celebrity of sorts. Plenty of interviews and bios for me to read online. Seemed the least I could do, being the daughter of the infamous Jefferson Lynch. Can't say I was impressed.'

Lynch reckoned he ought to have been insulted, but he felt a swell of pride. The eyes, button nose and high cheekbones might be his wife's, but the mouth and the brain behind it were definitely his. The kid had attitude aplenty. He felt a fresh pang of regret at how much of her life he had missed.

'Guess I walked into that one. I've made a lot of mistakes in my life. Dare say I'll make some more before I'm through. But you aren't, and never will be, one of them. So I guess I'm asking for a second chance. The opportunity to get it right this time.'

'Seriously? You think you deserve a second chance?' Christine wrinkled her nose. 'You stink of cigarettes and bourbon. If that hasn't changed, why should I believe anything else has?'

'You've every right to be angry. I get that. And I probably don't deserve a second chance, but I want to try and make things right anyway. Even though I can never make up for all the time I was absent, or for what I put you and your mother through. But I'm in a good place now. I've got a new book deal and a vidcast, and people are queueing up to interview me. I won't fu ... mess up this time.'

'I'm almost thirteen, Father. I've heard the word fuck before. And it's probably a little late to start trying to set an example now.'

'Ah. You're probably right. Aha!'

Lynch remembered the gift in his bag. He flipped back

the satchel's flap and took out a square package. Christine looked uncertainly at the supervisor, who still stood like a gaoler by the door.

'It's okay. It's been approved. Isn't that right?'

The supervisor nodded, and Christine accepted the box. Lynch had thought about wrapping it but had then decided the plain box would serve well enough. He watched as she unfolded the lid to reveal the pair of drones nestled in the docking station. The wings were folded, truncating the crudely applied Day-Glo legends of Truth and Justice. She picked up Truth and examined it carefully.

'Bamako Tech Corp X17 camera drones, running mil-spec security and encryption.' Lynch tapped the scar behind his ear. 'You're too young for an implant, but they'll run off an app on your com-unit synched to HUD glasses.'

'Are these the drones you had in Israel?'

'No. They got destroyed in Casablanca. But those are the ones I had with me throughout the Civil War. Recorded some serious history, they have. And got me out of a few jams along the way.'

'What am I supposed to do with a couple of beat-up drones?'

Despite her words, Lynch noted she hadn't let go of the drone. 'You could put them back in the box and leave it to gather dust on a shelf. Or you could spy on your neighbours. That'd be fun, right? Or maybe you could use them as part of a school project – make a documentary for media studies. Maybe you could go in search of the news.'

Lynch felt a constriction in his throat as he tried to read Christine's expression. Was she happy, indifferent, or insulted? He had thought about buying her a state-of-the-art com-unit but rejected it as a cheap move, even though he owed her several birthday and Christmas gifts. For a man who earned his living with words, he found himself unable to articulate what the drones represented to him and why it was important she should have them.

'Here, let me show you the app.'

Christine let out an involuntary gasp when she caught sight of the com-unit's desktop. The lapse in her defences was momentary. 'Did you load that on this morning?'

Lynch looked at the familiar image taken at his daughter's ninth birthday party. Until today, that was the last time he had been allowed to see her in person. He closed his eyes and saw every detail; the gap-tooth smile, long pigtails, red and blue floral pattern on her dress, the "I Am 9" badge.

'I've carried that image with me since the day I took it. God knows there were times I told myself it would easier to delete it, to forget all about you. You could say it became a kind of penance – a reminder of all that I'd lost. Then one day it became a symbol of hope. Now I had something to fight for. Maybe you think I'm spinning you a line here. Wouldn't blame you if you did. I know I've got a long way to go before I earn even part of your trust.'

The supervisor glanced up at the wall clock and unfolded his arms. His right hand seemed to fall casually onto the can of pepper spray on his belt. 'Time's up. You need to say your goodbyes, Mr Lynch.'

Lynch gritted his teeth and resisted the urge to give the jumped-up rent-a-cop a slap. He had to be on his best behaviour. 'I've really enjoyed our time together, Christine.' He shot the supervisor a venomous glance. 'Short as it was. If you'll see me next week, maybe we could have the full hour?'

Christine chewed her lip for a moment and then nodded. This time the constriction in his throat was accompanied by a pricking sensation behind his eyes. He gave his daughter a tight smile and motioned for the door to be opened.

'Wait! You didn't show me the app.'

'I'll send you a link. If you lift out the docking station, you'll find HUD glasses below.'

The supervisor stepped forward. 'Don't make me repeat myself.'

Lynch knew Christine wouldn't say the words back to

him, but he said them anyway. 'Love you.' He turned away to avoid seeing any negative reaction and missed the quiver of her lip.

Lynch's eyes were downcast as he left the room, and he didn't see the woman until he bumped into her. His apology trailed off as he recognised his ex-wife. There were a few extra lines on her face, and her blonde hair was brown at the roots, but otherwise Tabitha looked much as he remembered her. Well, not quite. At least she wasn't screaming at him. Not yet. He became aware of their proximity and hurriedly stepped back.

'Jefferson.'

The drawn-out enunciation of his name managed to contain anger, sorrow and pain. Probably best to rip the plaster straight off.

'I know this can't have been easy for you, given our history. But I'm truly grateful to you for agreeing to this.'

'Just remember, I did it for Christine, not you. And God as my witness, you better not hurt her.'

Lynch forced himself to look Tabitha in the eye. 'I know I can't ever undo it. There are some things there's no going back from. But believe me when I say I should never have raised my hand to you. I'm a drunk. An addict. All I can do is try not to be mean with it. I'm not the man you kicked out of your home all those years ago. The things I've seen …' A shiver ran down his spine. 'They change a person.'

Tabitha reached out tentatively. For a moment Lynch thought she was going to caress his cheek like she used to. Then her hand clenched into a fist and dropped to her side. He thought he detected a note of pity in her voice beneath the exasperation, which made it worse.

'When are you going to realise you don't need the drink and drugs, Jefferson? You're stuck playing a cartoon version of yourself, putting on a show for dumbasses who want the "Jefferson Lynch Experience", no matter how stupid or self-destructive. You say you want your daughter back? Then show her you can actually do something positive with your life.'

'Isn't that what I've been doing these last two years?' His voice was louder than he intended. 'I got the truth out there, didn't I? Often at great personal risk, I might add.'

'Jefferson.' Tabitha shook her head and smiled wearily. 'You caught the scent of a story and pursued it at any cost. Same as you've always done the twenty years I've known you. When we first met, I admired that grit and determination. But it didn't take me long to realise I'd always come second to the story. I might have lived with that, if only you'd thought to put our daughter first. Even once or twice might have been enough to show you had it in you.'

'I … I'm sorry.'

'I've waited a long time to hear you apologise and then I get two in one conversation. I can forgive you, Jefferson. But I'm not ready to like you. Not yet. Maybe not ever. But Christine wants to see you again, so I guess we'll keep doing this until either one or both of you gets bored. Or until I see proof you really have changed.' Tabitha tilted her head back as she looked up at him. 'Now *that* would be a story.'

CHAPTER 50

Jefferson Lynch shifted uncomfortably on the couch. The cushion sank alarmingly beneath his weight. The studio lights were hot, and he felt the first beads of perspiration on his scalp. His instinct was to wipe them away, but he did his best to settle his long, unruly limbs. He looked from the well-tailored lines of his host's suit to the faded black of his own cargo pants and the rose petal print of his nano-weave shirt. The latter had saved his life on more than one occasion and, given the nature of his planned announcement this evening, might be needed again.

He picked up the glass of water and took a sip. He was forty-two days sober. Was he supposed to feel healthier, nobler, or a sense of clarity? All he felt like was having a drink. Wasn't it supposed to get easier with time, or was that just some sponsor BS to make you stick with the programme? He took another sip and grimaced. They said you could get used to anything, given time.

The title music ended and Lou Bolger produced his com-unit with a conjuror-like flourish. He turned the screen to camera to display a book cover.

'Ladies and gentlemen, my first guest this evening is journalist, war correspondent, and former Free America rebel Jefferson Lynch.' A ripple of applause sounded from the audience. 'We'll be discussing Downfall, Jefferson's first-hand account of the of the campaign to liberate Jerusalem from the Caliphate, during which he was embedded with members of the Templar First Air Cavalry Brigade. Something, one would have hoped, that would make him uniquely qualified to comment.'

Lynch made a point of facing the camera rather than replying to Bolger directly. 'You have actually read it, Lou?'

Bolger nodded and smiled, revealing an impossibly white set of teeth. 'And I'm sure I'm not alone in finding it overly critical of the Israel campaign. Or that there appears to be no love lost between yourself and the leadership of the Free America movement.'

'Having been involved with both sides, I've come to realise there's little difference in their motives and methods. Although aid is pouring in through FA's allies, I don't think they should be entrusted with rebuilding America. Some say it's a show of unity that Pulaski chose Hopkins, a key player in the Gerrard administration, for her running mate, but it seems to me that they're just two sides of the same coin.' Lynch paused. Time to shit or get off the pot. 'That's why I'm giving you and your subscribers an exclusive this evening by announcing my intention to run for president as an independent.'

Bolger choked off his laughter when he realised Lynch wasn't joking. For a moment he looked flustered, but he was too much of a seasoned pro not to see the possibilities unfolding before him. What had started out as dull review piece now looked set to lead the majority of tomorrow's news. He forced a smile. 'I have to admit I didn't see that one coming. I guess the question uppermost in people's minds is what does Jefferson Lynch, non-conformist and rebel, stand for?'

Lynch licked suddenly dry lips as he summoned every drop of sincerity he could muster. 'People say it's long gone out of fashion, but I'm proud to stand for truth, justice and the American way. Some of your viewers are no doubt laughing, but it should be plain enough to all that there's no point rebuilding only to repeat past mistakes. To avoid that, we need to take a long and honest look at the problems affecting the country. A failure to prepare for automation, deliberate deindustrialisation and trade wars have resulted in decades of slow growth, low wages and employment insecurity. This toxic combination has been compounded by a prolonged underinvestment in public services and critical infrastructure by successive governments as a means to fund their ideological wars in the Middle East.

'Some economists say you can't borrow your way out of debt, but it's beyond dispute that right now this country needs investment in large capital projects, re-industrialisation, education and adult training programmes on a scale not seen since Roosevelt's New Deal. We need to get the economy growing in order to boost tax revenues and we'll only achieve that by investing in people. Don't get me wrong – this is no overnight fix. It will be the work of several governments. But we've all seen what happens when politicians peddle the snake oil of short-term fixes to long-term problems. As citizens, as a nation, we need to work together to achieve a better America for our children and all the generations that come after.'

Bolger raised an eyebrow to imply he wasn't convinced by Lynch's apparent Damascene conversion to moral champion. 'That all sounds very noble, and you've obviously thought hard about the issues, but they say the first rule of politics is to follow the money. So, who's funding your campaign? Because that's who's going to ultimately call the shots, right?'

'Wrong. The American people themselves will be backing my campaign. Here, tonight, I'm asking anyone who wants more open and honest politics, which truly serve the people, to donate money, time, or experience. Whatever they can best afford. All they have to do is believe that a better America is possible.'

Bolger shook his head. 'You can't possibly expect to win?'

For the first time that evening Lynch met Bolger's gaze. 'Maybe not, but it's the American dream, right? A person who believes in themselves and works hard can achieve anything. That's what I'm standing for. The American dream.'

APPENDIX A: TIMELINE

2030

Israel annexes the West Bank. International outcry follows and Jordan, Lebanon and the UAE sever diplomatic ties, leaving Israel increasingly isolated. Egypt admits thousands of Palestinians through the Rafah border crossing. US President Harris attempts to broker a withdrawal but fails to follow through on her threat to cut military aid in the wake of an increased threat to Israel from Iran.

American airstrikes target Iranian airbases. Iranian forces target American troops in Iraq, resulting in 53 fatalities. America seeks to legitimise war with Iran via the UN Security Council, but China and Russia use their vetoes. America responds by vetoing a resolution condemning Israel's annexation of the West Bank.

2031

China applies pressure to broker a peace deal after the escalating conflict closes the Straits of Hormuz, affecting trade. America reluctantly ceases military action against Iran in a bid to avoid a growing trade war with China.

2034

Hamas rocket attacks on Beersheba, Jerusalem and Tel Aviv kill 63 civilians and 11 IDF soldiers. Israel responds with airstrikes and a ground invasion of the Gaza Strip. Operation Bronze Spear lasts for three days, with 23 Israeli and 2,732 Palestinian fatalities. The operation destroys critical infrastructure, along with housing and hospitals. The US government again defends Israel's right to self-defence.

Defeated and destitute, much of the surviving civilian populace begins the exodus to Egypt.

2041

A resurgent ISIS in Iraq and Syria gains control of Lebanon and Jordan and cements itself as a new Islamic Caliphate. The USA deploys an additional 100,000 troops in an attempt to relieve Jordan and assist rebels in Syria. High casualties generate negative headlines in the US.

2043

Escalating tensions between India and Pakistan result in a minor nuclear exchange. Although targets are primarily military, civilian casualties are estimated at 250,000. Fallout affects areas of China and Afghanistan. China responds by sending relief aid and 'peacekeeping' troops to Afghanistan and Pakistan, strengthening the ties of the early twenty-first century Shanghai Cooperation Organisation.

The UN General Assembly attempts to broker an agreement on multilateral nuclear disarmament. China, Russia, the USA, Israel and North Korea refuse to sign. The UK, France, Pakistan and India disarm.

2044

The killing of 84 Turkish troops by Russian-backed forces in Syria results in escalating conflict between Russia and Turkey.

2045

Russian forces withdraw from Syria as part of an agreed peace deal with Turkey. The Islamic Caliphate takes advantage of the power vacuum to seize total control of Syria.

2047

American forces, brought to a standstill by the Islamic Caliphate, withdraw unconditionally from the Middle East. The withdrawal proves highly divisive with the American public, many of whom at a time of growing ecological disasters and global pandemics have embraced Creationist forms of Christianity

2049

No one admits responsibility for the aerial detonation of a nuclear device over the Arctic Circle. Opinion remains divided between terrorist attack and the mal-operation of a military defence satellite. Either way, it makes little difference to the victims of the tidal wave that follows the vaporisation of the Arctic sea ice. North America and Western Europe bear the brunt of the disaster, with large tracts of Alaska, California, Hawaii, Maine, Massachusetts, Rhode Island, New York, Connecticut, New Jersey, Delaware and Maryland remaining under water. England, Norway, Denmark, the Netherlands and the west coasts of Belgium, France and Spain are similarly devastated.

US President Santiago Garcia is killed by the tsunami. Vice President Kecia Williams assumes the presidency, but with much of the infrastructure of the northern states destroyed she is powerless to prevent the country descending into anarchy. A short and bloody second American civil war ensues when 26 American states ¯South Carolina, Mississippi, Florida, Alabama, Georgia, Louisiana, Texas, Virginia, Arkansas, North Carolina, Tennessee, Kentucky, Missouri, Delaware, West Virginia, Maryland, Oklahoma, Nevada, New, Mexico, Arizona, Utah,

Wyoming, Nebraska, Illinois, Indiana, Ohio), secede from the Union and form the Christian fundamentalist territory of the Religious States of America, with Richmond, Virginia as the capital. The secessionists' intention is to continue the decades'-long war with the Islamic Caliphate in the Middle East.

Construction of Europa City begins, to provide emergency accommodation for millions displaced by the Great Flood.

2050

Woody Lyndhurst is sworn in as the First President of the Religious States of America. The remaining US states request financial aid from the International Monetary Fund, while refugees flee across the border into Canada. With no functioning federal or state governments, the former US states became lawless no-go zones ruled only by the gun.

The RSA withdraws from the United Nations. Russia follows suit, together with a number of the former Soviet Republics, which proves to be a precursor to what follows.

2051–2053

Following the financial collapse of many of the eastern European Union countries, Russia steps in with financial and military aid, effectively annexing Estonia, Latvia, Lithuania, Belarus, Ukraine, Georgia and Kazakhstan into the Greater Russian Collective.

2052

Having requested direct military aid to restore law and order, South Dakota, Idaho and Oregon are formally admitted to the RSA.

2054–2055

Following the collapse of oil prices in the wake of green technologies, the majority of Saudi Arabia falls to the Islamic Caliphate. Oman and the UAE help preserve its southernmost regions. Diplomatic channels are opened with the RSA in the hope of securing military assistance.

2055–2070
A series of typhoons and rising sea levels devastate Japan, Taiwan, Singapore, Indonesia and the Philippines. An influx of refugees fleeing the damage allows North Africa to establish itself as a cyber technology capital, and the foremost supplier of the emerging nanotech market.

2056
In response to the expansion of the Islamic Caliphate, RSA President Lyndhurst signs off on the creation of a new military order of Templars. Drawn from existing special forces units across the military, they are an elite force dedicated to defeating the Islamic Caliphate. Like their predecessors, they take a vow of celibacy, believing that the lack of dependents will make them more willing to make the ultimate sacrifice.

2057
Templar forces establish operational bases in Jerusalem, Haifa, Tel Aviv and Eilat at the behest of the Israeli government.

2061
The Islamic Caliphate attacks Israel. Backed by the RSA and supported by an unprecedented airlift of vital supplies, Israeli forces hold out for two years.

2063
Caliphate forces finally overrun Jerusalem. A detachment of Templars covers the final air evacuation of Israeli forces. The Templars, led by Commander Maxwell Lewis, fight to the death. The Caliphate broadcasts images of their mutilated corpses worldwide.

2065

An accidental deployment of a targeted nano-virus kills in excess of two million people in the Khyber Pakhtunkhwa region of Pakistan before it is contained. In the wake of the disaster, governments around the world sign the North–West Frontier Accord, which outlaws all weaponised nanotechnology.

2066

First Crusade. Utilising Cyprus as a spearhead, the RSA launches a series of air strikes targeting military installations in occupied Israel and the surrounding countries of Lebanon and Jordan. A ground assault on Haifa led by Templar forces ends in a bloody defeat with sixty per cent casualties. The campaign is abandoned amid public outcry.

2069

Seeking fuel for its war machine and a staging point for future military action in the Middle East, the RSA annexes Kuwait, initiating a series of conflicts that will be known collectively as the Oil Wars.

2070–2075

RSA special forces engage in a series of covert actions in Iran, Iraq and Jordon, primarily with the aim of intelligence-gathering for a fresh crusade. Operations, including the assassination of high-ranking Caliphate officers, continue in these territories until the middle of the decade.

2071–2073

Second Crusade. Air strikes and a prolonged ground assault allow the RSA to take control of Israel and parts of Lebanon. Jerusalem remains out of reach and Islamic Caliphate counter attacks soon wrest back control of the territory.

2074

Kuwaiti insurgents rebel against the American occupation. The RSA's response is led by Templar Captain Isaac Vaughan. Vaughan takes less than three months to put down the uprising, executing its leaders live on air. Vaughan is promoted to the rank of colonel.

2075–2076

Dubbed 'Vicious Vaughan' and 'Colonel Killcrazy' by the tabloid press for authorising the use of heavy ordnance and fuel-air strikes against the civilian populations of Iran and Iraq, Vaughan is recalled to Richmond in August following an official complaint by the United Nations and asked to account for his actions before a Senate inquiry. Believing himself betrayed by a government that will not commit to a war of total attrition to defeat the Islamic nations, Vaughan resigns his commission and embarks on a public-speaking tour of the RSA to promote his book, The Enemy Within.

2079

Vaughan assumes the position of Chairman of the Board of the Tessler Corporation in Europa City. Over the next three years he triples its profits by using his military contacts in the RSA to secure contracts for the supply of experimental cyber-ware.

2079–2083

Third Crusade (Saudi Campaign). Having twice failed to take Jerusalem, the next Crusade focuses on liberating Saudi Arabia from the Caliphate and depriving it of the oil reserves used to fuel its war machine. Islamic Caliphate forces are successfully driven back to Syria and Jordan.

2089

Fourth Crusade. Bolstered by Christian recruits from Eastern Europe and the Greater Russian Collective, the RSA amasses an army of one million frontline troops.

Saturation bombing lays waste to Lebanon and the western borders of Syria and Jordan. RSA forces then launch a three-pronged attack through Lebanon and Jordan in the east, via Egypt in the west, violating Egyptian airspace to land ground troops on Israel's western border, and by sea with direct beach landings. A protracted and bloody ground war of attrition follows as they fight to retake Israel foot by foot, culminating in the bloody siege of Jerusalem.

With the city devastated by long range bombardment, the Templars, now joined by the Israel Defense Forces, launch a final assault on Jerusalem. No quarter is given or asked for as the surviving Caliphate forces are driven back to the Wailing Wall Plaza. Unwilling to sustain further casualties, the IDF deploys a targeted nano-virus to destroy the remaining Caliphate troops. Use of this banned weapon, together with the assassination of Caliph Abu Ahmad al-Nasr al-Qurayshi while he is at prayer in the famed Al Aqusa Mosque, draws international condemnation.

2090

Buoyed by their success in Israel, Templar forces launch a fresh assault, seeking to drive Caliphate forces from Syria and Jordan. However, with stories of atrocities continuing to mount, opinion is starting to turn against the Religious States of America, with both Europa City and the African Tech Corps threatening to embargo the supply of arms.

2091–Present

Templar forces seize control of territory in Syria and Jordan, forcing the Caliphate, now under the control of Marshal Ismail, to retreat. But the Religious States' success proves to be short-lived when Gina Pulaski, former US senator and leader of the Free America movement, calls for President Gerrard to step down and dissolve the RSA. Their demands unanswered, Free America launches a series of asymmetrical attacks, plunging America into its third civil war.

APPENDIX B: MILITARY ACRONYMS

APS: Active Protection System
AMPV: Armoured Multi-Purpose Vehicle
ARV: Armed Response Vehicle
AWOL: Absent Without Official Leave
COSCOM: Corp Support Command
CSS: Combat Service Support
CROWS: Common Remotely Operated Weapon Station
CUSR: Covert Urban Sniper Rifle
ECH: Enhanced Combat Helmet
E-SAPI: Enhanced Small-Arms Protective Insert
E-SBI: Enhanced Side Ballistic Insert
FASCAM: Field Artillery Scatterable Mines
GEMSS: Ground-Emplaced Mine Scattering System
GPK: Gunner Protection Kit
GSR: Ground Surveillance Radar
HAHO: High Altitude High Opening
HEAT: High-Explosive Anti-Tank
HEMTT: Heavy Expanded Mobility Tactical Truck
HUD: Head-Up Display
IFFN: Identify Friend, Foe or Neutral
IHADSS: Integrated Helmet and Display Sight System
IOTV: Improved Outer Tactical Vest

IRST: Infrared Search and Track
JLTV: Joint Light Tactical Vehicle
LTAS: Long-Term Armor Strategy
METT-TC: Mission, Enemy, Terrain, Troops available,
          Time and Civilian Considerations
MIA: Missing In Action
MILES: Multiple Integrated Laser Engagement System
MOUT: Military Operations in Urban Terrain
MRE: Meal, Ready-to-Eat
MSR: Main Supply Routes
NLAW: Next generation Light Anti-tank Weapon
NSTV: Non-Standard Tactical Vehicle
OCT: Observer, Controller, Trainer
OPFOR: Opposing Forces
POL: Petroleum, Oil, Lubricants
POW: Prisoner Of War
UAS: Unmanned Aircraft Systems
UCIW: Ultra Compact Individual Weapon
VTOL: Vertical Take-off and Landing

ABOUT THE AUTHOR

Leon Steelgrave is the author of the *Europa City* series — hardboiled science fiction that traces its genealogy back to the pulp stories of the 1930s. This dark and satirical world serves as a warning of the dangers of ecological disaster and totalitarian regimes.

Leon's early work includes articles and reviews for music fanzines *Take To The Sky* and *Glasperlenspiel*. But it was his attempt to secure a commission for writing one of a series of *Judge Dredd* novels published by Virgin Books that kickstarted his fiction writing career. Although ultimately unsuccessful, the editorial feedback was sufficiently positive and encouraging for him to complete his debut novel *White Vampyre*. He has published a further three books in the series and is currently working on the first of a new series set in the wider *Europa City* universe.

Leon is a member of the Alliance of Independent Authors and self-publishes his work through Ice Pick Books — fiction to make your ears burn!

Writing being a solitary profession, Leon loves to engage with his readers, so feel free to join his mailing list for releases, updates and exclusive material.

www.leon-steelgrave.com